Rockbound

Rockbound

Frank Parker Day

With an afterword by
Gwendolyn Davies

UNIVERSITY OF TORONTO PRESS
TORONTO BUFFALO LONDON

© University of Toronto Press 1989
Toronto Buffalo London
Printed in Canada

Reprinted 1997, 2004, 2005, 2006

ISBN 0-8020-6723-9

Rockbound was first published in Garden City, New York, by Doubleday,
Doran & Company in 1928; it was first published by University of
Toronto Press, with an introduction by Allan Bevan, in 1973.

Printed on acid-free paper

Canadian Cataloguing in Publication Data

Day, Frank Parker, 1881–1950
Rockbound

ISBN 0-8020-6723-9
I. Title.
PS8507.A96R62 1989   C813'.52   C89-093822-9
PR9199.2.D39R62 1989

Publication of this edition has been assisted by the Canada Council and the
Ontario Arts Council under their block grant programs.

Rockbound

CHAPTER I

With many a tempest hadde his berd been shake.
CANTERBURY TALES.

WHEN David was eighteen he heard from some of the Outpost fishermen that his great-uncle Uriah, the rich king of Rockbound, wanted a fisherman. Here was his opportunity; for weeks, in fact, ever since old Gershom Born had talked with him, he had wondered how he would get up courage to face the old man and tell him what he knew. In his yellow dory he set out from Big Outpost one morning of early summer. The sea was apparently oil-smooth, but a ground swell always runs among these outer islands, and the flood tide was against him. He tugged hard at the splintered spruce oars, which had seen two years service on the Grand Banks, lifting his elbows at the finish of his stroke in a manner peculiar to the Outposters. With slack water he gave himself a spell and drifted idly for a little, a yellow speck on an immense floor of blue.

He looked up at the sky half-conscious of his insignificance in the universe above him; then, feeling cold water about his feet, reflected that only a half inch of leaky spruce marked him off from the watery world below, where shadowy albercore dodged in and out between streamers of waving kelp. The Outposts and Rockbound, now almost equidistant, were dimmed and softened by summer mists. As he sat there resting, his oars half drawn in through the thole pins, he looked at first glance like a hundred other young fishermen along the coast. He was barefoot and clad only in a pair of ragged brown trousers and a faded blue buttonless shirt that fell open at the neck to reveal a bronzed and hairy chest. His hands that clutched the oars were calloused and split, and scarred with marks of salt-water boils and burns from running hand line or halliard. Sly but kind gray eyes shone out through narrow slits overhung with thick eyebrows; a hawk's nose gave his face a touch of fierceness; his head was crowned with a thick brown mop of uncombed hair. He was not unhandsome, and when he smiled the corners of his mouth twitched and drooped.

Though he looked it not, he was a man of destiny—in small things, it is true, yet in relation to the universe all things upon this earth are small—and this voyage in his yellow dory, a voyage of destiny, less spectacular than Jason's but requiring none the less courage and resolution. For Jason had with him forty heroes and had but to meet a dragon, while David was alone and had to meet Uriah. As he floated idly there and looked up at the pale smoky sky and across the shining turquoise floor, he was conscious of the throb of the great deep below him and felt himself in the grip of Destiny of "some strange consequence yet hanging in the stars" that he could not understand. Why not let Fate decide for him whether he should row on to Rockbound or return to the Outposts? he thought. He was a Jung himself, but a poor Jung, a gearless, homeless Jung; how dare he face and make demands of Uriah, the rich king of Rockbound, who had wealth in boats and land, and lofts piled high with herring nets and tubs of trawl? He was on a line between a clump of lofty spruces on the Metatogan Main and Lubeck Island Light. Let Fate decide! He pulled in his oars, let them rest from gunwale to gunwale, and for fifteen minutes watched his landmarks. The beginning of the ebb and a faint draught of offshore wind were setting him toward Rockbound. Fate had decided! Out went his oars, and he gave way.

When his stem bumped against the logs of Uriah's launch he sprang out and drew his dory up a little—he dared not draw her too far without invitation—and made fast the painter to a spike. The ebb was running fast now, and she would be high and dry in half an hour. Heart in his throat, his bare feet took the long strides from log to log, and he reached the door of the great fish house just as Uriah, a terrifying figure, waddled out, his yellow oilskins spotted with blood and glistening with sequins of herring scales.

"An' what might ye be wantin'?" said the old man, the king of Rockbound.

"I wants fur to be yur sharesman," answered David.

"Us works here on Rockbound."

"I knows how to work."

"Knows how to work an' brung up on de Outposts!" jeered Uriah. "Us has half a day's work done 'fore de Outposters rub de sleep out o' dere eyes, ain't it!"

"I knows how to work," repeated the boy stubbornly.

"Where's yur gear an' clothes at?"

"I'se got all my gear an' clothes on me," said

David, grinning down at his buttonless shirt, ragged trousers, and bare, horny feet, "but I owns yon dory: I salvaged her from de sea an' beat de man what tried to steal her from me."

Uriah's eyes showed a glint of interest.

"You ain't got no place for to live on dis island; no one won't take in a tramp like you."

"Yes I is."

"How's dat?"

"I owns one tent' o' dis island t'rough my grandfader old Edward Jung, same as you owns yur shares."

The boy stood trembling inwardly and with shaking knees, yet looking the old tyrant boldly in the eyes.

"Who's bin stuffin' ye wid dat foolishness?"

"It ain't no foolishness, it's true. Old Gershom Born, de keeper o' Barren Island Light an' de wisest man in all dese islands, tole me las' time he was on de Outposts; an' says he, if yur great-uncle Ury refuse ye, go before lawyer Kingsford in Liscomb an' claim yur right. Yes, he did."

Uriah grunted and glowered. Old Gershom Born's name was one to be conjured with. He read fat law books and wrote deed, will, and mortgage for the islanders as fair as the grandest lawyer. Moreover, the king knew in his heart that the boy was right.

"What ye do wid land?" Uriah had been growing tall timothy and fat cabbages on David's piece for ten years free of charge and was loath to give it up.

"Live on it, farm it same as youse do. Dat house where Mudder died's mine too," said David, grown bolder, and he pointed to a tumble-down cottage which Uriah used as a storeroom for lobster pots.

The king looked scornfully at the landless serf; David stood in the presence of Goliath.

"I'se got de same rights as Anapest an' de Krauses." Like many kingdoms, Uriah's was not whole and perfect, but troubled by invaders.

"Maybe you is got some rights, maybe you isn't, but ye can't be no sharesman wid me."

"Den I'll squat on my land an' live in my house and fish offshore in my dory." David had gone over all the possibilities of this conversation many times before.

"You, wid nair a line or net to git bait."

"I got a line an' I kin pick up squid an' caplin on de beach."

"An' where will ye land yur boat? Ye can't use my launch."

"I'll land on de sand beach in Sou'west Cove an' haul my dory out."

"One summer storm will make kindlin' wood o' your dory."

"Den I kin land on de Krauses' launch. Anapest will let me. Anyhow, yur sharesman or no, I sticks and stays."

The old fox saw he was beaten, and he liked the fight in the boy: after all, he was a Jung, though a beggarly one.

"I wouldn't take ye for no sharesman, 'cause ye couldn't hold up yur end wid my boys."

"Give me a mont's trial," said David. "If I can't ketch fish fur fish an' haul net fur net wid Martin, Casper, Joseph, I'll go back to de Outposts an'ask fur no wages."

"Done," snapped the crafty Uriah, who saw a chance of keeping the land and of getting a month's work for nothing. "You take *Phœbe* tomorrow, far boat on de launch; she's stood idle since we lost Mark. Haul out yur dory on de launch."

Thus was the first battle with the old king won, and thus the disguised prince set foot upon his own dominion.

David turned from the old man and walked up the pathway to his mother's house, that was well-nigh a ruin. The doorstep gaped from the sill, the sagging back door hung by one hinge of leather, the kitchen was half full of lobster pots, and as these had been pushed rudely against the walls, plaster and lathing were broken. Big slabs had fallen from the ceiling. The kitchen stove was yellow with rust, and the pipe entered the chimney at a rakish angle. There was no furniture save a long sofa, on which, he remembered, Richard Covey had slept out many a drunken spree, and a hand-made chair the old folk had brought from Sanford. To most people this dilapidated house would have been only a source of heartbreak; to David, who had nothing, it was a potential palace. It was his own, his first possession, he should live there, and his gray eyes twinkled and the corners of his mouth drooped as familiar objects awakened some half-forgotten childish memory.

First, two rooms must be cleared for kitchen and bedroom. He worked his way around to the dining-room door and began lugging lobster pots into parlour and front hallway. A front door and reception room would be superfluous to him for many a day. When kitchen and small room opening off it were freed of pots and trawl tubs, he descended into the damp cellar, and there, groping in a jungle of broken fishing gear, found a handleless shovel and the stub of an old broom. The dark cobwebbed cellar seemed a source of wealth that he would explore at leisure. Smiling fondly at his treasure trove, he returned upstairs, and clearing up plaster and dirt with shovel and broom, threw the débris out into the yard. From the stove he dug out the matted ashes and found among them a black twisted fork. More property! His eyes gleamed again with pleasure in his possession, then darkened as the fork reminded him that he had nothing to eat and no source of supplies. He ran down to the shore and returned with an armful of gray driftwood.

Evening was coming, and, after the work about his house and the long row from the Outposts, he was hungry. He looked across the fields toward Anapest's sombre house, where a lamp glowed yellow in the kitchen window. There was something friendly and inviting in that blotch of light. Dare he? He must not let Uriah beat him, and he could not live forever by hitching up his belt. There was nothing else for it; he must beg bread of someone; later he would show them he could repay and earn his keep. From the tribe of the Krauses, who like himself had established a foothold on Rockbound through Anapest's inheritance of a tenth share from old Edward, who had died intestate, he had had no sign of welcome nor even awareness of his existence, though every soul on Rockbound had known of his arrival ten minutes after he had landed. Krauses and Jungs were immemorial enemies: they grunted at one another but seldom spoke, sent their children to spy into rival fish pens, and lived in a tense atmosphere of envy and mutual ill-will. Uriah had never forgiven old Edward for dying without a will, nor Anapest for marrying Joshua Kraus, nor the Krauses generally for having invaded his kingdom, which, he felt, would have been perfect and complete without them. As Uriah was king of all the Rockbound Jungs, so Anapest was empress of the Krauses. She ruled a smaller kingdom but was none the less imperious; no fleet of nets was set, nor did any Kraus boat set off from the Rock without her sanction.

Still, David felt, as he stared at the yellow light, that there was more hope of obtaining bread from Anapest than from Uriah. He crossed the fields and knocked humbly at her kitchen door. Anapest, her thick black dress girt in at the waist with a man's belt, was bustling about the stove.

"Come in," she called harshly, and David's bare feet scraped the rough splinters of the kitchen floor.

"I'm yur nephew David Jung from de Outposts."

Anapest looked the vagrant over, her quick

dark eyes taking in torn shirt, frayed trousers, and bare feet. Her heart softened toward him at once; still, she guessed he had come to be Uriah's sharesman, and his lot was thrown in with the enemy. Christian, Nicholas, and Melcher, sons and henchmen, ate greedily at the kitchen table and did not so much as throw a glance in his direction.

"How's all de folks on de Outposts?"

"All right."

"What you doin' here?"

"Uriah's sharesman."

"Ury's sharesman. Ha! a lot ye'll have fur yur summer's work when Joe an' Casper has figured expenses."

"Beginnin' I'se 'll take what dey gives me; some day I'se 'll take what I wants. I don't expect no mercy, but I'm hungry an' I come to ask some bread off ye."

"Sit ye down an' fill yur belly. Arter all, yur my brudder's son, if ye is Ury's sharesman."

David sat down meekly at the kitchen table, for he was even more fearful of Anapest than Uriah. The Kraus boys looked up and grunted at him; any stranger was to them a potential enemy, and this stranger had allied himself with a hostile clan. Anapest was a grand cook and fed her men well. There was a steaming fish chowder made from a fresh-caught haddock mixed with onions, sliced potatoes, and fried pork scraps; there were fried herring roes and new potatoes in their rosy jackets, showing mealy where the broken skin turned back; there were high piles of thick white bread and mugs of hot tea. David made hay while the sun shone.

"I'se sorry to beg," he said after the edge was taken off his hunger, "but I'se 'll have to git de scatterin' loaf o' bread off ye, Aunt Anapest. I'se 'll pay when I gits my first mont's share; I'se got naught, but ye'll lose naught t'rough me."

"Why don't ye beg yur bread off Ury?" asked Christian brutally.

"I can't. He's too hard."

"Den, if ye gets no bread ye can't stay on Rockbound," remarked Melcher hopefully.

"Yes, I kin! I stays, I sticks, if I has to dig up de roots o' de field. I kin live on fish an' mussels an' an odd checkerback. Man, you'se don't know what I bin a-used to livin' on. I stays an' lives in my mudder's house."

"Dey's haunts dere," said Christian, "what'll twitch de clothes off ye nights."

"Haunts or no haunts, I stays. I ain't skeered o' no haunts. Why, on de Outposts I lived next house to de ghost catcher."

"What, Johnny Publicover?"

"Ay, Johnny Publicover, de same what ketched de fierce Sanford ghost," said David between mouthfuls. He had caught the Krauses' interest for a moment and must make the most of his chance and eat enough to keep him alive for the next two or three days. Then fortune would throw something in his way, he would have fish, at any rate.

"Ye'll have a hard go wid no bread," said Nicholas.

"And he won't go wid no bread," shouted Anapest, empress of all the Krauses, stamping her foot. "What ye talkin' so fur, ye great lumps, to yur own cousin? Has his house an' land done ye air a good? Isn't Ury gettin' free grass an' cabbages off dat land fur dese ten years? Bread ye'll have, boy; t'ree big loaves a week, if ye kin live on dat."

"Dat I kin," said David rising, "an' my t'anks to ye, Aunt Anapest. Ye'll find me in de years to come no grudgin' neighbour."

Then, tucking one of Anapest's great loaves under his arm, he went back to his own house, and in the darkness built up a fire of driftwood in the rusty stove and sat down before it to plan and dream. Though he had neither lantern nor candle, the fire cast a fitful glow on the rough floor and made a glimmer of light in the room. The summer fog, pushed northward by the inshore breeze, had enveloped the island and, with its damp blanket, intensified the darkness of a moonless night. The hateful, ill-smelling careys, who love such nights, squeaked and gibbered around the house, and he heard an occasional whir of nighthawks' wings. The gray driftwood cracked sharp in the stove, and there was some strange rustling among the lobster pots in the hallway. But though David knew that the footless nigger of Rockbound was abroad on such nights, he sat unmoved by the stove and stirred only to feed the fire with a fresh stick. He was used to loneliness, and fog had no terror for him. Though he knew it not, as he sat there reviewing the past, he had great capital wealth in the fact that nothing to be faced in the future could be worse than what he had endured in the past. Starting from zero, the meanest acquired possession would connote a worth out of all proportion to its intrinsic value.

He could not recall his father, lost at sea when he was but two years of age. His mother had died of consumption in the bedroom that opened off the dining room. Certainly her pale ghost would not haunt him! He remembered going often into her room, where she had raised a limp hand to

stroke his head and look at him with pity. Her
hand, he remembered, was so transparent that
the bones shone through. His stepfather had
been a bad one. After his mother had married
Richard Covey, Uriah's loud-mouthed sharesman, they had had nothing but misfortune.
Richard Covey was a luckless man: he had gone
fishing on the wrong days; when the nets of others
were white with meshed herring, his had but a
scattering of fish; sportive albacores slit great
rents in his fleets while the fleets of others were untouched; the seas rolled his lobster pots into the
dog holes, a tangled chaos of broken lath and
twisted head rope. David thought of what he
had suffered under Richard Covey's rough
hand: scarce a day had he been free from welts
on his legs and lumps on his head as big as a sea
urchin.

At seven he was taken in the boat and assigned
duties beyond his strength. He was useful to the
man, for his sharp young eyes could pick up net
or trawl buoys, white with a stripe of scarlet,
far quicker than the rum-bleared eyes of his
stepfather. He had learned to endure cold, fog,
and blows, and to sag on a hand line to the maxi-
mum of his little strength. It was hard work
when the cod ran heavy and they fished with
two snoods, for when he hooked a pair he could

not draw them over the gunwale, and this brought upon him blows and curses. When they sailed, Richard Covey held the tiller and he crouched as far forward in the eyes as he could get, a bit of the spare jib drawn over his bare legs. How he had blessed the sun when it shone warm; the sun had been his best friend.

He remembered well that awful gray dawn when he crept out to light the kitchen fire, his duty since the age of five. Richard Covey lay sprawling on the sofa his legs twisted in a queer position. He had paid little attention to him at first, but put rustling paper and kindlings quietly in the stove; he had been beaten sometimes for waking the man as he laid the fire. Morning light that sifted through the eastern window fell on Richard Covey's white face and showed lips that were blue, a mouth half open, and bleared eyes that seemed to wink. He had been terrified by the winking eyes: had he made too much noise with the rustling paper? Then a deeper terror had entered his little soul: there was no sound of snoring or deep breathing that Richard Covey usually made. With a courage he himself had never understood, he had walked over and touched the man's face; it was set and cold. He had rushed into his mother's room shouting exultingly,

"He's dead, Mamma, he's dead!"

His mother had roused herself listlessly.

"Go tell Uriah and the boys to carry him away," she whispered, sinking back upon her pillows.

Three weeks later his mother had died. She was to be buried on Big Outpost, as are all the Rockbounders, and, hardly knowing what he did, he climbed over the side of the whaler on the launch as they lifted in his mother's rough board coffin, that looked like a great fish box. No one said him nay as he clambered aboard, no one spoke a word of pity. The Jungs had hated and despised Richard Covey—he was pariah, no one lent him gear or bait—Uriah had never forgiven the boy's mother for marrying the man, and as a child he had inherited a share of the hatred.

He could never forget that sail to the Outposts: the wind was fair, and Uriah winged out the tan-sailed whaler. The rough white coffin lay on the amidship thwarts by the centreboard; in the stern sat Uriah at the tiller with his son Mark minding the sheets, both red-faced, big-nosed— the Jew of the Levys shone out in Mark—both fierce eyed. He had sat in the bow, a pale-faced, underfed urchin of eight, staring at the coffin or looking across the sea. No word was spoken in that four miles of water journey.

When the shallow grave had been filled in and heaped up in the Outpost cemetery and the few mourners had filtered away, he had been left alone. He had sat there a long time, stunned by the fact that his last feeble friend was gone, but he was dry-eyed, he could not cry. After a while he had gone down to the Outpost launch to get in the boat. Far out on the southern waters he had seen Uriah's tan-sailed whaler beating her way back to Rockbound. They had left him without a word; he was alone on a strange island among strange people.

After that, he remembered, he had begged a crust from door to door and slept in sail lofts, a piece of an old canvas wrapped about his legs. In the first winter he would certainly have perished had it not been for the kindness of Jennie Run-over, so named by some local wit, because her fat hams oozed over the seat of any chair in which she sat, no matter how capacious, as does rising dough over the edge of a pan. She sold liquor, was an unofficial harlot, and kept in her house four stout girls, who in September were visited by lustful fishermen, home from three months' durance on the Grand Banks. Jennie Run-over had picked him up one day as he stood on the beach staring out to Rockbound. Her heart, he supposed, must have been touched by

the sight of the pale-faced, forsaken, half-starved,
homeless mite of a boy.

At any rate, she took him to her house and
taught him to fetch and carry; he gathered driftwood, cut kindlings, brought water from the
spring, weeded the garden, fed the pigs, and
slept on a pile of shavings in the cellar. But he
had enough to eat; for the first time in his life,
all he could eat, every day. True, he was often
beaten by Jennie when she was drunk, but she
sometimes patted his head when she was sober.
For five years he had served Jennie and learned
a great deal about drunkenness and lust. As soon
as he was big enough, he had shipped as "boy"
on a banking schooner, and slept well up in the
eyes, where every night, his ear pressed close
to the planking, he had heard the lap of waves
against the stem. He remembered many a night
when lanterns hung from the fore boom, the
schooner's waist a welter of slippery cod, and he
had stood ready for anything, to sharpen a knife,
fetch a basket of salt, or let go the falls for a
homing dory. "Whar's dat dam' boy?" the
salters used to roar from the hold. "Send him
down wid water." "Whar's dat dam' boy?" a
splitter bawled on deck. "I wants my second
knife from B bunk in de fo'c'sle." Up he used to
climb from the cool hold to dive into the smelly

forecastle. He was every man's boy to fetch and carry and many a clip he got on the side of the head. Still, on the whole they had been kind to him, especially John Brooks, the coloured man, who looked like a pirate with his big gilt earrings hanging from pierced ear lobes. He was high-line and feared no man, and, sometimes, when he was steersman, John would let him do a trick at the wheel, and teach him how to hold a star on the rigging and keep the schooner on her course without staring in the binnacle.

Jennie Run-over had taken all his slender wages for his winter's board, and he wore cast-off garments that seemed always too large or too small. For three whole winters he had gone without boots. He had spoken truly to Uriah: that very day when he landed on Rockbound his complete worldly possessions were his shirt, trousers, a frayed cod line, and the dory he had salvaged and fought for. As he sat by the flicker-ing stove, he felt very rich in his new possession of house and land. They could not scare him off by tales of haunts or threats of hard work. How lucky that old Gershom Born had come to the Outposts and told him he owned a house and one tenth of Rockbound. He had faced down the old king in the first encounter, and wondered at his own courage.

He chuckled as he sat by his rusty stove and started from his reverie. He must get some rest against to-morrow's work. He walked over to the couch on which Richard Covey had died, and throwing himself down, drew a sack over his feet, and after the manner of all fishermen, who even on the darkest night fear that the moon may peep out and shine upon them sleeping, wrapped another sack about his head. He had no fear of Richard Covey's haunt; he was used to loneliness in dark corners. In two minutes he was fast asleep.

CHAPTER II

Allas! the shorte throte, the tendre mouth,
Maketh that est and west, and north and south,
In erthe, in eir, in water, man to swynke
To gete a glotoun deyntee mete and drynke!

CANTERBURY TALES.

WHEN David woke with a start it was still dark, but he threw off his rough covering and went quickly to the door. Away to the eastward dark mountains of morning clouds lowered, but the offshore breeze had pushed out the fog bank, and the stars twinkled through. As he had never owned watch or clock, he had learned to use the great bowl of the universe as an approximate timepiece. He looked up into the northern sky and saw the dipper, in relation to the pole star, hanging in the position of V on a clock dial, and knew from memories of previous nights that it was between two and three o'clock. There was no time to lose if he meant to show Uriah and the Jung boys his worth. He threw a bag about his shoulders, tied it at his neck with a bit of marline, tore off a thick heel from Anapest's loaf, thrust one half in his pocket for lunch, and gnawing the other half, ran for the launch, his bare feet scattering the dew from heavily bent grasses across the path.

Early as he was, he was none too early! A squat dark object moving swiftly from boats to fish house he knew was Uriah. Casper and Martin were not about yet—Casper, the farmer by instinct, was always last to get his boat off in the morning—but Joseph had shoved the *Lettie* over on her bilge and was greasing her keel. Neither spoke to him. David went over to the *Phœbe*, pushed her over on her side, fumbled in the dark for a stick, which he too dipped in the tub of stinking gurry, and greased her keel so that she would slip easily down the ways. As the seas often run fiercely even on the northern and sheltered side of the island, Rockbound boats never lie at a mooring but are hauled out high and dry as soon as they touch the launch.

Uriah waddled out of the gloom of the fish house with a basket full of herrings.

"Dere's yur bait, an' dere's an extry line, a box o' hooks, an' two odd sinkers."

David righted the *Phœbe*, lifted the basket into

her, and set it down by the centreboard without
a word.

"Got nair a pair o' nippers?" queried the old
man.

"I don't need no nippers. I'se fished on de
Gran' Banks, an' me hands is tough."

"You best foller Joe; he knows w'ere de big
schools o' fish lays dis season ob de year."

David grunted something in reply, but he had
no mind to follow Joe or any of them; he would
lead or nuttin'; he hadn't fished out o' de Outposts for naught; he knowed where de fish layed
well as Joe. He set his shoulder to the stem of
the *Phœbe* and started her down the ways. First
she moved slowly, then gathered speed, and as
his foot felt the chill of the salt water on the last
log, she seemed to be flying. With his left hand
grasping the jib stay, he gave a mighty spring
and rolled in over the port washboard. Joseph,
whose boat was already afloat, listened with
the malicious hope that he would hear a great
splash, betokening that, in the darkness, David
had missed the logs set at unaccustomed spaces
and been dragged off waist deep by the flying
Phœbe, as he had seen many a green sharesman
dragged before. But David, safely aboard,
grasped a sweep and rushed quickly astern to
fend her off the ledge and turn her head to the

westward; then, darting swiftly forward, he made
halliards and creaking blocks sing, and the big
brown mainsail rose and bellied to the puff of
the shore wind. Astern he rushed to shove his
tiller hard aport and rattle in the main sheet
till his sail was flat. Up came the *Phœbe's* bow
into the wind. Now, setting the tiller in a middle
notch, he darted forward again to hoist his jib
and belay the halliard, back astern again to
haul in and make fast his jib sheet. All his mo-
tions were swift and catlike; his bare feet gripped
the wet surface of thwart and washboard.

When he had time to look about him, he
noted that the breeze was from the northwest
and that he could just clear the dull black mass
of West Head by jogging the *Phœbe*. Joseph's
boat was a hundred yards ahead of him. He
tugged at the rusty pin of his centreboard and let
the chain go clanking down; it would slow the
Phœbe up a little, but keep her from drifting
to leeward in this light breeze. Joseph made a
short tack to the northward to weather the head,
but David held straight on.

"Don't go in dere, de water's shoal," bawled
Joseph.

But David pretended not to hear and held to
his course; there would be plenty of time to come
about when the iron centreboard bumped and

bobbed up. The *Phœbe* was handy, he knew, for from the Outpost boats he had seen her luff up and come about a hundred times before she turned over with Mark, and he knew her points as a jockey knows the strengths and weaknesses of his rival's horses. He cleared West Head just outside the breakers and passed inside the Grampus with Joseph's boat, in spite of her tack, still fifty yards ahead. He let main and jib sheet run now and stood away to the southeast. With a long-handled gaff he winged out his jib, pulled up his centreboard, and watched to see if he was creeping up on the *Lettie*. Joseph's boat held her lead. The *Phœbe* was fast but crank, and Uriah had loaded her with ballast since she drowned Mark: four hundred pounds of beach rocks lay along her keelson.

"To hell wid ballast, dat makes a boat hard to get up an' off de launch; I'll ballast my boat wid fish," thought David, and stooping he tossed two hundred pounds of beach rocks into the sea. Then the lightened *Phœbe* began to draw up on the *Lettie*, and as David sailed his boat close to the *Lettie's* quarter, to take the quick puffs from her sails, he was soon abreast of Joseph's boat and little by little drew ahead. Now he was leading the Jung boys, first of the Rockbound fleet; Martin's boat showed dimly outside the Grampus, and Casper's trailed far behind. Daylight was coming gradually.

When he was well ahead and well to the southward of Barren Island, he hauled in his sails flat and stood away again to the westward toward his favourite bank. A landsman who looks at the even surface of the sea and whose acquaintance with the bottom is limited to slightly pitched bathing beaches thinks of the seafloor as flat and level. Not so it appeared to the mind of David, who from frequent soundings with a cod line visualized it truly as composed of hills, mountain ranges, deep valleys, sharp cañons, buttes, and wide plateaus. It was futile, he knew, to drop his baited hooks in a valley, for on the tops of the ridges and shallow plateaus lay the cod, waiting for schools of herring and squid to drift over. The finding and exact location of these shallow plateaus called banks by the fishermen seems to the uninitiated, who sees only miles upon miles of waves that look everywhere the same, nothing short of marvellous. They are marked by alignments of distant islands, by cross bearings, and time courses run by the compass.

To his favourite bank in the open sea, southwest from Barren Island and south-southeast from Lubeck Island light, David steered the

Phœbe, that, lightened of her ballast, heeled over and put her lee washboard under in the freshening breeze. Presently he rounded his boat up, let the jib run, dropped the peak of his mainsail, but held fast the throat, so that the *Phœbe* would ride to the wind, and tossed over his grapnel. Over went his double-baited line, with his sinker he sounded bottom, twelve fathom, and he drew up a fathom to keep his hooks clear of the weeds on the sea floor. He began to saw patiently, but nothing happened; in half an hour he caught only two small rock cod. His heart sank; he could scarcely face Uriah on his first day with an empty boat. He would be cursed for not following Joseph as instructed. What was the matter? He had always caught fish on this bank before. Presently he ran forward, hove up his grapnel, hoisted jib and peak again, and stood farther to the westward toward Matt's Bank.

Again he anchored and tried. This time he was on the fish; ten seconds after his baited hooks reached bottom, a pair of big cod flashed over his gunwale and were snapped into the fish pen. The fish bit fiercely; as soon as the hooks were down came a tug on the line; then, after a few seconds of swift hand-over-hand pulling, gray forms with twirling white bellies showed dimly in the green depths. He gave himself no rest, but pulled and hauled, baited and rebaited for three hours. Once a strange boat drew up to him, and David, with two great cod hooked that twisted and tangled his snoods, let his line rest on the bottom.

"Air a fish?" hailed the stranger.

"A scatterin' rock cod," called back David lying stoutly. When the boat was well away, he pulled up his fish and repaired his snarled snoods. By nine, when the fish stopped biting his fish pens were two thirds full and the *Phœbe* had but a streak and a half clear.

The breeze dropped, and the sun shone warm to dry his shirt and trousers, soaked from the spray of the hand line. He squatted tailor-wise on his bit of deck by the jib stay, and though both hands were bleeding from the run of the burning hand line, he felt happier than he had for many a day. On the sea he was a free man and his own master. The corners of his mouth drooped in his quizzical smile as he thought how Joe, Martin, and Casper would curse when he came in high-line on his first day. And high-line he certainly would be. He drew out his heel of dampened bread and devoured it ravenously, washing it down with deep draughts from the *Phœbe's* water jug that Uriah had stuck in the

bows. Uriah was mean and greedy, but he knew
how to fit out a sharesman, thought David, and
he kept his boats tight.

As he ate and looked about him at the sunlit
water and enjoyed the sway of the boat that
rocked him as if he were cradled—little cradling
had he had as a child—he saw a great swirl and a
dozen splashes dead astern to the southward.
Then black backs flashed on the surface.

"Playin' pollock," said David to himself. He
knew what to do for them. He stuffed the last
crust into his mouth, seized his line, cut off the
heavy leaden sinker, and, wrapping both hooks
with guts torn from a fat herring, let his line
trail astern near the surface. Snap, and he was
fast to two pollock! Over and over again he repeated the operation, till he dared not lay another fish aboard the *Phœbe*, clear only by half a
streak from the gunwale. He tried his pump till
she sucked clear. It was a pity to leave those
tens of thousands of playing pollock; if an Outposter came near he would hail him. However,
no boat neared him.

In the offing far to the eastward, he could see
the black specks of Joseph's, Casper's, and
Martin's boats bunched near the Rock. It
would be a long, hard beat home; the little breeze
that remained, puffy and variable, still hung in

the nor'west. Far out on the sea rested a thick stratum of fog bank, through which a three-master loomed, with spars unearthly high. He rested patiently, awaiting a breeze, knowing that the wind often hauled at noontime. Before twelve came a draught from the sou'west; luck favoured him that day. He let out his mainsail to catch the quartering breeze and rested happy at the tiller. Then the other Rockbound boats made sail and stood in. By their speed he judged them light; they would be home long before him.

The southwest breeze had caught the fog bank half an hour before it touched the sails of the *Phœbe*, and the fog travelled faster than the boats. Presently the sun sickened, the islands dimmed to a dull gray, and black specks that meant boats were blotted out. David took a course on Rockbound before the fog shut out the island, and kept his ears alert for the sound of breakers. The deep-laden *Phœbe* moved sullenly, her jib flirting from side to side of the stay with a vixenish snap. Now, had David had a draught of rum, or even pipe and tobacco, he would have been comforted, for the stoutest heart is lonely on a fog-shrouded sea.

In two hours time he heard the smash of surf and, standing close in and staring eagerly, made out the black form of sou'west gutter rock. He

steered west now, hugging the dim black of the
cliff, and dared again to round West Head inside
the Grampus, lest he should lose touch with the
shore. Then he jibbed, hauled flat, and stood for
the launch, letting out a great "Hallo." Uriah
was at the launch with the oxen, and, as his prow
took the logs, hooked the wire cable into his
stem ring.

"Go easy," yelled David, "she's deep."

"I'se hauled out boats while you was yet
suckin'," retorted Uriah, starting his oxen with a
mighty "Gee Bright."

"How much do ye hail?" queried Uriah as the
boat reached the top of the launch.

"Six quintal," answered David proudly. Casper came out and stared in his fish pens.

"Scale fish," said he contemptuously, handling
the pollock.

"No dey's not scale fish," said David. "Dere's
a few scatterin' pollocks on top, underneat's all
big cod."

Uriah said naught to David; silence and absence of complaint were ever his loudest praise,
but he had a word to say to Joseph, Martin, and
Casper in a corner of the fish house. David hailed
more that day than the three brothers put together. In all his years on Rockbound, he never

had a better day's fishing nor a greater triumph.

When David had been fishing a fortnight off Rockbound, the dogfish came and drove in the boats from the Rock and adjacent banks. It was no good trying for cod when dogfish were about—even Uriah admitted that—they chased the cod and did nothing but tangle and destroy the fisherman's gear. Still, the boats went out each morning in the hope that the fisherman's pest had vanished; a few unavailing trials, and they returned early. David had hoped for some afternoons of rest and leisure, but that was not part of Uriah's plan, who put him to work tanning nets.

About noon on one such day, Joseph, the sly one, went to Cow Pasture Hill on the west end to stake out his young bull. When he came to the cliff's edge and looked down from the height into the green water, he saw that Sheer Net Cove was alive with herring. They darted to and fro or lay by millions on the yellow sand of the cove's bottom. That could not long be kept a secret, and he knew that the Krauses had their nets and seine laid in their seine boat, whereas the seine of the Jungs was in the upper loft. If the Jungs started to get out their herring seine, the Krauses would see them, launch first, and get round the fish. He thought for a moment, ruffling up his black hair, then ran through the thick spruces on the back of the island, and, bending low to escape observation, dashed across bar and sand beach and made his way into the thick woods on the eastern end. After a moment's pause to catch his breath he came running down the road from the eastern end bellowing: "De herrin', de herrin' is in on de shore in millions."

What a hurry and scramble was there then! Uriah puffed to the loft and tore down the herring seine; down the stairs stamped Casper with an armful of ropes, grapnels, and net buoys; Joseph followed with two baskets of sinker rocks; young Gershom Born ran to and fro, shouting and waving his arms as he gathered up equipment, with Noble Morash following sullenly in his wake; David greased bottoms of seine boats and dories. Do what they could, the Kraus boats were off first, but the Krauses, deceived by Joseph's ruse, pulled madly for the eastern end. Only when they were well out of hearing Joseph said:

"Quick now, de herrin's in de Sheer Net Cove an' we kin git dere first."

Casper, who excelled in net fishing, led the fleet of Jung boats around the western end of the island. One man tugged viciously at the oars, and another sat straddling the bows, peering down into the green water, not more than three fathom deep, for the edge of the herring school. Young Gershom Born, the most powerful oarsman, pulled the boat in which Casper was the watcher; David pulled the second boat with Noble Morash in the bows, and Martin, the weakest oarsman, trailed behind with Joseph straddling his bows.

"Here are herrin'! Here are herrin'!" Joseph and Noble began to shout from the rear boats.

"Not enough yet," bawled Casper from the leading boat. Over the yellow sands the green-backed herring raced in schools so thick and opaque that the sea floor was hidden.

"Shoot here, shoot here," yelled Joseph in his anxiety to beat the Krauses. "Lot's o' herrin' here, ain't it!"

"Not yet, not yet!" shouted Casper.

When the boats came to the mouth of the rocky Sheer Net Cove, Casper raised his hand as a signal to shoot. He took his boat close to the breakers, cast over the end of the seine, tying on rock sinkers with a swift and adroit hand as he paid it out, while Gershom Born, the great blond sharesman, strained at the oars and tugged the heavy seine boat, heavier now with

the drag of the seine, westward to sea. Then, at
a signal from Casper's hand, he made a sharp
turn northward to the right, again a signal, another sharp turn to the eastward, and millions of
herring were penned in the cove. The ends of the
seine were brought together and tied; now it
floated in a great corked circle, the vibrant
water within crowded with herrings, a tumult
of blues and greens. At the first rush of the imprisoned fish against the outer twine, the seaward corks went under.

"Quick, Dave, quick man, git on de buoys,"
bawled Casper, "or de fish will git ober de top."

The seaward head ropes were dragged up on
the prows of boats to hold up the seine till the
white fir-wood buoys could be tied on, and
Joseph and Martin ran out moorings and grapnels to north, west, and south, to hold the seine
against the rush of the tide.

Still, in spite of the light fir-wood net buoys,
the seaward head ropes dipped under, for the
seine twine was now white with meshed herring;
the smaller fry darted through the meshes and
to sea again.

"Quick, now, Dave, wid de nets," bawled
Casper. David was everyone's slave; everyone
called orders to the newest and lowest sharesman.
He did not care for this herring fishing, where

there was little chance for individual action: his great moments were when, on the open sea, he was alone in the *Phœbe*. As long as the herring were in, he knew that the boat he already loved because it gave him freedom would lie dry on the launch.

Over the head ropes went dories and seine boats, and the inside of the seine was circled with a fleet of nets that were drawn into a smaller circle. Gershom Born, blue-eyed Viking, hurled in the jiggler, a stone tied with a rope to pieces of white wood. This he flounced up and down, to scare more fish into meshes of net or seine. Noble Morash, the gaunt, black-bearded, silent sharesman, and David darted their spruce oars to the bottom, and when they bobbed from the surface like the sword Excalibur, caught them neatly by the handles, to drive them down again among the frightened fish. Once Noble Morash drove his into deep water, and when the oar handle did not reappear in the usual rhythmic time, he peeped over the gunwale to see if his oar blade had caught in a cleft of the rock bottom. Whereupon the oar handle shot out, caught him between the eyes, and knocked him flat and half stunned into the bottom of the boat. There was a yell of laughter in which David joined. That was a first-rate Rockbound joke to be recounted for many a day. Noble Morash rose, mopping the blood from his nose, and glared savagely at David with his narrow, sinister eyes. He would show the new sharesman if he could laugh at him, even if he were Uriah's kinsman.

"Herrin'! Herrin'!" they screamed at one another as if they had never seen a fish before.

"We got two hundred barrels, ain't it?"

"We got five hundred barrels."

"Chuck in dat giggler."

"Souse her up an' down."

"De herrin's not bin in on de shore like dis fur twenty year."

David caught the spirit and like the rest became a wild fisherman, intoxicated with the great catch of herring, shouting, gesticulating, taking his turn with the heavy giggler, driving down the oars. Presently the Kraus boats hove up alongside; the Krauses had taken no fish and eyed the Jungs resentfully, though they had not got to the bottom of Joseph's ruse.

The inner net, heavy with fat, gleaming herring meshed from both sides, was hauled now, each end in a separate boat. David and Noble Morash in their boat dragged in head and foot rope and shook the fish into the boat's bottom a half bushel at a time, or tore out those that stuck fast in the twine with a rending of gills and sometimes the loss of a head. When they strode from bow to stern now, they waded knee deep in herring. Lower and lower sank seine boat and dories, till only single streaks were clear. When the net was picked, it was again circled within the seine. Outside giant albacore in pursuit of the herring splashed and swirled the waves into foam.

"Bring in de spare boats," bawled Casper, and in they floated over the head ropes.

David glanced up from his work once in a while to admire the little cove in which these Jungs shouted and toiled unmindful of any beauty about them. It was closed to the eastward, and partly to the northward and southward, by sheer cliffs of slaty black and iron-red rocks, seamed and fish-boned with cracks from some pre-historic fire. The slanting afternoon sun filled these rocks with light and cast deep shadows in the clefts. Above the cliffs ran in a fine curve a narrow margin of green turf crowned with masses of stunted wind-blown spruces crowding like horses in a gale, tails to the sea wind. The cliff-fallen boulders at the foot were clad with raw-sienna rockweed, and among these the green sea washed with a bang and a roar, lashing itself, even on this comparatively calm day, into a fury of foam and creamy lather.

It seemed like a dream to David, and that he was dreamer and a part of the dream.

There they laboured together, great shouldered, red faced, clad in yellow oil pants, shouting, gesticulating, pulling on head ropes, hurling the giggler, darting oars, balancing on thwarts or gunwale with all the grace of athletes, tearing out shining fish tangled in brown meshes, wild with greed and excitement, though they had done this a hundred times before. Beneath the yellow dories that were down close to the gunwales the sea, patched in green and black, was vibrant with backs of frightened herring, racing madly about nets and seine in their effort to escape.

Again they hauled the fleet of nets and picked them. The sun was low over Flat Island now, and the boats could carry no more. Reluctantly Casper gave the order to set a fleet of nets about the remnant of the school and to take up the moorings of the big seine, which they dared not leave overnight so close to the shore.

Home they rowed in the twilight, deep-laden seine boat and dories dragging wearily. Uriah was waiting at the launch with his oxen to draw out the boats. From him came no word of praise.

"You got to be quick now, boys," he cried. "It's Saturday, an' I neber works on de Lord's

Day, me nor my fader before me." And to David, "Git a snack an' be back quick. Dese herrin' got to be dressed by midnight. Quick, now, we don't want no loafers on Rockbound." This, after he had fished on the Rock before daybreak and tugged at the heavy seine through a long afternoon.

David, with back and shoulders aching, rushed off to his house and tore ravenously at a crust of bread and a piece of salt fish. He would show the old man if he was a loafer; in five minutes he was back at the fish house, just as Joseph was coming down the road. Uriah was waiting for him, Uriah the king, who neither ate nor slept while fish were on the floor.

"You boys is awful slow. Why, in de ole days me an' my brudder Simeon stood on yon beach an' gibbed eighty barrels of mackerel an' never stirred from dere from tree one afternoon till sundown nex' day. Men could work in dem days. Here you, David, look alive, run dat spare dory down de launch an' fill her wid water while I fetches de cattle."

CHAPTER III

Poverte is hateful good, and as I gesse
A ful greet bryngere-out of bisynesse,
A greet amendere eek of sapience
To hym that taketh it in patience.
CANTERBURY TALES.

ANTERNS hung from the thick brown beams made spots of yellow light, but dimly illuminated the dusky corners of the great fish house which Uriah's father and uncle, George and Edward Jung, had built from the wreckage of vessels lost on the Rockbound shoals. In the southwest corner was the salt bin, holding hundreds of bushels of wetted yellow salt taken from the bankers in September; along the southern side stood row upon row of puncheons full of pickled cod, mackerel, and herring, the mackerel and herring to be packed in smaller barrels and carried to the main from time to time, and the cod to be laid on rocks and flakes, when the September sun came with

42

heat enough to make the fish without burning them. On top of the puncheons were piled nets, hand barrows, trawl buoys, decoys, and lobster pots, in a welter of confusion. About the beams and in niches of wall or studding were hung or stuck articles of fishermen's use—cotton gloves, nippers, hanks of cod line, finger stalls, and spare splitting knives. In the east end of the room was the flat salting table rimmed with a strip of wood and piled high with yellow salt and gleaming herring. The floor of beech and maple planking, salvaged from a wrecked ship, still showed the trunnel holes and was soaked with the brine and blood of seventy years. In mid-floor stood big tubs, half puncheons, some filled with sea water for washing the fish, some to catch torn-out milt and roe, and some to receive the herring guts, these last to be carried out and spread upon the new-mown timothy land. Tiny spots of light were caught and reflected from thousands of fish scales that sequinned tubs, blood-empurpled floor, and yellow oilskins.

Beneath a swaying lantern, where he could watch and command all, sat Uriah, his swift, keen knife ripping open the bellies of herrings, his horny thumb, unprotected against sharp bones by glove or stall, tearing out entrails or roe to be thrown into the appropriate tub.

"Dese ain't de fish dat was here in April; dese is he fish mostly; dey's full o' milt." He kept up a conversation to make the boys forget their weariness and to drive them on to work.

"My body's good but my legs's gone," said he in apology for sitting on a box. "But I kin still split fish wid ere a man. Me an' my brudder Simeon stood on yon beach an' split eighty barrels o' mackerel from tree one afternoon till sundown nex' day an' never stirred nor eat 'cept when de women folks poked a piece o' bread in our mouf. Dere ain't no men kin work so now'-days, ain't it!"

"Men's jus' as good now'days, Fader, but times is changed," growled Casper from the salting table.

"Jus' as good, is it?" jeered the old man. "An' here's dis crew wonderin' if dey kin gib fifty barrels o' herrin' 'fore midnight."

Uriah, the king, a man of seventy, wore a battered straw hat; his squat figure was clad in yellow oilskins and rubber boots. He had a short grizzled beard, his right eye drooped, and an upward twitch in the right corner of his mouth suggested that some day he would suffer a stroke of paralysis. He was rich, avaricious, and had a passion for work; he slept little, was tireless, and drove everyone before him. He ripped open fish with lightning darts of his swift knife and tore out guts with remorseless hand.

"Jus' as good, is it! Jus' as good, is it! I'd 'a' liked to seen you boys keep yur end up when me an' my brudder Simeon was young men," he jeered. "Ain't it, Sim?" yelled Uriah, for Simeon was deaf.

"Ay, so it be, Ury," answered old Simeon, though he had heard never a word of the preceding conversation.

Simeon, the old dotard, worn out with seventy years of incessant labour, sat in a dim corner gibbing feebly. His head bobbed to and fro as he split, a perpetual fond smile was on his face, and saliva drooled from the corners of his mouth. Only the shadow of a man, still working from habit of work, remained.

Joseph, Uriah's son, and Noble Morash, the gaunt black sharesman, emerged from the darkness lugging a barrow piled up with herrings from the boats, and dumped them with a smack on the soaked floor, to add to the great slithering pile already there.

"More work fur de women an' ole men," said Joseph gaily.

Uriah snorted and began, "When me an' my brudder Simeon . . ."

But Joseph waited not to hear; he was always

in a hurry; he never walked, he ran. He was
avaricious and loved money like his father, and
was already the slave of labour. He hustled
Noble Morash out into the darkness again to
fetch water from the drawn-up dory for the
washing tubs. Joseph was a huge fellow with
broad shoulders and slim hips and legs; he had a
hawk nose, brick-red face, and piercing blue
eyes. He was clad like the others in yellow oilskins, long boots, and sou'wester. His nostrils
were well cut up on the side, and his face had
somehow a strange Turkish or Oriental caste.
Uriah had married a Levy from Little Outpost,
and the Levys, time out o' mind Baptists, had
once been German Jews, though none knew
what had converted them, unless it had been the
wearisome argument of the sea. Joseph was a
money maker, a shrewd bargainer, who peddled
cabbages and mackerel through the streets of
Liscomb when there was no sale on the wharves;
he kept the wooden box into which the Jungs
put their common earnings to be divided at the
end of each month with much acrimony and
mutual distrust. He darted to and fro in the
spotty light, sousing the split herrings in the
washing tub, transferring them to the second
tub, or scooping them out in a dip net, to carry
them and smack them down on Casper's salting

table. While he kept up a foolish chatter, his thoughts ran thus:

"Fifty barrels at six dollars a barrel is three hundred dollars cash money, and a fifth part of that will be mine, and I'll put it in the bank with the rest. Sixty dollars more for me, and some day next autumn I'll go to the bank in Liscomb and get the cashman to count my money all over for me and tell me again it's all there."

It was a Saturday night, and Uriah knew in his heart that they could not gib the fifty barrels of herring before midnight.

"Me and my brudder Simeon nor my fader before us neber worked on de Lord's Day," he said to spur them on.

"Did us, Sim?" he yelled.

"Dat's a fac', dat's a fac'," babbled the old dotard.

Uriah's thoughts, however, were as follows: "T'ree hunderd dollars fur dis lot; what a pity to-morrow's Sunday! If de leas' sea gits up, de herrin' will go off in deep water, an' we'll have to use sunk nets. My boys is tough, dey don't need no day o' rest, an' dey can't shoot de seine till broad daylight on Monday, for you can't see a herrin' on de bottom till two hours arter sun-up. The Lord should give me a big jewel in my crown for laying dis crew off to-morrow. T'ree hundred dollars gone!" and he groaned inwardly.

Uriah's wife, the Levy from Little Outpost, sat in a darkened corner gibbing silently. She was a big woman with a placid face, who had endured many hardships with fortitude. She was by fifteen years Uriah's junior and had borne him fourteen children. Eight of them had died at birth, for when the fish came plentifully she had worked every night in the fish house, or toiled in potato and cabbage patches even when her time was approaching. Everyone must work on Uriah's island from long before sunrise to dark. She listened not at all to the babble of conversation; she had heard it all before in a hundred variations, and understood Uriah's drift. She sat thinking of the time when she had been a little girl, of her grandfather's long gray beard, and of a big black book with curious printing he used to read in. She thought, too, of the time when she had first seen Uriah, as her father's boat passed close to his in the ships' channel between Big and Little Outpost, and how he came soon after to court her on Sundays. She had been proud to be courted by the best fisherman on the whole coast; then Uriah was daring and a wonder in a boat, now he had become mean and cautious and seldom ventured on the sea.

Near her were two of her daughters, Ruth and
Tamar, girls still in their teens drafted into this
forced labour. The herring must not go soft or
spoil, though men and women wore themselves
out. They chattered and giggled to themselves
and cast eyes at David, the new ragged sharesman, who, working like a trojan, sat with downcast glance listening to all and saying never a
word. His shoulders ached, his hands bled from
deep cracks, for all the week before he had
fished with squid bait, but he squatted on his
heels near the herring pile, working furiously and
disdaining a seat as if he were a man of iron.

Fanny, the potato girl, and Gershom Born,
the blond Viking, kept up a continual banter.
Gershom was obscene in his remarks when he
was sure Uriah and his wife were not listening.
Fanny slept in the loft with the sharesmen, since
there was no other place to sleep, and Gershom
was often the companion of her bed. In fact,
Fanny refused none of the great sharesmen,
though Gershom was her favourite, her only
proviso being that they washed themselves and
put on a clean shirt before coming to her. Fanny
was pretty, of moderate height and stoutly
built; she had yellow hair, blue eyes, and a
kindly, placid face. As she threw back to Gershom Born some chat none too proper, her

white teeth flashed in a pleasant smile. David looked shyly at her with wonder. As yet he knew nothing of women except Jennie Run-over and the trollops she had kept in her house on Outpost. He kept on glancing at Fanny out of the corners of his slitty eyes and found pleasure in her beauty. Tamar caught his sidelong glances and nudged Ruth and giggled.

Fanny was certainly a fine creature, but her morals were those of the birds. She came from Big Outpost to hoe Uriah's cabbages and potatoes, since the men had no time to work about gardens. Moreover, gardening was distinctly woman's work. All day long she hoed and weeded and gave a hand at night in the fish house, as did all the island women when a run of fish came. She trudged home from the fields in the late afternoon, hoe over her shoulder, whistling blithely. Before supper she always went to the beach, stripped and washed herself—little cared she if the men peeked—and put on a clean shirt and a fresh dress of blue and white in tiny checks. Her dresses, scrupulously washed and ironed, were kept in her father's sea chest in the loft by her bed. In the midst of all the dirt, stench, and disorder, she had an instinct, well-nigh a passion, for tidiness. In another setting she might have borne herself with the

greatest lady in the land. She was great-hearted
and could never refuse a strong fisherman half-
crazed with lonely passion. When the women
talked to her and said: "A little of dat's all right
maybe when you'se young, but if you keeps on
you'se'll never git a man," she used to reply,
"We was made for de good of mens, an' mens is
going to have me." If Uriah and his wife, she
thought, cared so much for morals, why had they
put her and Leah Levy to sleep in the loft with
the sharesmen?

Sure enough, she never got a man, but she bore
three daughters that grew into stout lasses,
knowing no more than Fanny who were their
fathers. In after years Gershom used to say,
"I t'ink de pretty one wid de yaller hair mus' be
mine, but de dark ugly one favours Noble
Morash." Fanny saved her pennies and looked
after herself, and when she was too old to work
bought a little white cottage in Liscomb. When
she was very old and felt herself at the point of
death, she sent for her three daughters, but they
refused to come. They had all married and were
ashamed of their mother. One morning the
neighbours found her dead on her clean-valanced
couch, even in death smiling bravely upon a
world that had taken her all and paid nothing
in return.

But that is going far ahead of this story, for the Fanny who bickered with Gershom Born that night in the fish house was only a wild, gay girl of eighteen. She wore, like the others, oilskins spattered with herring blood, and a sou'wester to protect her yellow hair.

The stench, a strange mixture of odours from gurry tubs, ancient fish heads, lobster shells, wetted salt, and gore-drenched floor, almost intolerable to a stranger, was hardly noticed by these tough Rockbounders. Smells, noxious or pleasant, are like everything else relative—there is a fine nuance from a delicate perfume to an ugly stench—and matters of habit and custom. Indeed, the crafty old king, unconscious of the noisome odours, was thinking, as his knife flashed in and out and his facile thumb gouged the bellies of herrings:

"De rent's comin' due dis quarter on my house in Liscomb. Dat'll make more money to go in de bank. What's dat fool woman mean by wantin' a backhouse off de kitchen? She mus' be crazy! Does she want to stink up de whole place? Dey don't need no backhouse, anyhow. Why can't dey go on de beach like us?"

Casper, at the salting table, a great-shouldered giant like Joseph, kept seizing a split herring in each hand and pushing them together through the salt pile till their bellies were crammed with salt. Then he laid the fish in piles, and when the piles were about to topple, he grabbed the salt-stuffed herrings and packed them in a puncheon.

"Quick, Dave, my boy, more salt," he cried, wishing to show his authority. "Quick now, look alive; we ain't got all night."

Casper was the oldest of the Jung boys, but Joseph was the natural leader, a driver, the joy of his father, though for some strange reason Uriah loved Martin, the youngest boy, best of all. David, at Casper's call, stuck his knife in a strip of studding, darted for the salt bin, and emerged in a moment with a bushel basket heaped with salt, which he carried swiftly across the room and dumped on the salting table. Then he was back at his place in a flash, splitting, flashing his knife in and out, gouging out entrails with thumb and fingers, his back and shoulders well-nigh numb with fatigue. No one gibbed more herring than David that night. He would work till he dropped dead, he resolved, before a Rockbound Jung should see he was tired.

Uriah did not like Casper for a number of reasons. In the first place, Casper had never married, while Joseph and Martin had buxom wives both present splitting fish, who had borne them several children. Moreover, Casper argued with the king, and worse than that, he had lost money for him. Ten years earlier Casper had had one grand adventure: he had gone West with the harvesters. Uriah perhaps resented the fact that Casper had dared to leave his kingdom, or dared to prefer any other place to Rockbound, more than the loss of his money. In the West, some crafty real estate man had shown the grasping Casper how to treble his money quickly. It was such a sure thing that Casper had written to Uriah to send him a thousand dollars, meaning to pay the old man well and keep a snug commission for himself. Then land went flat, Casper lost everything, and in a year or two straggled home by hard stages. Before his departure, he had kept the money box, but on his return he had found Joseph ensconced as banker. In his heart he feared and hated the sea and dreaded rough foggy mornings near the Rock; he was a farmer by instinct, happiest when he drove his slow yoke of oxen afield to bring in the hay, or to haul a load of sea dung from the beaches. In spite of Uriah's jibes, his boat was always the last off the launch of a morning, and the first in, if a wind breezed up or fog shut out the islands. He could read and write and knew more of the outside world than any man on Rockbound. By nature, however, he was envious and argumentative, and in recent years had developed, through reading the Old Testament, a curious antireligious tendency that angered Uriah, whose heart was set on acquiring all the money he could on earth, and insuring a crown of glory in heaven. As Casper stood under the yellow glow of his swinging lantern, his hands flying to and fro as he pushed salt into the bellies of herrings, he was thinking:

"If I had e'er a wife and kids, I wouldn't have dat Ole Testament round de house. It's full o' tales o' concubines and kept women and old whorin' stories. Why, if e'er a child o' mine brung home a book wid stories like dat in it, I'd burn de book and whip de child."

Strangely enough, Uriah, as if conscious of Casper's thought, stood off on a theological tack. He often got the boys stirred up over a religious discussion toward eleven of a heavy evening.

"Ain't Egypt to de east'ard o' de Promised Land, Casper?"

"Dat it is, Fader, from de maps in de books," replied Casper readily but inaccurately, wondering what his father was driving at. Casper did not know that Uriah's wife had been reading to

him the night before of the captivity of the
Children of Israel.

"I t'ought so."

"Why you t'ought so, Fader?"

"'Cause I does," said Uriah, wishing to pro-
long the mystery and get full credit for having
thought out this particular bit of exegesis.
"'Cause I does, from meditatin' on de captivity
o' de Children o' Israel."

"An' what might ye o' bin t'inkin', an' what's
it got to do wid Egypt bein' to be east'ard o' de
Promised Land?"

"Well, don't de good Book say de Children
o' Israel went *down* into Egypt, an' don't we say
go *down to de east'ard* to Marmot and *up to de
west'ard* to Liscomb?"

"Dat up an' down don't mean nuttin',"
muttered Casper.

"It do, it do," shrilled Uriah.

"De folks on de Outposts, dey says *up* to de
east'ard and *down* to de west'ard. Don't dey,
Gershom?"

Gershom, deep in an undertoned amorous
conversation with Fanny and unaware of the
general drift of the argument, bellowed in his
booming voice:

"Us Outposters says *down* to de bottom o' de
sea."

Then he laughed his great laugh to think how cleverly he had avoided partisanship, for he liked neither Uriah nor Casper, and went on telling Fanny one of his adventures at Jennie Run-over's.

"De Outposters is wrong about eberyt'ing," shouted Uriah. "Dey don't know how to work. Why, me an' my brudder Simeon, when we was young mens . . ." and then, suddenly recalling that the argument was theological, reverted to his *down-east* theory, "Us here on Rockbound says *down to de east'ard*, jus' like de good Book says."

"Dat *up* an' *down's* child's talk," retorted Casper stubbornly.

Noble Morash, the gaunt, iron-gray sharesman, stood erect, split his fish viciously, and looked about him with scorn and hatred. His heart was black with hate that night. He hated Gershom with his gay boisterous laugh and booming voice because he was monopolizing Fanny, and because Gershom was Fanny's favourite. Too seldom he himself got Fanny's favours. He hated the hoary Uriah, who goaded him to work without end, Joseph, spit of his father, and the apple-faced Casper who gumbled at the salting table. He despised the women because they made him a matter of jest. He hated David Jung, the new sharesman, because he was Uriah's kinsman, and because in the boat that day he had dared to laugh when the oar bobbed out and caught him between the eyes. "I'll take it out on dat young bugger," he thought viciously. Both his eyes were blackened, his nose swollen to twice its normal size, and his evil temper was not sweetened by the fact that Ruth nudged Tamar and giggled whenever she glanced his way.

David, in obedience to a swift-flung order, stepped out into the darkness to fetch buckets of water to replenish Joseph's washing tubs. Noble Morash slipped out after him, barged against him in the darkness, and upset him and his buckets over a tub of rotten gurry. David groaned with pain and anger as the edge of the tub caught him in the ribs, but by the time he had picked himself up and found a stick, Noble Morash was back at his splitting table gibbing herring, with a gleam of sardonic pleasure in his sinister eyes. David dared not start a fight in the fish house, so he filled his buckets with water, carried them in, and emptied them in the washing tubs with never a word. But he thought, "I'll bide my time, Noble Morash. Ye'll pay for that push. I can't lick ye yet, but wait till I gits feed up an' set."

A few mornings later, when Noble Morash pushed off his boat in the dark and tried to hoist his sail, the halliards kept slipping through his hands, and when day broke he found they had been greased from end to end with the rottenest fish gurry, as his nostrils had made him suspect on the first encounter. But it was not until a year and a half later that David met his mortal foe, one twilight, at the head of the launch, and engaged in deadly combat to pay off a long score of cumulative insults. Had the ubiquitous Uriah not caught sight of them as they rolled in a death grapple under the logs of the launch, he would have been short a sharesman on Rockbound, and that probably a gaunt and black one.

Snip, snip went the fishing knives, splash fell the flung entrails into the tubs, the swaying lanterns flickered wearily, eyes drooped and backs sagged. It was midnight, though no one dared look at watch or clock, and still huge piles of herring gleamed on the floor. Even now some were soft and had to be flung aside. Uriah would not work on the Lord's Day if anyone told him the Lord's Day was come. There must be no talk of time.

"Speak us a piece, Gershom, speak us one ye made yur own self," cried Joseph.

This was long before Gershom had made the ballad on Joseph in which he referred to him as mud-rat Joe; that was the outcome of a quarrel

not yet born. Gershom was a great teller of tales
and a famous maker of ballads. Nothing loath,
he began now in his great voice to speak one he
had made against Israel Slaughenwhite, at the
instigation of his cousin Dennis Born, who had
been publicly insulted by Israel. Gershom
boasted that this ballad had become so popular
with the Outposters that it had driven Israel
off the island.

"O 'Lord above!' poor Israel cried,
As he humbly knelt at Sophie's side,
'O Lord! look down and hear my prayers,
And cut off Gabe and all his heirs;
And save the land old Jake has given
To Tim and me and Liza Jim.'
Again he prayed to His Majesty,
'Oh, keep me safe on life's rough sea,
And keep my loving Sophie pure,
And guard her from the tempter's lure.'
But a pair of horns for a marriage dot,
Was the only answer Israel got.
Again he prayed, he prayed in vain,
He prayed like one who prays for rain,
He prayed and prayed till his knees were sore,
He prayed till he vowed he'd pray no more.
He vowed that he no more would pray,
Till Gabe and Jake was took away,

And the land give back to him and Tim,
And a deed of the house to Liza Jim.
And then he'd pray with all his might,
To the Lord who doeth all things right,
But until his heavenly prayer was heard,
In prayer no more he'd utter a word."

Uriah shook his head gravely, but enjoyed the slander just the same.

"It's a gif', it's a gif'," said the old king, his open left eye twinkling. "Now, Gershom boy, if ye could only gib fish as good as ye kin make verses, ye'd be a great sharesman."

Gershom laughed his great laugh. "I keeps my end up. I don't try to pull an' haul my heart out like dat new David boy. I enjoys life, I does," and he winked amorously at Fanny.

David listened to the ballad open mouthed. He knew all about the Slaughenwhites and their fight with Dennis Born and had heard the ballad chanted by the fishermen, but it became a new thing in the mouth of the maker. It was astonishing to him that anyone should have such learning and be able to string words together so that they bobbed in time like the net corks on a gentle sea. Young Gershom got his brains and gift from his father, old Gershom Born, philosopher, wise man, and keeper of the Barren Island Light.

"Young Gershom'll be a mighty man an' a wise one, too," thought David. "I'se'll stick close to him." He remembered now that the folks on the Outposts said of old Gershom, "He's nigh crazy, but wise. He sits out on de cliffs an' talks to de sea an' de moonlight." Wise man, yes, he was! To him he owed his foothold on Rockbound.

It was long after midnight, yet no one spoke of time. Joseph and Noble Morash still lugged in barrows of herring, and dumped them in slithering piles. Uriah told the story of the footless nigger that haunted the field below Rockbound Light, of the unseen force that had three times pushed him off the path into the tall timothy, and when these tales failed to hold their interest, tried to involve them in an argument about the advantages of Rockbound as compared with the main. But no one responded; even the blond Viking, Gershom Born, flagged. Joseph still ran from salt bin to washing tubs, but he was silent as he ran.

Then, in the midst of all this disorder and weariness of work without end, when the flickering lanterns cast but a sickly light on the oilskin-clad, blood-bespattered figures bent with fatigue and glittered feebly on knives that flashed in and out and on the hateful piles of fish that seemed never to diminish, in the midst of all the dirt and confusion and stench, with an accompaniment of the northeast night wind that hummed about the eaves and the rhythmic mutter of the surf that alone was tireless, Fanny, the potato girl, despised and rejected by the women of Rockbound, Fanny, who slept in the loft with the sharesmen and who had the morals of the birds, lifted up her voice and sang in a sweet, clear treble:

"'There's a land that is fairer than day,
And by faith we can see it afar;
For the Father waits over the way
To prepare us a dwelling place there.'"

One by one the tired islanders joined in:
"In the sweet," sang Fanny.
"In the sweet," boomed Gershom Born's great bass.
"By and by," rang alto and soprano.
"By and by," answered bass and tenor.
"We shall meet on that beautiful shore."
All were in accord now and forgetting their weariness, except Noble Morash, who scowled darkly about, and Casper, who thought, "I don't want to meet on no *beautiful shore.*" Like John on the isle of Patmos, he sighed for a place where there should be no sea.
David was too shy to sing at first, though he

knew both tune and words of the familiar hymn, but bending his head to escape observation he made the words with his lips and swayed his head in time with the others. But when Fanny came to:

> "'To our bountiful Father above,
> We will render a tribute of praise,
> For the glorious gift of His love,
> And the blessings that hallow our days'"—

David, with an eye upon Ruth and Tamar, who might laugh at him, joined in more boldly. As he sang he felt rested and refreshed. Through to the end they carried the hymn, and then repeated it over and over.

Some time after two, Uriah threw down his splitting knife. "Put de res' in pickle. It mus' be gettin' on fur midnight; me nor my fader before me ne'er worked on de Lord's Day, an' I won't begin now. Put de res' in pickle an' all hands to bed, says I."

Off they staggered, except David, who was ordered to remain and help the tireless Joseph scoop heaps of unsplit herring into pickle tubs. That last labour over, he, too, staggered along the pathway to his house, where he threw himself on the kitchen couch and pulled sacking over head and feet. For a moment, as he lay there, he regretted that he had left the Outposts, a place of poverty but comparative ease, for this hell of driving work; in the next moment he was in a sleep like death.

CHAPTER IV

Eterne God, that thurgh thy purveiance,
Ledest the world by certein governaunce,
In ydel, as men seyn, ye nothyng make;
But, Lord, thise grisly, feendly, rokkes blake,
That semen rather a foul confusioun
Of werk than any fair creacioun
Of swich a parfit wys God, and a stable,—
Why have ye wroght this werk unreasonable?

CANTERBURY TALES.

HE level sun streaming through the eastern window shone on David's face, and the strange warmth woke him with a sudden start. He was on his feet in a second; it was broad daylight; his heart was in his boots, the Jung boats were long since near the Rock. Then he remembered that it was Sunday and sat down with a smile and a sigh of relief. "T'ank de Lord fur Sundays," he muttered. He bestirred himself and built up the fire to make some tea, but when

66

Anapest saw his smoke she came to her kitchen
door and called: "Come ober, come ober, David."

"You'll be needin' some real food arter a day
an' night like dat," and she sat him down to a
mountainous island of oatmeal porridge in a sea
of creamy milk. Anapest knew that Uriah was
trying to break with labour this boy who of necessity fed himself badly, and she was moved to
supply David with good food once in a while,
not only because of the goodness of her heart,
but because she wished to circumvent the old
tyrant.

The Kraus boys, who had had no catch of
herring, lounged sullenly about the kitchen in
their clean underclothes.

"How come Joe Jung come down from de
eastern end yesterday?" queried Christian Kraus.

"He were stakin' out his bull, I guess," answered David.

"An' de bull's staked on Cow Pasture Hill; I
seed him dere last evenin'. How come he runned
from de eastern end wid de news o' herrin'?"

"I don't keep no count o' Joseph's movements," said David, squirming uneasily. He
made up his mind that the Krauses would not
pump him.

"It's God damn queer, dat is," said Nicholas.
Joseph's ruse had not yet penetrated their

thick heads, though David felt they were peril-
ously near a solution, and he resolved to eat all
he could before the Kraus boys put him out. The
porridge bowl pushed aside, he attacked a high
pile of mellow toast and washed down Anapest's
scrambled eggs with three mugs of hot coffee.

He rose from the table a new man, and with a
humble, "T'ank ye, Aunt Anapest, you'se de
only frien' I got," went out quickly before the
Kraus boys could quiz him further. He recrossed
the fields, entered his own house, lay down again,
and slept intermittently till four in the afternoon,
when he yawned, stretched, yawned again, and
then sat up really rested and refreshed, with the
wonderful resilience of youth.

He stripped, washed himself in his tin basin,
and wished for clean Sunday clothes such as
other men put on. He had none and had to take
it out in wishing. Some day, he resolved, he would
acquire everything the others had and a great
deal besides. He was in good heart after his long
sleep and Anapest's food, and felt he could endure any task Uriah might put upon him.

He pulled on ragged trousers and frayed shirt
and strolled out in the warm afternoon air to
walk around the back of the island. He crossed
the low bar, climbed the cliff, and on the cliff's
edge lay down on the thick matting of crowberry

vines, through which spikes of cranberries pushed
their pink petals. From this vantage point, he
could look southward to the rim of the sea and
survey the panorama of broad bay, scattered
islands, and the dim headlands of the main.
Though the ground swell smashed in at the cliff's
foot, the sea was comparatively calm, and he saw
that the herrings were still in the coves, for in
the deeper water he marked the swirl and splash
of albacore that had followed the fish. That
meant that to-morrow would be another day of
toil. Well, let it come; at any rate, they would
do no line fishing, but shoot the seine soon after
sunrise and get through most of their gibbing by
late afternoon or early evening.

From his rocky height he looked in leisurely
fashion over the rich kingdom of Rockbound,
where, from land loaded with sea dung and fish
entrails, hay, potatoes, strawberries, and vegetables of all kinds grew in profusion. The island,
elliptical in shape, was but a mile long and perhaps a half mile wide in its widest part, and con-
sisted of two rounded spruce-clad knolls, at
eastern and western ends, with a cleft between
them. In the northern end of this cleft or shallow
valley stood the fish houses and dwellings of
Jungs and Krauses. Throughout the valley,
from sea to sea, were fields of rank timothy and

rich garden plots of growing potatoes and cabbages. Two of the hills on the western end had
been cleared and turned into hayfields, and
named respectively Crook's Hill and Wilson's
Hill, after two old pioneers who had broken their
hearts in the clearing, and gone back to the mainland bent old men defeated by cold, hardship,
and the savage sea. In rough weather, when
winter seas broke on the southern bar, spray and
blown spume flew clear across the valley to the
northern shore. Always the sea snarled and
gnawed at the bar.

"Some day," thought David, as he lay on the
cliff's brink, "she'll wash t'rough, an' den dere'll
be two little islands in place o' one, an' some
day maybe she'll wash de whole t'ing away, an'
de chart'll be marked t'ree fadom, dangerous fur
mariners." Dimly he grappled for a moment with
nature's fierce and contemporary desire to create
and destroy.

Far off to the eastward he could see the dark
looming cliffs of Metatogan, part of the main,
to the north the masses of Big and Little Outpost
—Big Outpost shaped like a half-submerged
whale—and the blue ship channel between them
on which the afternoon sun glittered. By straining his eyes he could even catch, through the gap
of the Outposts, a dim flitting glimpse of Friendly

Island Light. To the westward were stretched
out for him Big and Little Duck, Flat Island, the
Raggeds, and very dimly Lubeck Island, marked
by its pillar of white lighthouse. To the southward was the flat sea, the only speck upon it
Barren Island, where old Gershom Born lived
alone and kept the light. It was the last outpost
and, like Rockbound, a mass of upheaved,
twisted rock over which was spread a thin matting of turf and grass.

David wondered as he lay there what had made
all these islands—there were some three hundred
of them scattered about the bay—and why and
how they had been made. Certainly they were
not perfectly made for fishing stands, since in
the sea between them were many treacherous
shoals; even on this calm day the Bull snorted
to the eastward, the Grampus showed a bone
in its teeth, and the Rock sent up from time to
time a curtain of white spray. Only last September, Ed Swim and Morehouse Young had run
their boat over the Grampus in a fog, swamped
her, and lost their lives. He had heard of the
omnipotent God who created the world and
punished those who disobeyed His laws. Why
had he not made the world a perfect, happy
place? he wondered. For it was not perfect, and
he could not get the idea out of his head that

dreaded shoals had once been green islands, and
that these islands now around him would one day
be ugly reefs, cutting the top off the breakers.

He was vaguely conscious of a force beating
beneath him, perhaps the rhythmic impulse of
the sea at the cliff's foot, and of the unending
restlessness of the sea. It seemed to him that God
and the devil were in a gigantic struggle, the one
building up islands and continents for men to
live on, the other personified by the sea, growling,
roaring, and gnawing away what God had made.
He had heard the old men tell how much the
sea had encroached on the islands in their life-
times. Yes, the devil was in the sea destroying
islands and mainland. Sometimes he seemed
asleep on a sunny, windless day, but you had to
watch him, for he sprang at you treacherously
out of a fog bank, or in a dead calm sent a sudden
roller against you to swamp your boat, low down
with fish. And the devil seemed stronger than
God! How could that be? He must ask old Gershom Born.

Were the islands made, he wondered, when
the sea washed away soft parts of the main, or
had they popped up suddenly from the sea floor
expelled by some earth force? Certainly all the
twisted cliffs around him that now stood slanting
and on end looked as if they had been once laid

down in flat layers. If the rocks had popped up from the sea floor, how had trees and flowers and grass got on the islands? Perhaps the sea wind had blown some fine sand dust into a rock crevice, and into this a sea bird had by accident dropped a seed, or perhaps a high wind had blown seeds from the main. He had often seen thistle-down twirling its light parachute far out at sea. Then a plant had grown and spread its seeds and rooted, and more plants had grown, and fine sand had tangled in their roots. But what a long time it must have taken to make even as much soil as there was on Rockbound! Ages and ages! Jennie Run-over, when maudlin with drink, had sometimes talked to him of God, the great lover of men. Why, he wondered, if men were His children and He truly loved them, had He made things so rough and hard? Why had He made sharks, dogfish and albacore, which played havoc with the nets, and in one night sometimes destroyed more than a man could earn in a month? Why didn't he stop that treacherous devil in the sea that sent stout boats to the bottom and forever ate up the land He had made? On the Outposts were many widows whose little children ran wild, ill-clad, and half fed. Why was the God-fearing Uriah so grasping, and why did the Rockbound Jungs kill themselves with labour to get money when they had plenty already? He knew why he wanted money: to repair and paint his house, to get himself some clothes and gear, to buy himself a fast, stout boat, every timber his very own—Ezra Goudy, the best builder in all the islands, should make her—to buy some day a fiddle and learn to play jigs on it like Cutter Westhaver, and above all to escape slavery. For he realized that he had always been a slave, and that he was still a slave, driven to and fro at every man's beck and call. Wait till he got some money! Perhaps he could some day build his own launch and fish from his own fish house.

So he lay on the matting of soft crowberry and dreamed and rested, thanking the good God for the Sabbath, till the sun's disk touched the rim of the Ragged Island cliffs and twilight came softly, and the light on Barren Island began to wink. Old Gershom Born had trimmed and lighted his lamp, and it repeated over and over: five seconds flash, five seconds occult, five seconds flash, five seconds occult, twenty-one seconds flash, nineteen seconds occult, saying to mariners on the high seas: "I am Barren Island Light. I warn you from the Rock, the Grampus, and the Bull. Keep well to the eastward of me if you want to make Minden by the inside passage, or well to the westward of me if you want the ship's channel between the Outposts to Duren Bay. After you leave me, you will pick up the fixed lights on Rockbound and Friendly that will guide you to safety."

It seemed to David that the light was marking off time; a complete revolution meant a minute. "There's another minute gone," he thought, "and how am I changed, or how am I better off than I was a minute ago? I am one minute nearer to being dead, and I am still Uriah's sharesman." Time never stood still, but flowed by him like the tide through sou'west gutter. Only the tide ebbed and flowed, while time had always flowed from somewhere in one direction, and its flood made into a limitless future. It was like space, bigger than the sea, stretching out in all directions without limits. Could the world be round? The coloured man on the banker, who taught him to steer, had told him so. But how could water stick to a round ball, and why didn't it drop off the under side? Certainly it looked flat enough, though when he thought a while he remembered that on clear days he had seen the upper spars of vessels that were still hull down. Yes, there must be some curve even to the surface of the sea.

When the stars peeped out, David lay on his back and looked on them. He had lived so much alone that he had learned to look and wonder. He marvelled at their multitude as the night grew darker, and saw that some twinkled and some shone copper red. Stars were useful things to steer a vessel by: you could hold one star on the rigging and keep her on her course, and without north star and dipper fishermen would fare badly. God must have stuck them in the sky, but surely there wasn't any need for so many stars to light the earth, especially those sprinkled like sifted flour across the middle belt of the heavens.

Day birds that had wheeled round his height— he knew them all from the great gannet to the flitting checkerback—now settled on rock or wave and their places were taken by carey and nighthawk, island birds of the darkness. After a while he stirred, stretched himself, and started homeward, rested, refreshed, and braced for the morrow's work.

The herring stayed on the shore for three weeks. Never had the Rockbounders made such a catch; every puncheon in the fish house was heaped up, and Uriah insisted on filling as well two old whalers and a dory that, when soaked up for a day in the sea, were still tight enough to hold pickle. In the last ten days of the herrings' stay, the old king ruled that the hay must be got. Uriah cut fifty tons in the rich valley and upland fields, which he loaded down in October with fish heads, entrails, and rotted kelp. Every morning of those last ten days Joseph, Martin, young Gershom, and David shot the seine and encircled a school of herring, while Casper and Noble Morash drove ringing scythes into the tall, overripe timothy, already becoming a little woody in the stem. By noon, when the fishermen were in with deep-laden boats, the farmers had made work enough for them. The women turned the hay and raked it up in windrows; the men gibbed fish till four in the afternoon and then rushed to the fields to haul in five or six great oxloads of hay, cut the day before. Time was precious, for the fog bank usually rolled in before seven. Everyone drove and hustled everyone else; everything was done in a rush. In a rush the hay was pitched on the carts, in a rush it was pitched off and stowed in the mows. Uriah, the general, was everywhere. Hay must go in, come sunshine or fog, though it steamed and heated in the mows, for it was within the range of possibility that a summer month might go by on Rockbound without a drying sun. Old Gershom Born used to say that he had seen Uriah and his sons making hay in their oilskins. One terrible afternoon, after a heavy catch of herring, they hauled in seven loads on the creaking wains and stowed them in the old man's barn. After a hasty snack of supper that night, men and women were back in the fish house, gibbing furiously in the swaying light of the dim lanterns.

David, almost broken with toil, prayed to the Lord who sent the Sabbath and gave the guiding stars that the herring fishing might stop so that he might take the *Phœbe* on the banks and again be his own master. When the hay was almost garnered, his prayer was answered: a summer storm came with big rollers, and the herring were driven off into deep water. Even the giant sons of Uriah heaved sighs of relief, but Uriah, who could not bear the thought of letting anything escape him, grumbled at their lack of industry, though every puncheon, dory, and spare boat was piled high with salted fish. Had all the fish in the sea been laid on the floor of his fish house, he would have been still unsatisfied, but would have set about praying the Lord to create more so that his sons might catch them.

CHAPTER V

For, al-so siker as In principio
Mulier est hominis confusio,—
Madame, the sentence of this Latyn is,
"Woman is mannes joye, and al his blis."

CANTERBURY TALES.

WHEN David was twenty-four and
had been six years on Rockbound,
he was still Uriah's sharesman.
Things had changed but little.
Age had not withered Uriah, who
was as active and driving as ever. True, his legs
had weakened a little each year, and bowed a
little further outward at the knees, but when he
sat on his box to slit open herring or mackerel,
his hands flew as fast as ever. Every night, as the
sun touched the western horizon, he trudged,
come sunshine, fog, or snow, to light the fixed
light on the cliffs of Rockbound, and he was
never happier than when he sat down to mend
net or seine, torn and tangled by dogfish or

albacore. He kept all the gear in repair for the
boys. He was too old to go fishing. "De boat
rutches my legs too much," he used to say. Every
year his bank account had grown, and as he
moved the livelong day from one labour to another he derived enormous pleasure from medi-
tating upon his wealth. The tenant in Liscomb
had given him endless trouble, but at last, to
quiet her clacking tongue and stop her letters.
he had allowed her a toilet off the kitchen.

Joseph still ran from barrow to barrow and
aided and abetted his father in hustling the
sharesmen, and Casper still grumbled and
grunted anticlerical argument at the salting
table. Fanny, the potato girl, as pretty as ever,
still whistled blithely over her cabbages and
potatoes, still raised the hymns in the fish house
of a heavy evening, and still served the needs of
the great sharesmen in the loft. Even David had
plucked up courage to invite her to walk with
him on the back of the island, where they reclined
on the crowberry vines and in the shelter of a
thick screen of spruces watched old Gershom
Born's light blink out the hours.

Old Simeon was dead at last, but he had
nodded his foolish head and gibbed in the fish
house on the very day of his death. Noble Morash,
too, the gaunt black sharesman, David's enemy,

was gone. Uriah had sent him to the Sand Cove to fetch dory loads of rockweed and kelp, which the islanders call sea dung. Having met with reproof from the old king for the smallness of a previous load, he had forked on to this last load he was to carry three forkfuls too much. A breaking wave swamped him as he rounded West Head; his dory turned over and threw him into the sea. He could not swim, as is the case with most of the islanders, and had clawed with numbed fingers at the smooth bottom of the upturned dory, till the icy water chilled him to the bone. He was lying stretched out on the sea floor, and curious fish were sniffing at him and peering into his staring eyes long before the boats that set out from the launch could reach him.

Young Gershom was as jocose, as noisy, and as full of talk as ever. He was merely biding his time with Uriah on Rockbound till he could inherit Barren Island Light from old Gershom. He had become David's inseparable friend and had taught the boy all the wickedness he knew. Gershom, an epicurean by nature, believed in wine and love as a relief from labour; his wine being the black rum smuggled in by St. Pierre runners, his love, affairs with any stout fisher lasses he could pick up on the islands. "Boy," he used to say to David as they fished near each other on the banks, "I'm savin' up my money, an' in October I'se goin' to de main to have two weeks of sinful pleasure." As he was courageous, strong as a lion, generous with his friends, and daringly rude to his enemies, a famous wit and story-teller, a great lover and drinker, he was welcome everywhere.

Though it was true that David was still a sharesman, he had advanced, for all that. Joseph had paid him a monthly share, though it was not his true monthly share, as David right well knew. He owned a boat, a stout fast clipper equipped with a gasoline engine. Uriah had at first derided the engine, things that he and his brother Simeon had never had, but gradually all the Jung boys had come to them; now even at the head of the launch was a stationary engine, with drum and wire cable for hauling out the boats. The slow-footed oxen had been superseded for that function, though they still dragged the plough, sagged in the great loads of hay, hauled the tubs of gurry to the autumn fields, and twitched logs in winter. David had a Sunday suit, four changes of woollen underwear, overalls, rubber boots, oilskins, sou'westers, cotton gloves, and nippers. His house he had painted, reshingled, and repaired throughout; even the upstairs rooms were finished and plastered. He owned

four fleets of herring nets now, and a half-dozen
tubs of trawl, a long-barrelled duck gun—he was
the best shot on the island, with Gershom a close
second—and last of all he had paid Selmar
Strum, the cunning workman of Hermann's
Island, twenty-five dollars to make him a fiddle.

The bottom of maple was made of a piece of
hand-hewn beam that Great-grandfather Strum
had put into his barn somewhere about 1760,
soon after the old folks had come across the seas
from Oldenburg; the top was of old, well-seasoned,
wide-grained spruce, the tailpiece and string-
board a cunningly inlaid strip of swordfish spike,
while the scroll was carved in the shape of a
leaping pollock. David loved to handle it and
to stroke the curves of the smooth, satiny wood;
already he had learned to play a few tunes on it.

In his six years on the island his friendship
for Gershom had steadily grown. Now he went
everywhere with the blue-eyed giant, who,
though ten years older than he, was a dashing
and lively companion. They pushed their boats
off the launch at the same moment and fished
on the same bank; sometimes Gershom was late
of a morning, and if David, urged on by Uriah's
taunts and jibes, was obliged to push off first,
he jogged his boat and waited for Gershom to the
southward of the Grampus. At lunch time on the

bank, they lashed their boats together and laughed and talked as they ate their bread and cakes. In this piece of comradeship, however, they were often interrupted, for David was such a lucky fisherman and had established such a reputation for uncanny knowledge of the whereabouts of cod that he had become the fish pilot for the fleet, and when the flash of fish over his gunwale was seen in far-off boats, Jungs and Krauses, aye, and fishermen from the other islands, circled his selected bank.

In late October of each year, after the last school of mackerel had gone south, the cod dried and the herring barrelled and sold, Uriah, in accordance with the fisherman's custom, had perforce to grant David and Gershom a fortnight's holiday. This they always spent with the Boutiliers, distant cousins of Gershom's, at Miscou, on St. Michael's Bay. Boutilier, himself a huge man, was a great lover of dancing, fighting, and drinking, and a fit companion for the sanguine Gershom and his disciple. Nearly every night they drove long distances to some country hall where a dance was in progress, kissed the pretty girls in dark corners, got very drunk, and fought with the local bucks.

At one such dance, where red-faced fishermen twirled their broad-hipped partners, David, flushed and arrogant with rum, insisted on taking the violin from the local fiddler and playing Outpost jigs and some strange airs he had learned from the sea. He swayed the dancers first to one mood and then to another, and won such applause that the established fiddler, Pierre Comeau, a strong man who could do more than fiddle, for he was a blacksmith by trade, challenged him to fight on the grass outside. A couple of lanterns were fetched, and out flocked men and women to see the contest. David fared none too well and carried home two blackened eyes, for Pierre Comeau was nearly sober and he half drunk; the fishermen stopped the fight after a few rounds, lest the artists should hurt their hands and thus make an end of the dancing. To eat heartily at leisure, to be drunk and go to a dance every night, to have numerous fist fights, to lie in bed late of a morning, seemed to Gershom and David the substance of an ideal holiday after the fever of work on Rockbound. Here, on the main with the Boutiliers, there was no hypocrisy of virtuous pretence, no one thought much about money or strove for stars in some far-off crown.

When they laboured on the island, Gershom and David always spent Sundays together. Sometimes they explored the Raggeds to pick

up some lobsters or scallops out of season, sometimes they took boat, visited the Outposts and
hung about Jennie Run-over's place. Jennie,
the buxom one, was just as hearty as when she
had picked up the gaffer David staring with
homesick eyes toward Rockbound. There they
learned all the local news and gossip of the islands,
for Jennie's place was a kind of clearing house
for such stuff, and met the Outpost girls, who
liked to slake their thirst on Jennie's foaming
black beer.

David had become Gershom's apt pupil; already Molly Biddle of Big Outpost attributed a
love child to him, and though David was none
too sure of the parentage, he ungrudgingly paid
her a monthly dole. Gershom, in a playful mood,
used to gird at him with, "Dat kid's de livin'
image o' you, Dave, but how come de red hair?"
But now, as well, he had a serious affair on his
hands: he was paying court to Leah Levy, old
Nathan Levy's daughter. Nathan Levy was
reputed to have eight thousand dollars in the
bank, and owned two hundred acres of good land
on Little Outpost. Most of his money would go
to Leah, as his boys were all married and established. With the reputation of being the best
fisherman in the bay, David was an acceptable
suitor for any man's daughter. His peccadilloes

in Miscou and the Outposts counted as naught against him with the islanders. Leah was comely, with her black hair, oval face, and olive complexion, and while David was not deeply in love with her, he figured that she would make a good wife and a means of pulling himself up in the world. She attracted him more than other island girls, for while she repulsed his advances she looked on him with favour and would not apparently disapprove an offer of marriage. However, something unexpected happened, which upset all of David's calculations.

Tamar Jung, Uriah's daughter, a young woman in her twenties, began to cast eyes upon David and to follow him about. For years he had seen her in field and fish house, but she had never attracted him, because she had Joseph's big nose and aggressive jaw. She was red-faced, strong, and healthy, and could take one end of a loaded fish barrow from boat to fish house when a man was missing, or pitch on hay over the high racks as fast as anyone on the island. Wherever he went in the fish house or loft she was at his heels, once she followed him into the salt bin and rubbed against him like a playful kitten. The wily Gershom, skilled in the ways of women, observed all this and one day said to David: "Dat Tamar's stuck on you, boy; don't miss a chance like dat."

So David walked with Tamar in the woods of
summer nights. She wanted him badly for a husband, but, in lieu of that, she would take him for a
lover. David was not in the least in love with
her; he preferred Leah Levy's dark face and soft
voice. Still, Tamar was affectionate in a rough
way and a great worker; she would inherit some
of Uriah's money and make a useful partner
for a fisherman. In fact, David was rather sick
of the sharesman's loft where he had slept for the
last two years, first because of his desire to be
always near young Gershom, and second because
there he was sure to be called by Uriah and get
his boat off among the first. Once he had over-
slept in his own house. Lately there had been
bedbugs in the loft, though to the credit of
Uriah's wife and the girls they did not last long
after their discovery, and Frank Richardson, the
new sharesman, befouled the air with his obscene
noises. Yes, David was pretty sick of the sharesman's loft and half wanted a wife, to complete
the house he had painted and repaired. Still, he
had no intent of marrying Tamar or even Leah
Levy just now; he meant to keep himself free
for a few more years, save some money, and
indulge in his annual riot with Gershom and Jean
Boutilier in Miscou.

It was one night in early September, when they

were beginning to lay the split cod to dry on the ledgy rocks of Sou'west Cove, that Uriah said to David, "Come wid, I wants to talk wid you." In silence he led him to the middle of the timothy field, now rank with second growth, on Crook's Hill. There Uriah turned on David fiercely:

"What you mean ruinin' my gal?"

"I didn't know as how she were."

"Well, she is, an' what does ye mean?"

David said nothing.

"You'se come sneakin' out to dis island what me an' my fader made, an' now you goes an' knocks up Tamar. What does you mean?"

"I don't mean nuttin'; I didn't go fur to do it: it's only natural."

"Natural, is it! Well, you got to marry her now, an' here's one o' Nicolaus Kaulbach's boys bin a-wantin' her dis two year, him what owns a fish stand an' forty acres o' good ground on Little Outpost."

"Let Nick Kaulbach's boy have her, den."

"What foolishness you talk, he won't marry her now," screamed Uriah.

"I s'pose not; I s'pose he wouldn't like to have a woman carryin' anoder man's baby."

"You s'pose right. You got dat t'rough yur t'ick head, has ye? Now, listen to me, boy, you'se got to marry her."

"I don't want to marry no one. I'se'll pay fur de doctor an' de keep o' de kid."

"We don't have no bastard in de Jung family. De Krauses is full o' bastards, but dere ain't none from my gals," shouted Uriah in a voice that might be heard over half the island. "You got to marry her."

"I'se not makin' money 'nuff yet fur to keep a wife on."

"Ye'd make more if ye worked harder."

Then a wonderful idea flashed through David's brain.

"I tells you what," said he. "I'se tired o' bein' a sharesman. I bin sharesman now fur six year, an' I'se ketched more fish than air Joe, Martin, or Casper. I'se got to git on in de worl' same as you an' yer fader did afore ye. I'se a Jung an' de same blood as you. If ye takes me into de firm on an even divvy, I'se'll marry Tamar."

"What!" screamed Uriah, purple with rage at David's arrogance. "You come here a beggar an' now ye wants in my firm what me an' my fader made. You certainly got de gall."

"Take me in de firm if ye wants me to marry Tamar, or raise a Jung bastard," repeated David stubbornly.

"Dat I won't," shouted Uriah, "an' ye kin get

off dis island. Ye can't stay sharesman wid me."

"Maybe I won't stay sharesman wid you, but I won't git off dis island. Maybe ye don't know Anapest sold me a strip o' waterfront abreast her fish house. Dere I'se'll build me my own launch an' fish house an' hire my own sharesmen in time to come. Dere's many an able lad on de Outposts ready an' willin' to fish wid me, as ye right well knows."

Uriah gasped, and his empurpled face swelled as if he were about to suffer an apoplectic stroke. Why could this beggar, once a landless waif, always defy him? He had got the best of everyone else and imposed his will on them. He hated David with a deep, bitter hatred as he stood there, and would have given half his wealth to destroy him. To dispossess him, he had tried all his wiles: he had tried to break him when a boy by heavy and unwonted labour; he had even hired Martin to roll beach rocks along his hallway and to play ghost round his house at midnight, in the hope of scaring him away. All to no avail, and even a money loss, for Martin, on his last ghosting expedition, had got three buckshot in the calf of his leg that necessitated a secret visit to the doctor in Minden and an expenditure of ten dollars. How did this boy dare to defy him, king of Rockbound, and what could he do? Nicolaus Kaulbach would never let his boy marry Tamar now. He saw he could do nothing but give way and make the best of a sorry bargain.

"I'se'll t'ink it ober," said Uriah savagely.

"You t'ink it ober. I don't wish Tamar no harm; she's a good girl, but she ain't de woman fur me. You t'ink it ober; if ye wants Tamar married, ye takes me into de firm on an even divvy."

"I'se'll tell ye what I'se'll do right now," said Uriah.

"Let's hear ye den."

"I'se'll take ye into de firm on de line fish an' herrin', but ye'll go sharesman on de mackerel."

"Why on de mackerel?"

"'Cause ye ain't got no mackerel gear."

"I'se'll t'ink it ober."

"No, ye says right now. Dere ain't no time fur delays. If you'se goin' to marry Tamar it's got to be right off. Den we kin spread de word 'twere a seben mont's' child."

David thought for a dubious moment, chewing a straw of timothy.

"All right, I'se'll take yer lay: an equal divvy on herrin' an' line fish an' sharesman on de mackerel. How about lobsters, old man?"

"Sharesman on lobsters, too."

"No," said David, "lobsterin' hard, heavy, an' dangerous work. I won't go dat lay; I wants my own lobsters."

"Den keep yur own lobsters what ye ketches in yur own traps what ye make wid yur own hands. What kind o' man is ye, anyhow? First ye knocks up my gal, an' den, instead o' bein' sorry an' repentant, ye drives a hard bargain over it. Ain't ye ashamed?"

"I'se a man what stands up fur my rights an' tears away what I kin git from people like ye in de world. Didn't ye try fur to keep me off dis island an' part o' it mine by right?"

"De island's mine by right an' would 'a' bin, too, if ye an' Anapest hadn't come sneakin' back on it. Me an' my fader made dis island what it is, ain't it?"

"An' my grandfader, he made it, too."

"Well, it's no good arguin' wid a t'ickhead like you. Is it a bargain, does ye marry Tamar?"

"I does if I gits a divvy on all but de mackerel."

"It's a bargain," said Uriah.

The old man and the young man stood there in the twilight, looking straight into each other's eyes, each busied with his own thoughts. A bargain was a bargain, both knew, and though there was no written agreement, for neither could read or write, the contract was sure and binding.

Uriah, full of wiles, cunning, and double dealing before a bargain, would stick to anything he had directly affirmed. His life amid hardship and danger had made that part of the moral code essential. His morals were purely matters of utility, since he knew that nothing could be accomplished unless men held to their contracts. In the boy, Uriah caught a glimpse of the hard battles and conquests of his own youth, and felt with a twinge of regret that David was a better man than any of his sons. The old man's heart was in a fury because he had been beaten, but he concealed his rage. David turned over in his mind in that short moment what he could get out of the bargain. Joseph, the keeper of the money box, would, of course, still cheat him, but, at any rate, he would get twice as much as he had received as sharesman. Tamar had some learning, she could read, write, and figure, and could make a useful check on Joseph by keeping account of the catch from day to day.

Uriah fetched Mr. Snow the Baptist minister from Sanford, and David and Tamar were married without delay in Uriah's big kitchen. They stood in front of the cooking stove with a background of shining pots and pans. David did not feel right in his heart, and mumbled the responses, but Tamar spoke loud and clear, for she had won the man of her heart. None of the Jung brothers was present, but their wives and children, egged on by curiosity, were ranged around the walls on the kitchen chairs. It was a rather gloomy ceremony. Uriah, to uphold the honour of the Jung family, and to conceal the fact that it was a forced marriage, tried to assume a gay and playful attitude and told several stories of how he had courted his wife on Little Outpost. Even the supper and hot rum punch did not thaw the hearts of Martin's and Joseph's wives, who glowered reproachfully at bride and bridegroom. They had heard nothing but wrath and invective over this affair from their husbands, and they faithfully reflected their attitude. Soon after ten the wedding party broke up, and David took home to his house the woman he did not love.

But David soon found that he had made no bad bargain. Rockbound women study how to be of use to their husbands. They work, for there is no one to hire to do the work that somehow is naturally expected of them and which seems right and proper to themselves. They rear their children, tend their houses, milk cows, feed chickens, hoe the gardens, help with the hay, and when necessary give a hand in the fish house. It is no

uncommon sight to see a couple of babies sleeping
in an old sail on top of the fish puncheons as the
mothers split fish. But in addition to this work
they are always watching from the windows.
As they go from duty to duty, they peer from
kitchen window, from front-room window, from
upstairs windows for the boats. Trust them,
they know every boat, every patch upon the
brown sails, the peculiar chug of every engine,
the curve of each stem, the sheer, the strip of
colour beneath the gunwale. Each watches for
the return of her man. Far off they see his boat
coming from the Rock and know from its depth
whether he has had a good catch or not. If his
boat is light and fish pens empty, he may be
angry and discontented. As in all conditions of
life, where men daily face death and danger, the
women occupy a secondary position and sub-
ordinate themselves to the men. They watch for
the boats so that the potatoes may be boiled and
the stew steaming hot, the biscuits baked, dry
socks and boots laid out, at the exact moment
when the boat's prow takes the first log on the
launch.

David enjoyed life with Tamar and grew
fonder of her as the days went by; for the first
time he lived in comparative comfort. It was
great to get in from the boats and find a steaming

hot dinner, to have a clean decent lunch of bread
and cakes wrapped in a white cloth and packed
in a tin box to take to the banks, to have fresh,
clean sheets on the bed, to find clean underclothes warming by the kitchen fire of a Sunday
morning, to have socks mended, sea boots
warmed and dried, and oilskins hung on their
proper pegs in the kitchen. "Yes," he thought,
"I'se made none so bad a bargain, arter all."

He was proud of being in the Jung firm, and
could bear with lightness of heart the ugly
glances and spiteful words of Casper, Martin,
and Joseph. They stuck together against him
since the wedding, though each month they
squabbled among themselves over the division
of the money. They tried to make David feel
that even as a partner he was an outsider and
hence inferior. He bore with them patiently, but
on one occasion, after a heavy day in the fish
house, when they were all weary and irritated,
he let out at them. As he was carrying a bushel
of salt from bin to salting table, he bumped
against Joseph and spilled a handful of salt
down his rubber boot. Joseph turned on him with
a snarl: "What ye do dat fur, ye clumsy Outposter? Ye don t belong here nohow. All de
world knows how ye wormed yur way into de
family." Whereupon, in the presence of the

sharesmen, David struck his partner in the face with a flung haddock and knocked him over his washing tubs. David and Gershom drew closer together. There was no envy in Gershom; he disliked the arrogant brothers and gloried in David's good fortune.

CHAPTER VI

So wel they lovede, as olde bookes sayn,
That whan that oon was deed, soothly to telle
His fellaw wente and soughte hym down in helle.

CANTERBURY TALES.

NE night some two months after the wedding, as David sat drying his stockings by the kitchen stove, he heard shouting on the pathway that led up to his house. He listened; it was Gershom's booming voice, trembling with excitement: "De light's out on Barren Island, de light's out on Barren Island!" David strode quickly to the kitchen door, Gershom joined him, and both stared across the bar to the southward. It was true, no light twinkled against southern sky, nor cast its yellow ray over black sea. Some disaster had befallen old Gershom; perhaps he had slipped over the cliff wall, or a sea had dashed him against the rocks and broken his legs. Both knew what must

be done without delay, and David turned back to the kitchen to pull on rubber boots and oil-skins. "De light's out on Barren Island. Me an' Gershom's goin' off. Should be back by day-break," he called to Tamar, who, after the manner of Rockbound wives, made no protest and offered no suggestion.

David and young Gershom ran a boat off the launch, rounded the Grampus, and through darkness and a long-running sea drove hard to the southward. Though there was no fog, it was a murky night, and only the great stars blinked dimly in the black bowl of sky. In an hour the draught of southeast wind brought to their ears the boom and roar of Barren Island surf, and they began to feel their way in cautiously, since nothing marked the rock-cleft landing place save a line of black in a curve of breaking white, and that, on such a night, they could only discern when close in. They shipped a sea over their stern, but made the launch, clambered to safety, and hove out their boat. As their feet fumbled for the pathway that led across the sombre island, careys swooped and squawked about their ears. Gershom, hooking his great arm through David's, said: "I wisht we'd brung air a draught o' rum wid, Dave."

The lighthouse towered dark and silent, the

south wind strumming an unearthly melody on its supporting wires. The two friends entered the kitchen and, with the quick spurt and flare of David's match, both started in horror. The table was overturned, and on the floor lay the old man, dead, a half-emptied rum jug beside him. His dog, cowering behind the stove, bared his teeth and growled at the intruders. "Looks like he'd had an awful struggle wid a haunt 'fore he died," said young Gershom, trembling with grief and terror.

They lit the lamp in the light tower, stood watches throughout the night, and with the first gray of dawn carried the old man's body to their boat, the dog snapping and snarling at their heels.

Old Gershom was buried on Big Outpost one bleak November afternoon, and young Gershom was drunk at his funeral, for, sober, he could not bear to see the old man he loved and feared laid underground. With David he stood at the grave's head, his great body shaken with sobs, the tears making clean channels down his salt-stained cheeks. There was many a wet eye, too, among fisherfolk who claimed no kinship. Old Gershom had been great hearted. To whom could they now turn for the writing of deeds, wills, and mortgages, or for advice on the cunning of

fish dealers or the sharp tricks of Liscomb law-
yers? "Old Gershom Born will be missed in the
islands," they said to one another sadly. "Young
Gershom is a bold strong man, but he lacks the
wisdom of his father."

Young Gershom, who had waited many years
to succeed his father as keeper of the light, was
given the post. Uriah, who on the event of old
Gershom's death had applied secretly for the
place for one of his boys, was full of envy, for the
keeper got eighty dollars a month, besides fuel
and lodging, and that was great wealth in the
islands. The old king also resented losing Gershom as a sharesman; it would be hard to replace
the young giant in the fish house.

As for Gershom, now that he was appointed,
he dreaded going to Barren Island alone. He
thought of marrying Fanny, the potato girl,
but his pride held him back; some wit on the
Outposts would surely make him the subject of
jest and scorn in a ballad, and that Gershom
could not endure. Finally he besought his friend
David to come with him and spend his two
weeks' holiday on Barren Island. "Till I gits used
to de place and masters some o' dem haunts,"
pleaded Gershom. Now, David had planned an
epic holiday with Jean Boutilier at Miscou, but
in the face of his friend's obvious distress he

agreed to go with him, if Uriah would give his
consent. Gershom broached the subject to the
old king, who cunningly turned the matter over
in his mind. He was envious of Gershom but
not without a certain pity for him. It was terrible
for a man to go to Barren Island alone. He knew
more about haunts than any man in the whole
bay, had he not seen the footless nigger flit a
score of times, had he not thrice been pushed off
his path by an unseen force! And Rockbound
haunts were mild, compared with those of Barren
Island! Yes, it was a fearsome place to go alone!
"De cod's made," Uriah thought, "de green fish
an' herrin's sold. Nuttin' to do now but peddle
de cabbages along de shore from Dover to Liscomb, an' Dave's no good at sellin'. Martin an'
Joe's de boys to drive bargains an' git de last
cent. Bes' keep friendly wid de keeper o' de first
light." Aloud he said to Gershom: "I kin ill
spare David now, but I'se'll let him go wid as a
favour, providin' ye'll agree to make a smoke
when wreckage goes floatin' by or ye hears air a
word of a ship ashore. An' you, David, be back
on de day set widout fail."

So, one morning in late November, David set
off with Gershom to install him as keeper of the
Barren Island Light. They landed at midday and
relieved the temporary keeper, who was glad to

be gone. The island was an eerie place, for one heard naught by day or night but the tiresome beat of surf, the moan of the sea wind, and the shrill screams of gulls and careys. Though David was an agnostic in regard to ghosts, he could not deny that there was something queer and unearthly about Barren Island. Even the government engineer—so ran the tale—who had built the light's foundation, had reported to the islanders that things were not as they should be. As the friends stepped out of the lighthouse one blowy night soon after their arrival, to make the round of the cliffs, Gershom gripped David's arm and said: "Listen!" From the northern end a hoarse, distant voice seemed to cry: "Help! Ahoy, there, ahoy!" and from below the cliff wall came sounds like the rattling of oars and the banging of a shattered boat, but when they reached the cliff's edge they could see or hear nothing. After nightfall they kept close together, for both knew that the old man's haunt would linger about the island for a little while.

Apart from ghosts, the bareness of the island depressed David; there was neither garden plot nor mowing field nor single bush or tree. Old Gershom had tried to raise vegetables in his early days on the island, but the roaring sea had flung too much salt spray upon his land. Even the coarse grasses were yellow and stunted. David claimed that the island had once been larger and wooded, for, on the slack of spring tides, his sharp eyes, peering through green water to the yellow sands below, had seen gnarled stumps of pine and maple, preserved through the centuries by sea water and perhaps half turned to stone. The bareness of the place was accentuated by the buildings: the stiff white lighthouse stayed with cables to support its crystal head, the tiny barn, the fuel shed, the outhouse weighed down with slabs of stone on the southern end, and on the northern end the long boathouse that stood above the cleft blasted through the cliff wall by government engineers for a landing stage.

Now that Barren Island was to be Gershom's home, the two friends explored it thoroughly. It was only seven hundred yards long and perhaps four hundred wide; nothing but a slatty rock protruding from the sea, over which was laid a mat of soil and turf varying from one foot to five in depth. At the light's foot, a great stone block, a natural pier, stood out boldly and defied the open sea. No ship ever warped up to that pier, for on the calmest days of summer a tireless ground swell broke there, and in winter mountainous seas lashed it without rest. Above this

natural pier was a slippery plateau inclined at a
slight angle to the sea's surface. The impetuous
winter sea had broken coffin-shaped blocks from
the stratified rock of the pier, that some ancient
wrinkling of the earth's crust had stood on edge,
and hurled them bodily upon the surface of the
plateau. There they lay scattered about at odd
angles like giant sarcophagi. Old Gershom, the
scholar, used to say that the plateau was like a
stone yard, where slaves had chiselled out coffins
for a Pharaoh's household, or like some place
where whip-goaded workmen had knocked off
for the noon hour in the midst of building a
pyramid. The old man had loved this place, for
on this gaunt plateau, it seemed to him that life
was stripped of all its shams and that he could
see things as they were. Among these grim coffin
stones he used to wander on moonlit nights, to
talk of immortality to the sea and to watch the
mist wraiths take strange shapes on the face of
the waters. Many a night, from this vantage
point, he had seen rough sea gods rise and gleam
as they sported in a breaking sea. The old man
had told David and Gershom weird tales of
things seen and heard on the plateau, and they
always shunned it after nightfall.

A turfy pathway that the feet groped for in
the darkness led through the island from light

to boathouse. The cleft, blasted there in the cliff wall, was narrow and a place of danger, for without cease the seas swilled into it, rattling beach rocks like pebbles beneath the logs of the launch. To land or launch a boat there was difficult on any day of the year, and on many days positively dangerous. Old Gershom never slipped a boat off when the Rock was breaking, but young Gershom, who had not the resources of his father, never held to that rule in his years on Barren Island. After lonely nights, his heart yearned for the chatter of Uriah's fish house. He was tired of reading, and he used to push off when the Rock was churning the sea white and spouting like a school of whales.

Besides haunts, David and Gershom found real sources of annoyance on Barren Island. Chief of these were the audacious herring gulls, that nested by myriads among the rocks of the western shore and with tireless pugnacity drove from their kingdom all alien birds, plover, curlew, checkerbacks, and even great ravens and gannets. Only the nasty careys escaped them, by burrowing in the ground, and a few swallows that nested under the barn's eaves survived through swiftness of wing. All day long, as David and Gershom mended nets or tinkered at the boats, the gulls screamed and, swooping low, circled about their heads. Sometimes they planed high in the air and scornfully let their droppings fall upon them. David and Gershom were something new to the gulls—the old man had not stirred abroad much by day—they regarded them as intruders in their ancient home and sought to drive them off as they had driven plover and curlew.

Not less provoking were the careys! When the gulls ceased their shrewish screaming at sundown, the careys, cursed birds of night, sallied forth to make darkness hideous. Barren Island, their favourite breeding place, was so infested with them that in thick weather homebound fishermen of the bay used to say to one another: "We's inside Barren Island now, 'cause de careys is left us an' gone home." David and Gershom had long since learned to hate these loathsome birds, and on the banks, in slack moments, had knocked them down by dozens as they fluttered and crowded behind their boats to pick up bits of fish entrails. In their burrowing the careys had so polluted the soil of the island with their malodorous scent of liver and gurry, that it was useless to have a well on the island. Because of them the island springs were defiled, and whoever kept the light had to depend for his water supply on rain water drained from the lighthouse roof into a cellar tank. It was on murky nights, when the careys were out in force, that the two friends heard that unnatural voice cry from the darkness: "Help, help! Ahoy, there, ahoy!"

During the first week of David's stay with his friend the government supply steamer puffed up on her annual trip, anchored near their launch, and lightered off to them bags of coal and flour, barrels of salt beef and pork, drums of oil and gasoline, coffee, tea, sugar, and a dozen other necessities against the imprisonment of winter. Gershom had ordered as well some luxuries for himself and David, chiefest and dearest among these two buckets of hard red and white candies. The inspector came ashore when the stores were landed, looked over the light, and with stuffy dignity instructed Gershom in the approved method of fixing and lighting the new mantles. While the instruction was in process, David made such comical faces behind the inspector's back that Gershom could hardly keep his countenance. "A hell of a lot he knows about keepin' a light! I'd like fur to see him here alone in one ragin' winter week. He'd holler fur mamma," said Gershom as the inspector's boat pushed off from the launch.

It took David and Gershom a whole day to move the stores by wheel and hand barrow from

the tarpaulin-covered heap at the head of the
launch to the shelter of fuel shed and lighthouse.
Cheeks bulging with candies, singing and laugh-
ing, they made a game of it and by turns wheeled
each other on the empty barrow. To upset the
rider, the barrow above him, into some damp
hollow was a bit of light humour that invoked
laughter and mutually warmed their hearts.
That day they paid no heed to the screaming
gulls that, outraged beyond words, were on their
worst behaviour. It was a great labour which
made them happy in its accomplishment, and
satisfied an instinct that man shares with bee
and squirrel of laying up stores against the
winter's cold.

The next day they set off to visit a rum runner
that they noticed jogging to seaward, awaiting
boats from the main. After the bargain had been
struck, two ten-gallon kegs were hoisted over
the side into their lurching boat and laid snugly
one on either side of the centreboard. Then the
captain, a burly red-faced Frenchman from
Miquelon, invited them aboard, and in the shelter of his warm cabin plied them with rum that
had paid no government tax. Gershom boomed
along, composing and enlarging upon the scandal-
ous gossip of the islands. David, aroused from

his customary shyness, told how the old ram, enraged by a vision of expansive and unusual whiteness in his green pasture, had butted Gershom over the cliff into the rockweed below, his hands full of roots and gravel, his trousers dangling about his ankles, and of the gentle rebuke the stranded Gershom had addressed to the ram on the cliff wall above him. "Tell him agin, Dave," cried Gershom, roaring with laughter. "Tell him agin what I said to de old ram." David repeated his profane encore to a delighted audience. "Now tell him de story o' de pipe an' socks," said Gershom. "He'll like dat one." And David told how Dennis Born had defiled Gershom's pipe as Gershom lay sleeping by the amidship thwart, and how Gershom had revenged himself by feeding Dennis on a stew in which two of Gershom's ancient socks were boiled. The Miquelon captain thought them capital fellows and pressed on them a bottle of champagne from his own private store. Time flew by. In fact, they lingered almost too long, for as they clambered down the runner's side the sun hung low in the western sky. The light must be lit before his red disk dipped behind the distant black rocks of The Ragged and haunted Sacrifice. The two reckless cronies crouched singing in the stern as

their boat slid through the darkness. As they
drove along, David thought:

"I'se happy now; I had bad luck in my young
days, and my gettin' married was nuttin' much,
but I'se a partner in de Rockbound firm, an'
Gershom's my friend, an' we'se'll stick togedder
always."

Luck was with them! They made the launch
in good time and hauled out their boat shouting
in unison:

> "'Oh, Shenando' I love yur darter,
>   Yo-ho, my rollin' river,'"

as they strained against the capstan bars.

Gershom prized up a loose plank of the boathouse floor with the tine of a rusty fish fork, and
on the rock ledge below he and David carefully
laid one of the kegs. It had been the old man's
hiding place. There was really no need of a hiding
place at all, since there was no one on the island
but themselves, and they could always mark the
approach of any stranger an hour before his arrival. But David and Gershom were only two
great overgrown boys, and hiding the rum cask
and pretending they were watched and spied
upon by the crew of the revenue cutter was the
ritual of a game they played with themselves.
They had another long drink from the remaining

keg before David drove in the bung and hoisted it upon his shoulder to carry it to the lighthouse. Singing, he went across the turf, while Gershom in his wake cursed the swooping gulls and threatened them with his stick.

Happy were the evenings of that holiday spent in the light tower together. Without, as darkness came, it was cold and blowy; within, snug and warm. Gershom rehearsed his endless adventures; they laughed and roared at each other in deep booming voices until far into the night.

On the last night of David's furlough, a gale, that increased in fury with the hours, blew up from the southeast. Gershom lit his lamp in the gray, lowering twilight, and was not a little worried by a crack in one of the big outside panes, through which a trickle of rain kept oozing. From the light tower he backed down the ladder into the third-story room, where he and David spent their evenings and slept. In this room were two hand-made chairs, a rough table, two cot beds, a Franklin stove, and a walnut desk littered with weather reports that Gershom filled out daily. Three bookshelves on the eastern wall held the old man's library. A hanging lamp that swayed with each furious gust of wind cast a bright circle of light upon the floor but left the corners in deep shadow.

"It's blowin' like hell," said Gershom, as his foot left the ladder, "an one o' de big outside panes is got a crack what's leakin'."

"Let her blow," answered David. "What cares us? No leak can't sink dis ship."

While Gershom had been lighting the lamp he had brought up from the kitchen a kettle of boiling water that, from its place on the stove, sang and sent out friendly puffs. In a corner lay the broached rum jug; on the table were a bowl of lump sugar, glasses, and a plate of sliced lemons that David had bought from the steward of the supply boat. Their last evening together was to be a grand one.

Without, everything jingled and rattled in the blasts of the gale; the light tower tugged at its windward cables as if it would tear them from the rock; the sea roared against the natural pier and flung its spray among Pharaoh's coffins. Careys, who love the storm, were out in force. Once some great night bird, dazzled by the light's glare, blundered against the glass and, with a squawk of terror, fell to the kitchen roof below.

"A rare night for ghosts," said young Gershom as he took a deep draught of hot rum and planted himself for the night's work.

"Ay," said David, "I lays de footless nigger is flittin' dis night on Rockbound."

"Dere's somethin' queer on dis island, too," said Gershom, "dough I don't understand rightly why, 'cause de Sanford folks tuk it away."

"How's dat?" asked David, though he knew the story well.

"You mind Johnny Publicover, de ghost catcher on Big Outpost?"

"I minds him well, 'cause I lived nigh him when I was a gaffer."

"Well, you'se heard how nigh de Sanford ghost was to ruinin' Sanford. He had all de women an' children skeert, an' de men, too, an' dey was dat skeert, dey was goin' to give up dere fish stands an' move to oder parts o' de main or maybe some o' de islands. Why, dat ghost use' to roll beach rocks down de front hallway when de men folks was away, an' naught but women and children huddled roun' de kitchen stove, and snatch gals away from dere fellers on dark roads, an' he were dat audacious he use to whang on de back o' de church at evening meetin'. One night he gits dat bold, he reach in t'rough de back winder wid a brown skinny arm an' put a glass o' rum on de side o' de pulpit when de minister was a-preachin' a sermon on temperance. Warn't dat audacious?"

"It were," replied David.

The query and answer were made for no

rhetorical effect, but for the purpose of allowing narrator and listener to pause long enough to take another draught of hot rum and hold it in the mouth a moment before letting the soul-kindling liquor trickle slowly down the gullet.

"He were a holy terror audacious haunt, were dat Sanford ghos'," continued Gershom, "but dat last ac' o' his got de preacher's back up, an' he called a meetin' o' all de men in de school-house. Fore dis, de minister he'd bin tryin' to quiet de people an' tellin' dem dere warn't no sich t'ing as ghos's. At de meetin', Hezekiah Slaughenwhite—he's de great man in dem parts, 'cause he were de high-line fisherman on all de coast in de days o' his yout'—he stud up an' says right off: 'Folks, de only t'ing fur to do is to send fur Johnny Publicover, de ghos' ketcher on de Outposts.'

"Den de preacher, he yells, 'No, Johnny Publicover's half a witch hisself.' An' dere he were right, for him an' his wife had de power o' makin' harness an' yokes break all to pieces on de cattle ploughin' in de fields, if dey had a spite on ye."

"Ay," said David, "dey worked dat on Nat Young's boys."

"An' dey could make barnacles grow all ober a boat's bottom so you could git ne'er a way on her. So de preacher he yells, 'No, let's exercise him by prayer an' de power o' de Lord.'

"Den Israel Slaughenwhite says, 'Us don't want to exercise no ghost, us wants to git rid o' him; he's gettin' exercise enough trailing round de Sanford roads an' fields.'

"Den de preacher, he begin to explain what dis here exercisin' really meant, but jus' at dat very moment dat audacious ghos' goes whang, whang, whang, wid a big timber agin de back o' de schoolhouse. He damn nigh bust in de rear end, dat time. Dat settled dat, de preacher was finished, an' Israel got de vote all round to send fur de ghos' ketcher."

Here Gershom paused as if his throat were dry and cast a reproachful look at the empty glasses. David made haste to prepare two more; the rounds of yellow lemon floated seductively on top of the steaming amber liquor.

"So Israel's boys, Mattew and John, was sent nex' day to fetch Johnny off Big Outpost. You knows 'em?"

"Ay," said David, "I knows 'em bot'."

"Towards evenin' dey landed back on Sanford, an' what ye t'ink Johnny brung fur to ketch dat ghos'? A net wid a handle an' iron ring like what we use fur scoopin' herrin' out o' a tub, his long-barrelled duck gun, a halibut

gaff tied fast to tree fadoms eight-strand
maniller rope, an' a big canvas bag wid a draw-
string. He had all dis gear harnessed ober his
shoulders an' de gaff rope lashed round his waist.
You know how wizened an' small an' scrawny
an' black Johnny is? Well, standin' on de beach
wid dem great hulkin' Sanforders—dey's extry
big men; air a one o' Israel's boys goes ober two
hundred—I guess Johnny cut some comical
figger. But he had de heart and de guts; he
warn't skeered o' no ghos', an' dey was.

"'Whar's dis here ghos' at?' Johnny yelled at
dem. 'Fotch me to him an' I'll capture him, same
as I did de wild savage ghos' on Rafuse Island.'

"'Us don't know whar he's at now,' said Israel.

"'How kin I ketch him when ye don't know
whar he's at? Whar did he haunt at last?'

"'At de meetin' in de schoolhouse las' night.'

"'Den have anoder meetin' dere to-night,
an' if he haunts, I'll ketch yur ghos',' said
Johnny.

"Sure enough, dey holds anoder meetin' in de
schoolhouse dat night, wid Johnny ambushed in
a big cleft o' split granite. Dey gits de preacher
to preach dat night, 'cause de ghos' delights to
aggravate him, an', hush, man, when de preacher
gits goin' on how de Lord fed de Children o'
Israel on manna, de ghos' fetches de back o' de

schoolhouse whang, whang. Den de Sanforders was some skeert an' nigh held dere breaths, till dey heard de bang o' Johnny's duck gun. Den dey heard some squawkin' an' yellin' an' runnin' t'rough de bushes, an' bimeby dey heard Johnny screechin' way down in de t'ick woods. Nair a one o' dem big Sanforders wentured out to help him, dey was dat skeered stiff. When dey heard Johnny's voice hollerin' an' hulloin' jus' outside de schoolhouse door, dey follered old Israel out. Johnny had somet'in' in de bag all right, dey could see it movin' in de lantern light.

"'Dere's yur haunt,' said Johnny, an' he guv de bag a kick, an' de t'ing flopped an' fluttered an' squeaked. 'Dat were a feeble haunt. I kotch dem worser nor dat.'

"'How you ketch him, Johnny?'" asked Israel.

"'Did ye no hear my gun go? I winged him wid dat shot, den I chased him t'rough de bushes, whanged de net down ober his head, gaffed him in de white o' de belly wid my halibut gaff, an' stuffed him in dis here bag, an' dat's dat.'"

"What you s'pose he had in dat bag, now?" interrupted David.

"I'm not supposin', I knows, 'cause de old

man tole me, an' you'll allow he warn't no fool. He had dat wery audacious Sanford ghos'."

"My God, de sout'easter is a-snortin' to-night," interjected David as a wild blast shook the tower and made the glasses on the table dance and jingle.

"Dere's one good t'ing about it, Dave," said Gershom. "We can't make no Rockbound to-morrow, not if Uriah pulls out all his whiskers, an' we'll have anodder day an' night togedder."

David grinned and nodded his head in approval.

"We needs some more hot water, I can't tell no yarns wid a dry t'roat," said Gershom. "You git it while I goes aloft and looks at de crack in de pane."

Up the ladder climbed Gershom, and down-stairs to the kitchen went David, peering into every dark corner for haunts. He was glad he had left a lighted lantern hanging in the kitchen. He refilled his kettle, made his way quickly up the dark stairs, and replenished the glasses.

"She's sure makin' de old light sing," shouted David as Gershom's legs became visible on the ladder.

"Ay, dat she is," rejoined Gershom seating himself and toying with his glass. "Let's see, where was I? Oh, yes, some o' dose big Sanforders wanted to mash dat ghos' in de bag wid beach rocks.

"'No' says Johnny, 'ye can't mash dis kind. You got to land him on a lonely an' uninhabited island. Dis kind can't cross water.'

"Now, what do you s'pose dat bugger Johnny done? He charged dem Sanforders five dollars fur a-ketchin' o' dere haunt."

"A power o' money fur one night's work."

"'Now,' he says to dem, says he, 'I won't budge wid him off Sanford till ye pays me five dollars more. I contracted,' says he, 'fur to ketch yur ghos', not fur to transport him about de high seas. An' I kin loose haunts nigh as good as I kin ketch dem.'"

"A sharp one is Johnny."

"Dat he is."

"So dey clubs togedder an' riz de extry five, an' de nex' mornin' Israel's boys, dey rowed him off wid de haunt still flutterin' an' squawkin' in de bag. An' where do you s'pose dey landed dat ghos'?"

"Where?"

"Dat bugger Johnny landed him right here on Barren Island. Dat were fore de light were built, an' dere warn't no human habitations."

"An' is dat ghos' roamin' dis island now? Gershom, what fur did ye take dis light?"

"Hush, man, till I tells you de res'. Dat ghos' were on dis island fur many, many years, yes, till after de light were built. When de ole man cum to live here, he often see dat haunt roamin' round, but de ghos' paid him no heed, 'cause he knowed he couldn't skeer ole Gershom Born. But I heard de ole man say dat, many a night, he seed dat ghos' in de moonlight stretched out flat on de coffin stones, a-moanin' like all possessed an' grievin' fur his ancient home in Sanford.

"Well, one fine Sunday afternoon cum some lads from Sanford to visit de ole man an' to ask him somethin' about air a deed or will. Along wid dey brung a jug o' over-proof rum, an' dem an' de ole man drunk dat strong rum de livelong afternoon. Dey got drunk, all right, an' laffed and ollered an' fought an' had a good time. Den, along towards sundown, de Sanford fellers allowed as how dey'd better make off fur de main. Down dey went to dere boat, de ole man follerin' an' singin' along de path. Ye mind how he used to sing an' use mighty big-soundin' words when he was right drunk?"

"I minds well."

"Dey launches dere boat in a calm sea, but jus' as de las' man clumb aboard, somethin' stepped into dat boat dat put her right down to de gunwales. 'Twere de Sanford ghos' leavin' Barren Island, de ole man said, an' travellin' to his ancient home on de main. Dem Sanforders got out dere oars an' rowed like crazy mens, wid de water lappin' dere gunwales all de way, an' when dey cum to de Sanford beach de ghos' stepped out an' de boat riz a foot outer de water."

"Didn't yur ole man see dat Sanford haunt no more on dis island?"

"No more he did, but he seen plenty o' queer small haunts, an' dey're round here to dis day."

It was long after midnight when Gershom had finished his story.

"Time to turn in," suggested David.

"Why turn in? You'se dead when you'se asleep. I wants to be alive always. Let's have a nightcap, anyway," replied Gershom.

The gale was now at the height of its fury; joist and rafter groaned as the wind whistled through the supporting cables and swayed the tower. When the nightcap had been brewed and drunk, Gershom lurched to the ladder and climbed it unsteadily to see if the light were burning true. When his legs, body, and empurpled face descended from the square of blackness he said: "Dat crack in de pane's worse, we got to stand anchor watches."

"All right," said David.

"You do de first hour's trick, an' I'se'll do de second. I'se de quickest man to undress in all dese islands." Gershom slipped the braces from his shoulders, and letting his trousers fall in a huddled heap on the floor, sprang into his bed all standing. He puffed at his pipe for a moment, as he always did before sleeping, then laid it down carefully where it could be seized at the instant of waking, and in a moment was snoring.

David, left alone, listened for a while to the fury of the wind and hoped that no vessels were close inshore that night. He crossed the room to the bookshelves and tried to amuse himself by looking at the pictures in old Gershom's books. He regretted deeply at that moment that he had never learned to read. In one large book he found pictures of devils being forked onto burning coals, and of hideous dog-faced men standing neck-high in frozen ponds. He knew it was a bad book to look at on such a wild night after hearing Gershom's story of the Sanford ghost, but the pictures fascinated him, and he kept on turning pages that revealed worse horrors. Suddenly, in the light tower above his head came a terrifying, an awful noise. A ripping and rending was followed by a crash as if someone had dumped a ton of glass down the stairs.

"Up, Gershom, up," stammered David. "De light's all smashed to hell."

Gershom leaped out of bed and ran up the ladder, his shirt bellying out behind him. David followed close at his heels. They stared at one another in amazement; the light was burning calm and clear. Except for the trickle that oozed through the cracked pane, naught was amiss in the light tower.

"What's de matter wid you, Dave?" asked Gershom in high dudgeon as they descended. "Is dat drop o' rum gone to yur head? Can't ye carry yur liquor no more?"

"Hush, man, I ain't drunk. Dere certainly were one awful crash and bang up dere."

Gershom turned in without another word, but scarcely had he settled his great bulk in bed and drawn up the quilt when again came a mighty thumping and a crash of shattered glass. Up sprang the undaunted blond giant to run up the ladder and again find the light burning without flaw or flicker.

Gershom came below slowly and pulled on his pants. "No sleep fur us to-night, lad; one o' dem minor haunts is workin' on us."

So they sat close together through the night, sipped rum, and paid no further heed to the wind demons that ramped and roared above them.

Toward morning their eyes sagged wearily, and David felt a new thrill of terror when Gershom, in an unearthly voice, began an obscene address to a black and yellow dog that he said lived under his walnut desk and came out only on the wane of the moon. When the eastern sky was gray with dawn and the rim of the sun peeked above Metatogan, they put out the light and slept.

When they awoke, they found that the gale had blown out its fury, though big seas still romped among the coffin rocks of the plateau. About noon the wind hauled to the northwest and laid the waves the southeaster had raised. As the sea abated, David knew that Uriah would expect him and that he must go. In the early afternoon, he and Gershom got the boat ready and pushed off into the sea. They were both sad and low at heart. David hated to leave his friend, whom he would see but seldom; Gershom dreaded being left alone on his island. On the passage to Rockbound they scarcely spoke to each other.

"Ye'll come and have Christmas dinner wid, Gershom," said David as they rounded the Grampus.

"Ay, lad, dat I'se'll be glad to do, if dere's no ice," answered Gershom.

They shook hands and said good-bye on

Uriah's launch. Then the great-shouldered Gershom pushed off alone, and standing in his boat's stern kept turning and waving his hand till the point shut him out. David, at the launch head, duffel bag in hand, stared after him, thinking his two weeks' holiday on Barren Island the freest and richest period of his life and that he had now sealed a friendship with Gershom that nothing could ever break.

CHAPTER VII

Now welcom, somer, with they sonne softe,
That hast this wintres weders over-shake
And driven a-wey the longe nyghtes blake.

THE PARLEMENT OF FOULES.

AS DAVID, on his return from Barren Island, strode up the pathway toward his house, he was surprised to find his heart beating faster. Tamar was waiting on his back doorstep, to welcome him without a word of complaint. He dropped the dunnage bag from his shoulder, threw his arms about her, and gave her a hearty kiss. Tamar, who had never been greeted thus before, was delighted, for she loved her man. David's heart glowed as he stepped into his neat, warm kitchen. In spite of his regret at leaving Gershom, it was indeed a grand thing to come home to a house and wife of your own after pigging it for two weeks on a ghost-ridden island. "Poor Gershom," he thought, "out dere alone wid nair a wife nur kids to talk wid.

Eighty dollars a mont' an' grub ain't wort' it."

Uriah set him to tanning nets the day after his arrival, and with that labour accomplished he had work enough of his own to do. Knee-deep in snow, he cut trees on his wood lot and sawed and split a high pyramid of firewood. From storm-strewn beaches he hauled load upon load of sea dung, kelp, and rockweed and cast it into his barn cellar, to rot with the barn manure for his garden patch of potatoes and cabbages. In the long winter evenings by the kitchen stove he patiently mended rents that dogfish and albacore had torn in his nets, and shaved out big net buoys of dried fir wood. Orange he painted them, so that his searching eyes might catch them readily against the black waves, and Tamar, with deft brush, made a blue D on one side of them and a J on the other. They smiled at each other and looked proudly upon the gay pile of buoys that glistened in mid-floor. It was a symbol of their partnership.

But what a mess he had made of Tamar's kitchen with paint pots, brushes, splinters, shavings, and bits of net marline! That set him to thinking: he must have a "building," as every well-equipped fisherman had; a place that would be all his own, where he could go when he wanted to be alone, keep his gear and shave, paint, and whittle to his heart's content. Tamar had made no complaint, but it was hardly fair to a woman to clutter up her kitchen. Yes, a building he must have that would be all his own! For the convention of Rockbound decreed that a "building" was unlike dwelling, barn, or fish house; it was sanctuary, a man's very own, a place that no woman set foot within, just as no Rockbound fisherman dreamed of demeaning himself by entering a wooden backhouse, a place for women and children.

He knew well that neither Jung nor Kraus would aid him, but Gershom would come, when the sea permitted, to help him raise the frame. He confided none of these plans to Tamar, but when he began his trips to the main, on days of moderate calm, to fetch swamp spruce for his lobster-pot bows, he carried home as well a load of boards and studding. It was a mild open winter with little drift ice in the bay, and almost daily his boat returned to the launch gunwale-deep. The sills, joists, and rafters he hewed out of spruces cut on his own wood lot.

When the materials were ready, Gershom came one frosty day to help David raise his frame. The giant made a great noise, as was his wont, blew upon his fingers, and picked up one end of a sill as if it were a match stick. Krauses

and Jungs came to look on, stamping the snow
with their feet and making jeering remarks on
the open joints and general crudeness of the
workmanship, but Gershom's tongue was sharp
and bitter, and they often went away crestfallen.
In early March came a long spell of bad weather,
and Gershom was, for that time, imprisoned on
Barren Island. Then David laboured on his
building alone, singing as he drove home frosty
nails, while Tamar within the house smiled as she
heard his hammer ring, and cut and stitched tiny
garments for the baby she expected.

The snow melted in the cleft between the
knolls, the ice on Nigger Pond broke into cakes,
sea ducks were bedded near the Rock, and the
raw winds of spring began to blow. April was a
rough month; every day the rollers thundered
on the sand beach, crashed into the dog holes,
and made the cannon rock roar and spout, but in
spite of wind and weather David tended his
lobster traps daily, venturing out when no other
Jung or Kraus dared run a boat off the launch.
"He'll come home keel up one o' dese days,"
they said to one another with lowering brows.

One gray dawn in late April, as he was pulling
on his sea boots preparatory to setting off for his
traps, Tamar called to him from the bedroom:
"You'd bes' be askin' Anapest to step ober, I

feels de pains comin' on me." Anapest was the island's midwife and, in spite of her hatred of Uriah's brood, had delivered every infant born on the island in forty years past. Her heart melted with compassion at the sight of a Jung woman in labour.

David crossed the fields to Anapest's house and delivered the message before setting out. That day he had to make his long route around Barren Island shoal, and he had promised Gershom to bring him a bundle of papers, if it were smooth enough to make a landing. It was a day of bad luck: his boat stuck on the launch and, to his deep chagrin, he could only get her off by enlisting Casper's help, and three of his moorings had chaffed off and gone to sea. That meant loss of both mooring and lobster trap. By the time he had hauled and rebaited his remaining traps and paid his visit to Gershom—for a landing had been effected—it was late afternoon, and when his homing boat rounded West Head and stood in for the launch, dusk was falling. As he came up the logs of the launch, some weight seemed to press upon his heart; all was not well on the island, he knew that some evil thing threatened him. Quickly he threw his lobsters into the floating crate and hurried up the path to his house.

Anapest met him on the back doorstep. "De baby's come—it's a boy; but yur woman's right sick."

David hurried into the bedroom where Tamar lay, whitefaced. She was in great pain and but half conscious. To his deep distress, she did not know him.

"Is air a man gone fur de doctor?" he queried.

"'No," replied Anapest.

"Why de hell not?"

"She only come on bad two hours gone. De sea's risin' wid de night, an' a fog shuttin' down. Dey say it's too big a risk makin' Minden dis night."

"I kin make Minden in any weder if her own brudders an' fader can't. I'se'll be back wid de doctor by dawn. Stay wid her t'rough de night an' mind her an' de kid good," and he was off. In a moment of emotional stress he had dared give an order to Anapest, and she had accepted it without resentment or protest. He was as good as his word; he drove the *Phœbe* through fog and sea and fetched a shivering, unwilling doctor by dawn, but it was too late, Tamar was dead.

As David stood by the bedside of his dead wife, in the sad light of morning, the doctor muttering words of attempted comfort, life seemed hopeless and futile. Life was like the sea that began the destruction of an island as soon as it had made it. It seemed to him impossible, that Tamar, yesterday full of strength and vitality, could be lying there as lifeless as a stone. Childbirth was regarded by him and by every soul on Rockbound as a simple function of nature. From his dead wife upon the bed his distressed glance wandered to the tiny red mite that Anapest had wrapped in swaddling clothes and laid in a box near the stove, and thinking of his own wretched childhood spent in that very house he uttered a vow in a solemn voice.

"By God, Tamar lass, dat kid, if he lives, won't have to endure what I done. I'll promise ye dat, lass! He'll have learnin', he will, and he won't be beat up by me, nor no oder man on Rockbound, nor in de whole world."

With his own hands, David shaped Tamar's coffin of white boards, bought for the sheathing of his building. Sick at heart, it gave him some comfort to perform this simple office for her. Though his courtship had been without romance, though he had never loved her deeply, he had spent with her his first period of clean and comfortable living, and his respect and affection had grown for her steadily. She had been a good housewife and a grand worker. She had looked after his interests in the Jung firm and had daily checked the fares in the fish house. Now helper and comrade were gone.

With Tamar dead and Gershom on Barren Island, he was alone, and he felt that the fierce struggle of life, forgotten through that one winter, was to begin all over again. His conjecture was right. With Tamar dead, Casper, Joseph, and Martin became more spiteful than before. It seemed to them, now that his wife was gone, that he had won his way into the firm without paying the price, and by day and night they bedevilled Uriah to find some crafty pretext for throwing David out. But old Uriah could not be persuaded. "A bargain's a bargain," he hurled back at the nagging Casper, though he did not reveal to him the true inward working of his mind. He knew that if he put David out of the firm David would set up a fish house on the land he had bought from Anapest, that he would lose his best worker, and the Jung firm be out money. The old king could see farther than any of his boys, and though he turned their arguments over in his mind and shared their dislike of David, he revealed none of his thoughts but simply mumbled over and over: "A bargain's a bargain," and delighted in the impotent rage he saw in Casper's face. Casper, in a dark corner, whispered to Joseph and Martin: "What's de matter wid de ole man? He's gettin' soft in de head. We'se 'll have to push him out. A bargain's a bargain! He never stuck to no bargains in de past 'less he had to."

Tamar's baby was named Ralph in accordance with Tamar's wish; Anapest undertook to rear him, and Fanny, the potato girl, who was nursing a baby of her own and who made herself useful in every emergency, volunteered to feed him. David, as a relief to his feelings, crossed the fields to Anapest's house whenever he was through his day's work, to look at the infant. He lifted him sometimes in his great hands, held him at arm's length, and while Anapest and Fanny laughed at his clumsiness, stared at the child with wonder. The fact of the child's existence sobered David and made a decided change in his way of thinking and general attitude toward life. He was no longer, he felt, a free and irresponsible individual. Nor did he forget the vow he had made at Tamar's bedside: the boy should have education and a chance to escape this island of hatred and do something in the world. After these interviews, he used to wander back to his lonely kitchen and sit there thinking through long evenings alone. He needed company, but he could not bring himself to go back to the shares-

man's loft now that Gershom was no longer
there. His loneliness was accentuated by memories of the past and by the fact that all the Jungs
were against him. He dreamed sometimes of
establishing a fish stand with Gershom on
Barren Island, though he knew there was no
wood there. He longed for peace and quiet, to get
away from the hell of driving work, from greed
and hatred, and the perpetual quarrels and
nagging recriminations that were carried on
between the rival families.

But he could not escape the strife. In fact, the
summer after Tamar's death was a particularly
hateful one, a summer of unending quarrels.
First there was the business of building a schoolhouse. The world was advancing, and in spite of
all that Uriah could do, the land breeze carried
ideas even to remote Rockbound, and the third
generation of Jungs and Krauses began to think
that their children should learn to read and
write. They met in general conclave in the loft of
the Jung fish house, and there, seated on trawl
tubs and bundles of nets, listened to Casper,
the traveller, talk on the necessity of education for their children. Uriah and Anapest were
not present at this meeting, for the two heads of
the rival clans never met when meeting could be
avoided; but Anapest was represented by Chris-

tian, Nicholas, and Melcher, while Uriah, through his agents Joseph and Martin, fiercely opposed the establishment of a school. Had the brave old Jungs, who made Rockbound, been readers and writers? They had had no time for such foolishness. Anapest at first was luke-warm, but hearing of Uriah's violent opposition to the school she became a zealot in the cause of education. After several sullen meetings, Casper, backed by David, who thought of little Ralph, and by the Kraus faction directed by Anapest, carried the day, and it was forthwith voted to build a one-room schoolhouse on the road to the light, and that all the men of the island should labour on it jointly.

For the first time in Rockbound history Jungs and Krauses attempted something in coöpera-tion. What endless arguments they had about the size of the foundation, the height of the plate, the pitch of the rafters! With the frame up, they abandoned coöperation and agreed that the Jungs should build the north gable end, the east side and roof, and that Krauses should con-struct the rest. There the Jungs outdid the Krauses, for the front door came in their south-ern gable. Jungs sawed and hammered on the eastern side of the roof and ignored the Krauses who sawed and hammered on the other side. So great was the family rivalry that the schoolhouse was built with expedition, for Krauses would not let Jungs outdo them in quantity of work, nor would Jungs let Krauses outdo them. By the very nature of their isolated lives, they were skilled workers with tools and knew how to build curved boats with graceful sheer. And if one knows how to build a boat, the construction of a straight-lined schoolhouse is a matter of ease. Uriah shook his head as he stamped up and down the lane and prophesied that the school would bring evil upon the island, and in that the old man was right, though he thought only of the immediate and not the distant future.

With the schoolhouse completed, the trouble really began. David stood as far apart as he could from the quarrels, but it was inevitable that he should often be enmeshed. Because he wanted the school for his boy, he had to throw his weight now on one side, now on the other, and as a consequence he was trusted by neither faction. There was a secretary-treasurer to be elected, a teacher to be hired, and assessments to be made in accordance with each man's property holdings. Uriah, who owned eight tenths of the island, and upon whom the bulk of the assessment fell, stormed, raged, and refused to pay, until Anapest threatened to have the law of him. Casper assured him that he would assuredly lose in a law trial, and the old king bitterly cursed the Krauses, David Jung, and his false son Casper, as he fumbled with the lock of his money box.

On the eve of the election of secretary there was tense excitement in both camps. The two bosses lined up their electors and dictated policies. With Casper as chairman, Uriah saw that the Krauses would have an advantage in numbers unless he himself was present and voted. He could not depend upon David, who straddled the party fence.

Anapest and Uriah mutually surprised each other by coming to the great meeting held at evening in the new school. It was inevitable that the great question should arise, can a woman vote? This question was settled once for all on Rockbound, while suffragettes were still chaining themselves to the palings of the House of Parliament, and buffeting policemen in the streets of London.

Uriah opened the ball with: "Women ain't got no vote in dis meetin'."

"Dat dey is," answered Anapest.

"It ain't nateral, it ain't allowed in no land," retorted Uriah.

"Natural fur women to have no say, is it? Den how come dere's women queens?"

That was a bomb! Uriah had heard of Victoria, and Casper of Elizabeth. There was a moment of tense silence.

"We ain't electin' no queens to-night," was all the old man could think of to say.

"No, we ain't electin' no queens, we'se electin' a secretary, an' don't I own land an' pay fur de teacher same as de res' o' you? Can't I haul a line an' lug a barrow good as air a man on Rockbound? Tell me, does pants make ye vote? Many's de warm night when I wears nuttin' but oil pants in de fish house."

When David brought the hat around, Anapest cast in her ballot defiantly, and Casper the chairman announced after the count that Christian Kraus had been elected by four to three. One vote had been discarded by the chairman, who thought himself entitled to the secretaryship, but whether it was David's vote or Anapest's no man knows to this day. Anapest was satisfied with her victory and flounced out of the meeting. Uriah tore a handful of hair from his beard, and throwing his straw hat upon the floor trampled it into fragments. Christian Kraus was to collect and hold the school money and pay the teacher.

Gershom Born was the only person who got any
fun out of the new school; he wrote several
ballads about it and carried the news of the con-
flict to a circle of eager-eared gossips in Jennie
Run-over's place on the Outposts.

But the wrangling over the schoolhouse,
though longer in time, was a mere nothing when
compared in intensity with the quarrel over the
hole in the road. A road that ran north and
south over the narrowed part of the island from
launches to Southeast Cove marked the bound-
ary between the properties of Anapest and
Uriah, and by some ancient and immemorial
treaty the Krauses were bound to keep in repair
the north end, the Jungs the south end. Now,
what did some demon of discord do one day but
scoop out a hole in this road at a point equidistant from launches to beach. The summer was
a rainy one, and though the hole grew deeper
daily, neither family would mend it. Krauses
said it was the Jungs' job; Jungs said it was the
Krauses' job, and the ox carts of both families,
hauling sea dung from the cove, foundered hub
deep, to their mutual discomfort.

Uriah, stung by his defeat in the matter of the
school, met Christian Kraus one day and flatly
ordered him to fill the hole with a cartload of
gravel, and that without delay. A wordy dis-

pute followed, and Christian departed in a rage to report the whole story to his empress mother. Anapest listened to his tale, stamped her feet upon the kitchen floor in anger, and, girding up her belt, sallied forth upon Uriah, who was spreading a net in a field to the westward of his fish house.

"What you mean givin' orders to my boys?" she shrieked.

"I means dat puddle's got to be filled in."

"Den let some o' yur own spawn fill it in, or fill it in yur own self. It ain't on my land. Who you t'inks you is, anyhow? A king dey calls ye. Well, you'se an ugly king, an' ye may be king on yur own land, but ye can't boss my boys. I owns my own lands, an' you an' yur boys keep to hell off dem."

"Dat puddle's got to be filled in," shouted the old man stubbornly, "an' I ain't got no time to stand here argeying wid no woman."

"A woman, a woman," yelled Anapest. "Don't ye call me no woman, ye old bugger, or I'se 'll pull de whiskers off yur face, old as ye is. I knows what you t'inks a woman's fur, to raise a flock o' kids an' be worked to deat' in yur stinkin' fish house. If I was yur woman, I'd show ye."

"I'd sooner have air a wild beast in de house nor you."

Then Anapest flung her cap upon the ground, tore down her hair, and began to weep with rage. Her yells and sobs could be heard over half the island. Crouching low and bending forward, Anapest advanced upon Uriah opening and closing her fists, as if in anticipation of the moment when they would close upon the old man's hair and whiskers. She was a terrifying object in her position of attack, with her hair hanging in tousled strands about her face. Uriah was no coward, but he was bewildered as to his plan of action. It was impossible to join in fisticuffs with a woman; the news would spread quick as fog from island to island and make him an object of laughter and general derision. He decided on retreat, and, waiting till Anapest got within reach, he threw the net over her head and ran as fast as his old legs would carry him for the shelter of the fish house. He barred the door and waited. Peeping through a chink, he saw that young Gershom Born had landed from Barren Island and seen and overheard all. He was annoyed to think that the news of Anapest's shameful attack and his retreat would travel fast to the Outposts. Gershom might even make a ballad about it that would be sung all over the islands. He never forgave Gershom for having landed at that inopportune moment, and for having witnessed his disgraceful encounter with Anapest and his ignominious flight to the fish house. For Uriah had been a stout man in his day, and he had a deep sense of the dignity of his kingship.

However, the old man had not much time to reflect on Gershom's opinion, for Anapest, entangled in the net like a giant albacore, let out a flood of curses and abuse that would have done credit to the stoutest fishwife of Billingsgate. Freed at last from the meshes, she advanced toward Uriah's fish house and pounded upon the barred door with a broken oar handle.

"Come out, ye hoary old robber, an' I'se 'll teach ye to order my boys around. A woman, is I? Ye dat snatches a crust from de moufs o' widows an' orphans."

But Uriah made no response from his secure retreat, and when Anapest had spent most of her fury in wordy abuse, she burst into tears and retired to her own domain.

Entering her kitchen she found David there looking at the infant Ralph.

"Git out o' my house," she screamed at him. "Git out o' my house. You'se a Jung, too. I won't have nair a Jung in dis house."

"Why you talk like dat, Aunt Anapest? Ain't you a Jung by blood, too?"

"I'se not no Jung, I'se a Kraus. Git out o' dis

house. Ye works wid dat gang. I don't let no Jung enter dis house nur cross my land."

"I got fur to enter yur house an' to cross yur land fur to see my child."

That must have touched Anapest's heart, for she sat down suddenly at the kitchen table and began again to cry, pulling her gray hair over her face.

"I didn't mean fur to say dat, David. Ye can come an' see yur child, an' I'll rear him well fur ye, too. We can't take nair a spite out on dat innocent."

By this time the Kraus boys, alarmed by Anapest's shrieks, arrived in the kitchen and glowered at David.

"Dere's a curse on dat branch o' de Jungs," cried Anapest, raising her head, "an' I'se 'll tell ye why now. Dere's a curse on George's branch, an' dat's what makes dem so greedy an' mean. Ole George, Uriah's fader, were cruel an' mean jus' like Uriah, but our grandfader Edward were gentle an' kind. An' I'll tell ye all now how de curse come on George's branch.

"One winter night, long 'fore us was born, a brig from de West Indies busted in on de dog holes to de soudard o' de island. A white man an' a nigger come ashore. De nigger's legs was broke off below de knees, but de white man had life in him. Edward were off de island, but ole George an' his sharesman carried de bodies to de house, where de old folks lived, an' laid dem on de kitchen floor by de stove. Den ole George got right skeered o' de bodies, an' de women an' children began to yell, specially when dey sees de nigger wid no feet. So he carried out de bodies an' laid dem in de eel grass by de pig pen. Dey was both froze stiff in de mornin', an' den, sure nuff, de white man had no life in him. George buried 'em bot' in de sand heap by Nigger Pond, an' two days arter, when de nigger's feet come ashore in his boots, he buried dem in de field below where de light is now. Dat's how dem Jungs brung de curse on Rockbound. You might say as how ole George murdered dat white man. It's dat nigger dat can't rest dat goes flittin' foggy nights lookin' fur his feet, an' it's de haunt o' de white man what had life in him an' dey froze dat pushes Uriah off de path into de tall timothy."

Anapest finished her epic and stood up to twist her hair into a knot. Suddenly she turned on her boys.

"What you standin' here fur? Ain't dey plenty o' work on de land or in de fish house?"

David started out with the others, but Anapest called to him: "You come back, David, fur to see

yur kid whenever ye wants. You'se a good Jung
an' sprung from ole Edward's line."

In the afternoon of the day of the great
quarrel, David took wheelbarrow and shovel
and filled in the hole with beach rocks and gravel.
For this act Uriah denounced him in the fish
house, before the brothers, as a traitor to the
Jungs.

You's half in league wid dem bloody Krauses,
the old man stormed at him.

That night, as David sat in his kitchen, he
wondered if there were people in the world who
lived in peace and quiet. Would he ever reach
such a place? He and Tamar had never fought.
He had half a mind to sell his place to Uriah,
who would be an eager buyer, and try living
among folk on the main. But perhaps it would be
the same there. The Boutiliers of Miscou, he
remembered, had sometimes quarrelled fiercely
among themselves. Moreover, why should he be
such a coward as to sell his mother's place to
Uriah? The old urge to stand fast by his rights
asserted itself. He was heartily sick of Rockbound, but he must stick it out and stand as firm
as Uriah and his boys. In the darkness he cried
aloud: "O God, if dey is a God what cares fur
men at all, give me some peace an' quiet in my
life afore I dies."

CHAPTER VIII

For hym was levere have at his beddes heed
Twenty bookes clad in blak or reed
Of Aristotle and his philosophie,
Than robes riche, or fithele, or gay sautrie.

CANTERBURY TALES.

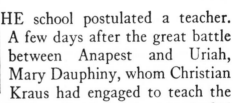

HE school postulated a teacher. A few days after the great battle between Anapest and Uriah, Mary Dauphiny, whom Christian Kraus had engaged to teach the Rockbound school, arrived on the island. Old Jean Dauphiny brought her in his boat from their home in Bay of God's Mercy, and having landed Mary and her possessions and bespoken her a boarding place, stopped for a little while to talk with Uriah, whom he had known in days gone by.

Mary Dauphiny, a pretty girl of twenty, came of fisherfolk on the main. She was of moderate height and strongly built, and as she had worked with the men in fish house and hayfield, she knew what was expected of women by labour-driven fishermen. When she had been allowed to go to school in the winters, she had shown such quickness and aptitude in reading, writing, and arithmetic that the local schoolmaster had told her parents that she should be trained as a teacher. At this announcement, old Jean Dauphiny had hummed and hawed, wagged his head, and said that learning was no good for a fisher lass. But his pride had been touched, none the less, and eventually he consented to send Mary to the county academy at Liscomb, where she took her B certificate with credit, and afterward to the normal school at Landor for her teacher's licence. Old Jean was proud of his girl's success and began to urge her on. He could very well spare Mary from farm and fish stand, for his money box, hidden at the foot of a brown rafter, was well filled, and besides her he had eight growing children, and a second wife, a shrewish Surette from Fond du Baie, who nagged and laboured from dawn to dusk.

Mary took to learning greedily, read a great many books not on required courses, found out much about life that had been hidden from her parents and those before them, but never lost her sense of values nor became ashamed of her

antecedents. Pale-faced, thin-shouldered men of
the inland towns she compared to their disad-
vantage with the bronzed, deep-chested fishermen, who moved with catlike grace and ease
to let go sheet or halliard. When she came home
for vacations, she would gib herring, rake hay,
and even go on the offshore banks with her
father, if he were short a sharesman. Of all his
children, she was beyond doubt old Jean Dauphiny's favourite, and he often boasted of her
when a little drunk. "Dere's a lass fur he," he
used to say to his friends. "Larnin' hasn't sp'ilt
her. She kin do a day's work wid air a lass on de
coast, an' she plays de organ somet'in' beautiful.
Larned it all by herself, she did."

Rockbound was Mary's first school. One has to
begin at the beginning in school-teaching, and
Rockbound, with its illiterate adult population,
stood near the bottom of the scale. On the day
after her arrival, she opened the school and felt a
strange sinking at heart as the children took
their places before her. There were no established
school conventions or traditions to strive against;
still, she was a stranger from an outside world,
and hence, at first, an enemy to the children of
Rockbound. Her gracious fairness soon won
their hearts, and she in turn began to enjoy the
task of sowing in virgin soil.

As she walked up the lane to the schoolhouse on brisk September mornings, her cheeks glowing, the tassel of her red stocking cap bobbing in the breeze, she was undoubtedly an attractive girl. David thought so, as he looked at her from afar. He liked the way she carried herself and her earnest intent in going about her business. She had a decided trace of French vivacity, for the Dauphinys had been established on this coast when the whole region was known as La Tuque. Yes, even before that, when the bay was known by the old Indian name Merlegash, bay of milk-white waves, and that was a good century before the landing of the Germans, Dutch, and Flemings in 1750. True, the Dauphinys of Mary's time had forgotten their patois, and perhaps even their origin, but, along with the Houblys and Boutiliers, they retained a few French traits that made them different from their neighbours. In Mary the inherited traits were marked. Her kind brown eyes were wide apart; she showed white, well-formed teeth when she smiled; but the real charm of her face lay in a short upper lip and a slightly tilted nose that gave to her face at times a saucy and almost impish expression. Young women are not marked, as are men, by the station in which they are born, and such was Mary Dauphiny's bearing and natural dignity that, had she been beautifully gowned, she would have graced the finest assembly in the land.

All Rockbound approved her within a month. She was, perhaps, the islanders first object of general approbation. Fanny, the potato girl, looked at her shyly and sighed for something she had missed in life. Mary, in turn, who listened to no gossip, liked Fanny better than any of the younger Rockbound women. They spent their lives watching for the boats, or in peering beneath a drawn blind to see who was going down the lane, and were mere reflections of their husbands' partisan opinions. Fanny, at any rate, tidied herself and put on a clean dress after each day's work, and that appealed to Mary's sense of order. Mary went out of her way to talk with Fanny, invited her to sing while she played the organ, and volunteered to teach her reading and writing. Uriah's only comment on the new teacher was, "A new broom sweeps clean," but that was high praise coming as it did from Uriah. Casper dropped his long chin and formed his lips into what he considered a smile of friendship whenever he met her, and Anapest, the old empress, stood behind her as a tower of strength.

On afternoons, when David got in early from the banks, it used to do his heart good to see the little children flocking up the school lane at the clang of the bell. For in the tiny belfry perched on the ridgepole the Rockbounders had hung a bell, a ship's bell with a fine clear tone, salvaged years ago by Uriah from the wreck of *The Lady of Gaspé*, and from it a rope dangled to the schoolroom below. At the first stroke of this bell, children darted from near-by houses to run up the lane and crowd into the schoolhouse, where Mary stood awaiting them. Little Jungs and little Krauses played games together at recess and sat side by side in the schoolroom, to con their lessons from the self-same book. "Dey won't fight and quarrel an' be so full o' suspicions 'bout one anoder when dey grows up," thought David, as he stood watching with his arm hooked over the prow of his boat. He wished, in such moments, that he had had a chance to learn reading. Reading would take away the loneliness of long winter evenings, and perhaps make a man wise, like old Gershom Born. Could a grown man learn it? he wondered. Someone would have to help little Ralph when he started school, and in his present state of ignorance, he felt himself a poor kind of father. A seed of desire was sown in his mind. "Why not ask her," he thought, "if a grown feller like me kin learn readin'?"

One afternoon, when the children burst out of school with shrill cries, and made their way homeward, he summoned all his courage and walked up the lane to the schoolhouse. Mary, seated at the teacher's desk, was making up her register in neat figures. She heard the strange footstep and looked up as he entered.

"Good-evenin'," he said. "I wants fur to ask ye somethin'."

"What is it?"

"Do ye t'ink dat a feller as old as me could learn readin'?"

"Of course you could."

"How does ye start fur to do it?"

"First you have to learn the alphabet."

"De A, B, C's?"

"Yes."

"Well, den, could I buy a primer off ye?" said David, pulling out a well-worn purse. "De kind de littlest kids use."

"I haven't any to sell, but here's one I can lend you."

"T'anks, I'se 'll take good care of it."

"Here are the letters," said Mary, opening the book at the first page. "You'll have to copy them over and over, till you know them all thoroughly."

"But how does I know dere names?"

"I'll go over them, three or four times, with you now. The first is A, that you know already, the second B, like a bumblebee, the third C, like the sea, the ocean."

"Dey's a string o' dem, ain't it?"

"Twenty-six," said Mary, "and after you've learned to make the twenty-six big ones, there are twenty-six little ones. Copy them over and over, and if you get stuck on the names or sounds, come up any afternoon when school's out, and I'll help you. On the next page are simple words with pictures: see, Rat, Cat, Dog. When you've learned your letters, you can begin on these simple words."

"I'se'll sure give her a good try," said David.

"Look here, I'll make a copy of your name and the names of the boats. There it is, David Jung. Your boat is *Phœbe*, isn't it? And Joseph's *Lettie*, Casper's *Gannet*, and Martin's *Sea Gull*."

David was much interested in this bit of applied learning.

"S'pose I kin larn?" he queried boyishly. "I got a baby, you know; Anapest's raisin' him fur me. Some day he'll be a-comin' to school."

"Of course you can learn. My dad says you've been high-line fisherman of this bay for three years. A high-line fisherman can learn anything.

Fishing takes brains and judgment; of course you can learn."

"I'se'll give her a try, hard as I fish," said David, departing, the primer gripped in his big hand, hope clutching at his heart.

At the kitchen table that very night he began his education. As if in anticipation of a rough and dirty job, he rolled both shirt sleeves high above his elbows, exposing his swelling muscles. He got paper, a stub of pencil, opened his primer, and after much squaring of elbows and puckering of brow, began to copy the big letters straight down the list. These crooked signs were mysterious to him; he felt as if he were learning magic. He wondered what great man had invented them. "Perhaps," he thought, "dey was a gift o' God to men, an' t'rough dem I kin find out somethin' good." The letters seemed to him fixed, unchanged from the beginning, inevitable. He little dreamed how they had been battered about the world, from Egypt to Crete, from Crete to Greece, from Greece to Rome, from Rome to barbarous Britain; a hard line given by a long-faced Egyptian, a graceful curve by some smiling Greek, a dignity of form by some pompous Roman, a dot and quaint twirl by some mincing clerk of Britain.

From the wearisome task of writing the alphabet over and over, he was led astray to copy
the sheet Mary had made for him with his own
name and the names of the boats. "David Jung
the *Phœbe*," fifty times he wrote it, till his
conscience pricked him, for it seemed hardly
fair to take up advanced work till he had con-
quered the straight and crooked letters.

At his right elbow, as he worked, stood a paraffin lamp with a mantle that cast a glaring white
light upon table and floor and made mocking
shadows dance on the ceiling. The lamp had a
history. David had bought it from a preacher,
not a regular preacher, but a kind of missionary
or aquatic circuit rider, who had spiritual juris-
diction over the outer islands. The grasping
islanders were willing to pay little in money for
their chance of salvation, and the poor preacher
was driven to selling them patent lamps to eke
out a slender income. David, whom Gershom had
taught to be a kind of agnostic, had no great
regard for the words of the preacher, but one
day, when the stout little man had come through
a rough sea to visit a sick woman and baptize
a girl of the Jungs and received but seventy cents
in the collection plate, he had issued from the fish
house and said: "Hi, there, parson, I wants one
o' yur lamps," and to the deep disgust of Uriah

and the brothers had handed over seven dollars to the man of God.

Every evening, by the light of his glaring patent lamp, David laboured away, and felt more tired at the end of two hours' wrestling with the alphabet than if he had spent that time in hauling heavy lobster pots in a rough sea. Still, he realized that it took his mind off the quarrels of the island, the greed of Uriah, the hatefulness of the brothers, and his own loneliness. He was spurred on, too, by a desire to exhibit his learning some day before Gershom. Sometimes he sat biting the end of his stubby pencil and dreaming of what he could do. Next year he would begin to take the Liscomb paper and learn what the world did from day to day and when little Ralph was grown, he could hold him on his knees and teach the child all he had learned. He made frequent afternoon visits to the schoolhouse to consult the oracle in regard to the sounds and shaping of letters. Uriah noted this and wagged his old beard. Already he had begun to think that Mary might make a useful wife for Casper, and that something in the way of dowry might be squeezed out of old Jean Dauphiny.

But not only did David work at learning in the kitchen. When he steered for the banks in gray dawns, the primer lay snugly tucked in a

pocket beneath his oilskins. When he stopped
fishing to eat his lunch, or if there came a period
when, because of the run of tide, cod would not
bite, out would come his precious book for a review of cat, dog, rat. Tailor-wise this scholar at
the beginning of things squatted upon his bit of
sun-touched deck and by turns frowned and
smiled upon his book. In part, it had taken the
place of Gershom, his old fishing comrade. Sometimes, as he steered for home, he held tiller in
one hand and primer in the other, glancing up
from the magic symbols to catch beneath his
main boom a quick glimpse of Rockbound or
Barren Island. Once, when so engaged, he jibbed
the *Phœbe* before a following wind and carried
away a back stay. Then his eye swiftly circled
the sea to ascertain if any fisherman had noted
his boat's misdemeanour—for to jib a running
boat is a matter for great scorn among fishermen
—and judging that no Jung or Kraus had seen
looked down again and, smiling, patted his book.

One Sunday, as he sat by his boat at the
launch's head looking across the sea to the Outposts, Mary, who had been making the round of
the island, came up to him. Her cheeks were
glowing in the sea wind, which made the red
tassel of her cap stand out stiffly and then dance
and bob.

"She's like none I've seen before," thought David sadly.

"How are you getting on with your lessons, high-line fisherman?" she asked gaily.

"Poor," answered David. "I guess I'se dumb at books."

"It's always harder to learn when you're grown up."

"Ay, dat it is. De trouble is, I doesn't rightly know when I'se right an' when I'se wrong."

"Look here," said Mary suddenly. "I'm teaching Fanny to read and write in the evenings. Why couldn't I teach the two of you together?"

David's heart gave a great throb of joy, and Mary would have been astonished could she have sensed the flood of generous and grateful thoughts that, at her offer, flowed through the mind of that simple man, who had had few favours in life but had won his little all by hard fighting.

"Dat would be great," he gasped, scarce able to speak for joy. "But I kin pay, I don't want ye to do it fur nuttin'."

"Never mind pay. You can do me a favour in return. Some day I may want to go to Bay of God's Mercy, and you can take me in the *Phœbe*."

"Dat I'se'll gladly do, an' as often as ye likes."

"All right, I'll come up to your house—it's too noisy in Christian's—three nights a week, Mondays, Wednesdays, and Fridays, and bring Fanny along with me."

Thus the winter night class was begun. David's kitchen stove, stuffed with spruce knots, glowed, the patent lamp cast its glaring light, in the distance the sea grumbled along the beach. Fanny, the potato girl, clad in clean blue-checked gingham, her wistful blue eyes shining gratefully, and David, brawny high-liner, sat on one side of the kitchen table, and like two little children conned their lessons from the *First Royal Reader*. Mary sat on the other side and, with the zeal of a young teacher, checked or encouraged them, as the occasion demanded. If, for instance, David spelled out painfully the story of brave Bobby and his gallant rescue of the child from the ravenous shark and commented in passing: "Dat's plum foolishness—a dog in de water ain't got no show wid a shark." Then Mary would rebuke him sharply as if he were a little boy: "Now, David Jung, your business is not to tell me what a dog or a shark can do in the water. Perhaps you do know more about codfish and sharks and dogs in the water than the man who wrote this story. That doesn't help much with your reading: your business is to know the words 'dog' and 'shark' when you come to them in print. And what's more, you and Fanny have got to stop saying 'wid' and 'dat.'" And Mary put her tongue between her closed teeth and showed them how to say "th." "Just as if you were going to spit and changed your mind," she explained concisely.

Then David and Fanny each had to say "that" and "with" fifty times with much spluttering, spitting, and suppressed laughter, before they were allowed to go back to the story of brave Bobby and the shark, which David still read with a cynical twist in the corner of his mouth.

After the lessons David walked home with Fanny and Mary. Fanny they dropped at the old loft house; with Mary alone he had a hundred yards across the stubble field to the home of Christian Kraus, where Mary boarded. David walked as slowly as he dared, to make those precious moments last as long as possible. Sometimes they looked out across the sea to the flash of Gershom's light and spoke of his loneliness; sometimes they looked up at the burning stars, and Mary told him the names of the constellations: the Pleiades, Orion, Cassiopea's Chair, the Great Bear, which, though formerly nameless to him, he had noted through a thousand nights.

It was inevitable that David should fall in love with Mary, for he was lonely, and by instinct his heart responded to gentleness and beauty. He had no desire to handle her, as he had handled other women; he desired only to be near her as a worshipper and to drink in her wisdom and beauty. Her words were balm to his troubled mind. He gave her the loyalty and affection that a dog of the Rockland breed gives his master. He had dreamed of no one who approached her perfection; she seemed the acme of wisdom and beauty. Tamar and Leah had been but women; Mary was something apart.

But he was wise enough to keep his feelings to himself. He knew the strict tradition and convention of the islanders, who, while they paid little heed to morals and regarded love children with slight disapproval, had somehow fixed on a two-year period of widowership before a man could begin to court another woman in honourable fashion. "Perhaps," thought David, "at the end of two years, I might ask her." But surely it was arrogant to think of asking anyone so far above him.

But David was not Mary's only lover. It was obvious that such a pretty and clever girl as Mary Dauphiny would be courted by the single men of Rockbound and the neighbouring islands. Uriah had, in fact, picked her out as a suitable wife for Casper. He detested Casper and merely wished to marry him well because he was a Jung, who should beget a brood of children who in time could work and outdo the Krauses. "She kin read an' write," he thought, "an' kin keep some books fur us. Dat'll keep de boys from wranglin' so much at de end o' de season. It's gittin' hard fur me to remember eberty'ing t'rough a whole month. She's a stout lass an' kin lend a good hand wid de fish when we'se pinched, an' after she's married, she kin keep right on teachin' school jus' de same, an' any money Christian Kraus collects will be turned ober to us in de end."

This last thought pleased the old king so much that he chuckled and rubbed his hands through his beard. Uriah broached the proposal to Casper and began to urge him on. In fact, Casper needed little urging, for his narrow, greedy eyes had followed Mary since the day of her landing on the island.

David hardly feared Casper as a rival, yet the fellow became a source of annoyance, for he used to come hanging about David's house on lesson nights to take Mary home. Along toward half-past eight, in the midst of their lessons, the red-faced Casper would arrive clad in his Sunday suit. If it were mild, he stayed without, whistling and stamping his feet on the doorstep, but if it were bitter cold he would, perforce, enter the kitchen and sit scowling at David and Fanny till the lesson was over. He could not comprehend, as he sat there, why Mary bothered with such low trash. Fanny's record was patent to every soul on Rockbound, and many a time he'd heard the Outposters graphically describe David and Gershom as "hellians fur women." "He knows not a scrap o' de Bible," he thought, forgetting that he himself derided the Old Testament. "Look what he done to my sister Tamar. If I was de Lord God, I'd wipe dat David an' his bully Gershom Born right off de eart'. A fine friend, birds o' a feather, a drunken whoremaster, dat's what I calls him. As fur David, nuttin' would do my eyes so much good as to see de *Phœbe* come round West Head bottom up. I wish she'd sarve him as she sarved Mark."

So he sat by the stove, patiently waiting for Mary and mingling his ugly thoughts with reflections on his own virtues and his ever-growing wealth. When Mary glanced his way, and that was but seldom, he quickly changed his lowering scowl into an ingratiating grin. The four walked down the lane together as far as the fish house;

then David stood alone, cursing softly but none the less bitterly as he watched Casper and Mary across the fields to Christian's house.

But Casper was the lesser of David's rivals, for Gershom Born fell in love with Mary too, and on every possible day drove his boat on some pretext to Rockbound to see her and perhaps have a word with her. Casper and Uriah had many a conference about Gershom in a dark corner of the fish house. Casper was all for denying Gershom the right to land his boat on their launch. But Uriah said, no, that could not be done; Gershom had been too long their sharesman, and such a denial was against the custom of the islands. The old man disliked Gershom but feared his bitter tongue and the opinions of the fishermen in the bay. Moreover, as Uriah pointed out, Gershom could land on the Krauses' land and see Mary in spite of them. The Krauses would be glad to aid Gershom in anything against the Jungs. Sometimes Uriah would turn fiercely on Casper with: "Why doesn't ye take de woman if ye wants her? I never let no man stan' in my way wid a woman when I was young. Ye'd do de same if ye had de spunk o' a louse. If dat David or Gershom gits her away from ye, ye kin git to hell off my island."

When Casper attempted to point out that

Mary Dauphiny was different from the women
Uriah had dealt with in the days of his youth,
the old man's eyes blazed with fury. "Women,
women," he muttered, "dey's all alike. Trouble is
de men's too like women, now'days. When I were
a gaffer, men what was real men took what dey
wanted."

David felt that he could easily compete with
Casper as a rival—the Jungs would hate him if
he won her from Casper; that mattered little
since their hatred was already bitter—but when
Gershom Born entered the lists as Mary's apparent suitor, hope sank low in his heart. One
Sunday afternoon he walked to the southern
cliff top. He carried his long-barrelled duck gun,
and his dog followed close to his heels, but though
a flock of blue-wings sheltered from the sea in
Southwest Gutter within easy range, he fired no
shot. The cranberry vines were covered deep in
crusted snow. He stamped a place clear, brushed
off a log, and sat down to think, his dog curled
at his feet. Below him was the angry winter sea,
its black surface checkered with floating ice.
Far off to the southward stood up Gershom's
lonely tower. His peace of mind had been of brief
duration. Now he was plagued with an aching
love for Mary, yet he must stand aside while
others wooed her. He dared not ask her for al-

most two years, and who knew what might happen in that time? How could he wait so long? Against Casper he knew he had a good fighting chance, for while Casper was backed by the wealthy Uriah, he was so cowardly and mean spirited that David felt a clever and sensitive girl like Mary would quickly see through him. Yet you never could tell what women would think or do; they were as sharp as fine steel in some things and dull as blunted tools in their judgment of men.

But Gershom as a rival! Gershom was another matter! Gershom, keeper of the great light; Gershom, son of old Gershom Born, wise man of the islands; Gershom, who read poetry books and could himself make and sing ballads; Gershom, who had never needed marriage, since he carried women off their feet and won whom he chose; Gershom, the giant with ready wit, handsome face, and great booming voice. Above all, Gershom was his friend, his sworn ally, who had stood shoulder to shoulder with him in a dozen fights. He could hardly enter the race against Gershom, and if he did, what would be his chances? Life was vexatious, he wished he were through with it, and he groaned so deeply that the dog started up and looked into his master's eyes with wonder. Again his eyes crossed the sea to the stark loneliness of Barren Island. Surely Gershom, on that ghost-ridden place, needed a wife more than he. But who can give a lover any law? His reasoning, his intense affection for his friend, could not lessen his love for Mary Dauphiny nor lay the sorrow in his heart.

Rockbound promised him no peace of mind nor quiet of heart; the tiresome procession of years that stretched before him offered endless labour but no striving for a goal that seemed worthy of attainment. For a moment he stood struggling with the temptation to throw himself over the cliff into the dog hole and let ice and sea batter him to pieces. But a thought of little Ralph and of his vow to Tamar held him back. The child must not grow up a landless man and spend his best years winning freedom. He must learn to endure and wait in silence, though life was hopeless and impossible. Men were as cold and cruel as the winter sea that crashed the ice against the cliffs and roared into the cannon rock to send up mocking cries.

CHAPTER IX

Swich a tempest gan to ryse
That brak hir mast and made it falle,
And clefte hir ship, and dreinte hem alle,
That never was founde, as it telles,
Bord ne man, ne nothyng elles.

BOKE OF THE DUCHESSE.

FTER his decision on the cliff, the night lessons became painful things to David. He scarcely dared glance up from his book to meet Mary's brown eyes. Though he had learned a great deal, he suddenly lost interest in reading; the magic symbols had brought him no happiness but only further discomfort. He loathed the smug Casper, who lounged in silence by the stove, and was glad when the lobster season, with its attendant work by day and night, gave an excuse for the suspension of learning.

David was able to set about lobstering early, for it had been an open winter, with the bay unclogged with floes, which sometimes in intense and sudden frost knit the islands to the main. He had a better season than any man on Rockbound; when it was time to haul his traps and go after mackerel, he was some four hundred dollars richer, but his heart was low, and success brought him little happiness.

With the advent of spring, Uriah began to rush and hustle his underlings. Age could not break the old man's spirit, nor time deplete his energy or lessen his desire for gain. Spring, summer, and early autumn were seasons of heartbreaking labour, in which Uriah gloried. Season after season the mackerel advanced north in myriads like an invading horde, following the indentations of the coast, in the same invariable fashion as those that spawned them had done. La Tuque Bay they passed for no apparent reason, schooled into St. Michael's Bay, and there rushed into hundreds of traps and seines set to receive them. All night during the mackerel season, watchmen of the Jungs sat and dozed fitfully, by tiny fires on the cliff tops, and, waking, stared for flash of white foam on black water, that betokened schooling fish in the seine. With the seine full came the labour of getting the fish out, boating them to the fish house, and dressing them. The fish-house floor was piled ever higher, and men staggered to and fro, drunken through loss of sleep. When the mackerel passed north, came the haddock and the attendant labour of setting and hauling heavy trawls. If halibut were taken on the trawls, a long night journey to Minden, to market the fish fresh, was involved. Endless fields of potatoes and cabbages had somehow to be planted at odd moments of this busy season. The women could not do the heaviest of this work. In the midst of cutting the timothy came the herring close inshore, and codfish were always with them. When in the cool breezes of September the cod must be dried on rock and fish flake, the mackerel retreated southward from the arctic waters. Boats must be repaired, caulked, and painted, nets tanned, gear overhauled, and then winter leaped upon them.

It is no wonder that David, restless and unhappy, looked forward to such a programme with a sinking heart. For Mary, he could have endured endless labour; without her, nothing seemed good in his eyes. The sight of Gershom and her together pierced like an arrow to his heart. If he could but escape for this spring and summer this prison of slave labour and unrequited love! But there was no hope in his heart. Escape, however, was closer than he thought.

In late April a boat from the main brought

Uriah a letter, which he carried home to his wife for an interpretation. It was from Captain Johnny Westner, asking Uriah to let two of his boys go to the Grand Banks on the *Sylvia Westner*. Since the *Sylvia Westner* had been for three seasons high-line of all the Liscomb fleet, and first home, her decks kenched high with cod, this invitation was something of a compliment, which pleased the old man. Johnny Westner, smartest young skipper on all the coast, picked only the most skilled hand-liners and ablest men for his crews. The reputation of Rockbound had travelled far and wide; none excelled Rockbound men with the hand-line, and long stretches of work without sleep were meat and drink to them.

Now, with the exception of David, and that in the days when he had eked out a slender existence on the Outposts, no Rockbound man had ever sailed on a Grand Banker. To allow such a thing might be to admit that Rockbound was not the best fishing stand on the coast, and that was a matter of pride with Uriah. For several days, as the old man sat mending nets in the loft, he pondered over the proposal. Of course, it never occurred to him to ask advice or opinion of anyone involved; he was the king, he alone decided policies of importance.

To let two boys go would leave him short-handed for the summer's work. Still, Joe's and Martin's oldest gaffers were big enough now to give a hand in the boats. "Dis goin' to school an' listenin' to a woman talk about words an' letters is all flub-dub," thought the old man. "Make 'em soft an' weak. Let 'em git inter de boats an' larn somethin' real, larn to be tough men, way me an' George an' Simeon done." He could hire a couple of cheap sharesmen from the main, and he and Joseph could drive them to the limit for one season. If the *Sylvia Westner*, he reasoned, made three trips and came home again high-line, a sharesman on board would make twice as much money as anyone fishing off Rockbound in the best season, for Grand Banks cod were big and fetched a higher price than inshore fish. The money thus got would be thrown into the common chest, and his would be the lion's share. Upon this consideration Uriah ultimately based his decision to send two of his vassals in accordance with Captain Johnny's request.

He would gladly have sent the grumbling Casper, but was restrained by two reasons: he had set Casper hot upon the trail of Mary Dauphiny, and if Casper were on the Banks for a whole season, Gershom Born, or even David, might get an advantage with her; moreover,

Casper was the most skilled and experienced in shooting the seine, and he could not spare him in herring time. David and Gershom would have been the perfect pair to send—then Casper would have had a clear field for his love affair— but, alas, Gershom was no longer a king's subject. Finally, the old king elected to send David and Martin, his weakest linesman.

David sprang in the air, cracked his heels, and gave a great whoop when Uriah told him. Uriah scowled disapproval in his pleasure at the announcement, but David marked him not. His prayer had been answered: here was a chance to escape for awhile the turbulence of the island and the sight of Mary. Gershom, who was on Rockbound at the time, gripped his hand and said, "Wisht I could go wid." David's escape increased his own sense of irksome imprisonment. He little guessed how he stung David when he added: "Well, if I can't git away, I got to git a woman on Barren Island, an' dat soon. It's too damn lonesome fur a man like me. I'se 'll fergit how to speak now. Dat damn island'll kill me in de end."

Uriah himself was to take Martin and David in his boat to the La Tuque Islands and there deliver them in person to Hand-line Johnny. Martin made no demur when the decision was announced to him; he never resisted his father, and on the day before the *Sylvia Westner* was to sail he said good-bye to wife and children with a show of stoical indifference. David shook Anapest's hand and charged her to take good care of little Ralph, but he avoided saying a word of good-bye to Mary.

When he came down the path to the boat, however, dunnage bag, rubber boots, and oilskins upon his broad shoulders, he found Mary waiting near the parting boat's prow. Martin was already aboard, stowing his kit; Uriah stood impatient to push off.

"Don't forget your lessons," said Mary as David drew near. "Here's a book I've brought you to read," and she shoved into his hand a battered and well-thumbed copy of *The Tempest* that she had studied in school.

"Wid Johnny Westner, he won't have nair a time fur readin'," interjected Uriah.

"Yes, he will; there's going and coming, when he'll have his watch below, and Sundays. Take it, take it," she added, pressing the book into David's hands. "It's all about a tempest, a shipwreck, magic, and a pair of island lovers."

David took the book and stuck it in his pocket, but he was dumb. He looked into Mary's eyes for what seemed an interminable time, but his lips would not open to say either, "thank you" or "good-bye."

Uriah broke the spell: "Git yur dunnage aboard quick, an' help shove off dis boat. We ain't got all day fur startin'; it's a right long sail to de La Tuque Islands."

Uriah and David slipped the boat off the launch, and Mary walked to the top of Crook's Hill to wave good-bye till their sail vanished behind the rocks of Little Duck. She surprised herself in doing this: surely she was not in love with David Jung; he was too recent a widower and must be put out of her mind. "Perhaps," she thought, "I wanted to wave good-bye because I'm a fisherman's daughter and understand the dangers they are going to." In her heart she knew she would miss David from the island.

The boat, with Uriah at the tiller and David and Martin amidships, moved along quickly. David dozed, head on thwart, and with a start awoke from a dream in which Uriah, as a pirate, was selling him into slavery. Uriah spoke not a word to either of his retainers. It was a long sail to the La Tuque Islands, but the northeast land breeze on their quarter carried them along so briskly that by noon they came within sight of Hand-line Johnny's vessel.

She was a smart-looking schooner, painted

gleaming black, with a strip of scarlet along her scupper line from stem to stern. Through the clear water, her coppered bottom glimmered, and below her bowsprit was a gilded figurehead that some local artist had carved as a semblance of the young master's little girl, for whom the schooner was named. She had deep, graceful sheer, her spars raked slightly aft, and with a couple of guns mounted bow and stern she might easily have passed for a swift privateer such as sailed those waters a hundred years before her time. With the exception of the *Springwood*, she was the fastest of all the Liscomb fleet. Both her top masts were stepped—something unusual in a banker—her yellow dories were nested on deck, jibs were flapping loose, the peak of the mainsail hoisted to dry, and as the breeze yawed her to and fro on her cable, she seemed to David as buoyant and supple as a gannet riding a wave.

They were soon alongside, and David, at Uriah's order, hastened to put out a rope fender to guard the schooner's new paint from their gunwale. Hand-line Johnny appeared at the rail above them to shout a greeting. He was as smart as his schooner. Although only twenty-five years of age, he was known from Cape Brule to Marmot as a fisherman of great skill and judgment, an accurate navigator and bold sailing

master. He dared carry on in half gale, and his
reputation for daring, combined with his youth
and strength, won for him the admiration and
loyalty of his crews. Sailors and fishermen swear
by a master who will carry on sail. Nothing
warmed Captain Johnny's heart more than to
have both topsails bellying and the lee rail under.

David and Martin climbed aboard and carried
their dunnage to the bunks assigned them in the
forecastle. Uriah, after a second invitation, came
on deck to have a moment's crack with Captain
Johnny, who was a man after his own heart.
"Dat David'll bear some drivin'," he confided
to the young master. Then, waving his hand to
Martin and David, he clambered over the side
to beat his way back to Rockbound alone, a
weary, long beat against a head wind, one long
leg to sea, one short leg back toward the land.
If the wind held from the northeast he might,
he thought, make Rockbound by midnight, but
if it headed him off he would stand in to Bay of
God's Mercy and talk with Jean Dauphiny
about Casper's marriage with Mary. Jean Dauphiny had some money, he knew, and should
give dowry with his girl, as was the custom
among people of French descent along the coast.
He must not scare the Frenchman off by asking
too much. The best plan would be to get Dau-

phiny to name a sum and then demand a little
more. The grizzled old king smiled to himself,
and speculated on dowry and the amount of
money David and Martin would bring to the
common chest in September, as his sharp old
eyes peered under the main boom and his sea-
scarred hand steadied the kicking tiller. He had
no luck with the wind that day; it hauled farther
to the eastward and headed him off with squally
puffs before he reached the riotous Baker's
Dozen. He came about on the landward tack
and stood in for the Bay of God's Mercy, to
spend the night with the Dauphinys.

In the evening Uriah and old Jean sat in the
Dauphiny kitchen and, over glasses of hot rum,
talked of many things. Uriah pretended that his
visit was a chance and friendly one, made on his
way home from delivering David and Martin to
the *Sylvia Westner*. This statement was partly
true, since Uriah would have held on toward
Rockbound had the wind not headed him, but
old Jean was not simple enough to believe that
a driver like Uriah Jung wasted his time in
friendly visits when he had no ax to grind.

After much talk of boats and fishing the astute
Uriah led up to his subject by praising Mary.
In an unusual rôle of promoter of Rockbound
education, he told the fond father how well his

island subjects were pleased with Mary's teaching and general conduct.

"Dat's one fine lass," said the astute Uriah.

"Dat she is," replied old Jean, swelling with pride. "Dere's none like her on dis coast neider fur books nur work, an', hush, man, has ye p'r'aps heard her play on de organ?"

"Dat I has."

"She kin sail a boat, too, as good as air a one o' yur boys."

"Maybe, maybe," said Uriah, wagging his beard.

"One o' my boys, Casper, de eldest, has bin agoin' round wid."

"Ay," rejoined old Jean, "dat's de way wid young folks. Ye minds how we was, Ury, years ago, on de Outposts an' de main? Dem was fine free days."

"Dat I 'members well. But times is changed, dey marries more now. I reckon, Jean, dat when we was gaffers half de kids on de islands was love kids."

"An' grand mens dey maked, too! Where's such mens now'days?"

"Times is changed, times is changed. A man's got to have a regular wife now by de time he's t'irty to look after house and gear."

"Dat's right, but dey does rant round an' tie

ye down," sighed old Jean, thinking of his shrewish second.

"A good un saves house an' gear an' pays her
way."

"Ay, dat she does!"

"Now, my boy Casper's come to de marryin'
time. He's a strong man, de first one I begot wid
dis woman, an' dey're reckoned de best. He's got
house an' land an' money in de bank."

"Ay, Casper's an able man."

"He wants fur to marry yur Mary, if it kin
be arranged betwixt us."

"I reckons Mary won't t'ink o' marryin' fur
many a year, her mind's sot on bein' a high-line
teacher."

"What you t'inks o' all dis studyin' books,
Jean?"

"Mostly damn foolishness."

"Dat it is, 'less it helps a man keep books, an'
see de dealers don't cheat him an' weigh him
short. Mary's got 'nough larnin' fur dat now.
What's de good o' dat fine lass dat kin bear able
men bein' an old maid school teacher?"

"Dere yur right, Ury."

"Let's settle it now, den."

So the old men drew their chairs closer together
and mumbled in low tones. They were both
astute, but Uriah outdid Jean in craft. Old

Dauphiny was not unwilling that his Mary should marry one of the rich Rockbound Jungs. In fact, he knew that no better business match could be made on the whole coast. Uriah inflamed old Jean's greed by dwelling on the richness of his island's soil, its matchless position as a fishing stand, his wealth in nets and boats and endless gear piled high in lofts. Casper was his eldest son, dear to his heart, and some day would inherit much. So persuasive was Uriah that toward midnight old Jean not only consented but promised dowry. Not cash, of course, from the chest hidden at the foot of the brown rafter— that was too precious to be passed recklessly from hand to hand, but something in the way of equipment, a deep herring seine and a thirty-foot boat that was to be repainted and named the *Mary*. At daybreak on the following morning, Uriah set out in his boat, smiling grimly to himself at the thought of having overreached Jean Dauphiny, and with a favouring breeze reached his island kingdom before noon.

On the same morning the *Sylvia Westner* sailed, and young Martin got his first extended view of the coast, a little part of which he knew so well. He was young Martin in name only, and so called to distinguish him from his uncle in Sanford. Young Martin was not liked on board from the first. He was close-mouthed, greedy at table, and had all the pride and arrogance of the Rockbound Jungs. David, however, upon whom Martin really relied for help and advice, soon became a favourite. His bunk in the forecastle was narrow and cramping for a man of his stature, but that mattered little to him, he was inured to hard beds and by nature a sailor. There were twenty-five men aboard, rigging and paint work were in first-class repair, and the watches light. On the outward voyage he had a two hours' trick at the wheel and the rest of the day to himself.

On the second day of this outward voyage he found by the capstan a snug corner, screened from the shrewd April wind, and when he had made sure that no one was watching, pulled out the book Mary had given him.

"Werses," he muttered as he turned the pages. "Dat's nuttin' fur me. Werses is harder dan straight readin'." Still, the book had Mary Dauphiny written on the flyleaf, and for her sake he stumbled through the opening scenes. It was all about a ship in a gale o' wind, passengers buttin' in, dough dey knew nought o' boats and ships, about brave sailors doin' dere best, an' how at last de ship struck an' split. Though he did not understand all the words, his interest was awakened, and he read the opening scene again with growing wonder. "Dey was a lee shore; dey tried to come about an' missed stays; must er had too much forrad sail. Den dey tried to wear ship, hadn't room, and struck. Dat's exactly right; many's de wessel bin lost dat way. De feller what wrote dem werses were a sailor and knowed ships an' de sea. Caliban," he thought, "is like dat mischievous old ram o' Gershom's. Miranda might be Mary. I wisht I could go back to Rockbound a prince."

He had no time for reading verses when they reached the southern bank, where Hand-line Johnny, with his usual run of good luck, found great schools of cod. He loaded the *Sylvia Westner* with everything he dared carry, and was back in Liscomb from his spring trip in a little more than seven weeks. Young Martin got a day off while the vessel was refitting, visited his family, and carried Uriah their earnings, but David stayed by the vessel.

Then the *Sylvia Westner* set out on her summer trip, this time to fish the sandy banks to the southward of Sable Island, where shifting channels give grudging passage through the bars. Hand-line Johnny knew the ground well, and it was, of all banks, his favourite. It seemed a marvellous place to David, who could look over the side of his dory into deep green water, see the schools of cod, watch them take the hook or scatter in terror as the dark shadow of shark or albacore hung above them. Near him, the *Sylvia Westner*, her black sides now scarred and scrubbed by chaffing dories, yawed at her cable. The triangular riding sail was set aft, to keep her head to the wind, and around her, in a circle of a mile diameter, her yellow dories danced. Just like an old hen with a flock of yellow chickens, he used to think. When the fish were biting well, he could see captain, cooks, and boys hauling the flashing cod over the vessel's rail. No one idled on Hand-line Johnny's vessel, for he had a passion for loading his schooner quickly, beating all records, and thus proving to the world that hand-lining was a better method of fishing than trawling. To establish this principle, which was, perhaps, of as much value as principles that people accounted more important try to establish, he spared neither himself nor his crew.

On the midday summer sea the *Sylvia Westner*, encircled by her dories and yawing under her riding sail, was a fine sight, but when the long twilight began to fall, softening all lines, she appeared to David romantic and beautiful. Then she was like a pirate ship, with all the excitement and movement of battle. Dories deep to the gunwale bumped alongside, forkfuls of fish flew over the rail, unloaded dories tailed and elbowed astern, the schooner's waist was a welter of slippery cod, splitters flashed their knives by the flare of torches, boys dashed to and fro to fetch and carry, salters sweated in the hold as the split fish came tumbling down the hatchways. A babble of talk and laughter mingled with the smack of fish on the splitting tables and the splash in the washing butts. Hand-line Johnny led the way, and everyone went at top speed. Little wonder he took a crew of picked men! David's training on Rockbound stood him in good stead.

On Thursday, August the fifth, though there was scarcely enough wind to shake the leaves of the Lombardy poplars by Uriah's house, long swells with a crest of white began to roll in against the red cliffs of Rockbound. The islanders said to one another that there had been a great storm somewhere at sea. On Friday the sea increased, though only a gentle draught of wind came out of the southeast. By Saturday night mountainous rollers were smashing against the cliffs, filling the dog holes with curdy foam and making the cannon rock spout high with the roar of a big gun. Cranberry vines and wind-stunted spruces high on the cliff's edge were flecked with flung spray and festooned with kelp and seaweed.

The herring were on the shore, and though the sea was running high, Jungs and Krauses, along with fishermen from the main, left out their nets. Without a wind, they reasoned, a sea cannot keep up, and on Saturday night the sea's surface for a mile to the southward of Rockbound was checkered with lines of dancing corks.

By nine of that Saturday night came the wind in a sudden gale from the southeast with thunder and heavy gusts of rain. The rainfall had been light on Rockbound that summer; Uriah's tank was almost dry, and after the first squalls had washed the dust from his roof the old man attached the pipes to the gutter, and heard the water go gurgling into his cistern. He listened to the sound, smiling with pleasure; it was grand to get something, even water, for nothing. Then, as the southeaster whistled around his eaves and swirled in the branches of the willows, he frowned as dismal thoughts crossed his mind. "Good-bye, nets," he muttered. "Dat'll take de edge off de lobster an' line-fish money. De boys was dumb to set dem Friday, an' why is de Lord God so mean as to send storms to destroy nets? Doesn't He know dey costs good money!"

About twelve that night the wind hauled suddenly to the northwest and blew a living gale off the shore; by Sunday morning it was back again, blustering out of the southeast and driving mountainous seas against the cliffs. The centre of the storm had passed over Rockbound. By Sunday noon the storm had risen to the height of its violence and begun to subside. It had come by slow degrees but departed suddenly; by twilight only a moderate breeze was blowing, by midnight the wind was stilled. Next morning the islanders were able to visit their nets. The gale had taken a heavy toll in the bay; of nets nothing but moorings, head ropes, and handfuls of twine, was left; the Jungs lost eight fleets, the Krauses five, and many a Sanford and Outpost man everything he had. Ernest Bachman's big new boat went ashore in Deep Cove and was smashed to kindling wood. Rockbound boats were saved, for Jungs and Krauses had dragged them up until their prows were across the roadway, and even there waves clutched at their quarters and slopped the white of long breakers into them.

"You might 'a' knowed you'd 'a' lost dem," said Uriah to his group of wet, dejected Rockbounders, who stood sadly contemplating the tattered fragments of twine that clung to the head ropes. "Me an' my brudder Simeon wouldn't 'a' set no new fleets o' nets wid such a sea runnin' an' risin'. Us neber let no nets lie out ober de Lord's Day. De anger o' de Lord were in dat gale."

"Dere warn't no wind," ventured Casper sulkily.

"Do wind rip a net ur sea?" retorted the old king. "Us is fishin' herrin', not sea gulls, ain't it?"

"My dad says, nothing venture, nothing have," said a woman's clear voice in defence of the downcast fishermen.

Uriah wheeled sharply to see what woman had dared voice an opinion on such an important matter, and finding it was Mary Dauphiny who had spoken, his hard old face softened, and on one of the few occasions in his life he made a semi-generous remark: "I minds now, when I were a young man, I set two fleets o' nets when de herrin' was aplenty an' los' dem all but de head ropes in a risin' sea." And then he added with a note of triumph in his voice: "De poor fellers on de Sanford main and de Outposts is de ones dat 'll suffer; dey ain't got no more nets, an' us got plenty in de loft."

"What's de matter wid de ole man?" muttered Joseph to himself. "He mus' be gettin' soft in de head, or else he's up to some game."

That great summer storm which harried Rockbound had its origin in a rotating hurricane that whirled from the Caribbean Sea to sweep the whole Atlantic coast. It drove past Rockbound and in due time struck the *Sylvia Westner* as she lay riding to the southward of Sable Island. Hand-line Johnny had no wireless to warn him of approaching storms, but for several days he had noted the barometer's fall, and felt in his bones that a great storm was coming. Still, the fishing was good, the vessel almost loaded; given another week, and he would be homeward bound, hold full, and decks kenched high. Five miles to the north lay the *Sadie Oxner*, out of Minden, a trawler, a dangerous rival for his honours, and he vowed to himself to stay on the ground longer than her master dared. At all costs, he must be home earlier and with a bigger fare than the *Springwood*, the *Nova Zembla*, or the *Sadie Oxner*.

So Hand-line Johnny disregarded the strange windless waves, daily increasing in length and height, and with two cables out lay fifteen miles to the southward and in full view of that treacherous crescent of rolling sand dunes, whose horns stretch twenty miles to the westward and fourteen to the eastward, under the green water. At night he saw the two lights, one on the eastern, one on the western end of the giant sand pile, blink warningly at him, and midway between them the dim glow of the life-saving station.

When, in the early part of Saturday evening, the full force of the southeast hurricane suddenly struck the *Sylvia Westner*, her fish-laden dories were alongside, and those empty trailed astern on their long painters. The ninety-mile gale howled through the schooner's spars, and away went scraps and patches of the riding sail torn from spar and boom. The *Sadie Oxner* had long since slipped her cable and departed. Dories had to be got aboard, nested, and lashed, hatch covers fitted and battened down, cables keg-buoyed and cut—there was neither time nor opportunity to get the anchors—foresail lashed down with double stops, and away drove the *Sylvia Westner* under a scrap of double-reefed inner staysail.

Hand-line Johnny and old Caleb Baker, his next-door neighbour on the La Tuque Islands, held the wheel steady, though violent blows of following seas almost tore the spokes from their hands. David, whose trick it was by turn, stood behind them to render assistance if needed. He had no fear in his heart, but gloried in the fury of the gale. It was just like the tempest in his book of verses, rain, wind, thunder, and a lee shore. Would Captain Johnny, he wondered, try to bring her into the wind when close to the bar, or would he wear ship and try the other tack? Either plan would be hazardous. The wind tore the sou'wester from his head and whirled it through the flying spume of the sea. Holding fast to the main sheet, he stood bareheaded and smiling; this was the stuff to drive from his mind thoughts of hopeless love.

Captain Johnny, as he steadied the wheel, knew that it was impossible to haul the *Sylvia Westner* up in the wind and heave her to; that meant setting the peak of the mainsail, and that could not be considered in this roaring gale. To put her even for a moment in the trough of that mountainous sea might trip her, and even if the manœuvre were successful and he hove her to, she would eventually drift ashore. No, the only chance was to drive straight on before the gale. Darkness had come, but the weather was clear, and he could see the blink of the eastern light on his port bow. If he held his course he would run over the middle of the eastern bar. The tide was at the top of the flood, there were deep channels through the sand, perhaps God would guide him to one; in moderate weather, he had run over the bar many times before. As he dared not bring his vessel to the wind, he could only make out as far as possible to the bar's end without putting her in the trough of the sea. The double-reefed staysail cracked, bellied, and tugged desperately at sheet and halliard; if that went he must manage somehow to set a corner of a jib.

Four men of the watch, young Martin among them, were on the forward deck, lashed to stanchion or belaying pin, for the seas swept her from stern to stem. As Martin clung fast to his lashing, he bitterly resented the fact that his father had sent him from his island home. Fishing from Rockbound was by comparison safe; there was nothing like having solid ground beneath your feet at night. Another time he would resist the old man. He drove some fear from his mind by reckoning up his share when the *Sylvia Westner* sold her fish in Liscomb. All the other men of the crew were below in forecastle or afterhouse, companionway and forecastle hatch closed tight; they could do no good on deck and had boundless faith in the luck and skill of their "old man" Hand-line Johnny.

Now the seas began to break short with a peculiar ragged whiteness. "We're in shoal water near de bar," yelled Hand-line Johnny to old Caleb Baker. "God give us luck dis night." Wind furies shrieked, stays and halliards groaned with the straining spars, piled dories tugged at their lashings, a water butt broke loose and went

booming along the deck to crash into the forecastle hatch. A mountain of white water gathered
behind the *Sylvia Westner*, rose with slow,
malicious dignity, and crashed down upon her
poop. David clung with arms and legs to the
main sheet, but both steersmen were dashed
against the deckhouse. Captain Johnny's right
hand held fast the wheel spoke, but when the
sea washed clear and he staggered to his feet old
Caleb Baker was gone. At a sign from the young
master David stepped forward and took his place.

At that moment the *Sylvia Westner* struck;
Hand-line Johnny had no luck that night. All
was over in the twinkling of an eye. The vessel,
deep-laden, was travelling at the rate of twenty
knots, and a tooth of black bottom rock
whipped bottom and keelson from her as cleanly
as a boy with a sharp jackknife slits a shaving
from a pine stick. Two thousand quintals of split
fish and the unwetted salt dropped down upon
the yellow sands; out came the spars with a rending crash, and deck and upper hull turned over.
Within ten seconds of her striking, every man of
the crew was in the sea. Away they went, young
Martin still lashed to a bit of bulwark among
them, poor scraps of humanity, weighed down
with soaked clothing and long boots; a flash of
yellow oilskins, hoarse cries that made no sound

in the fierce tumult, and they were gone. Some swam a stroke or two, some clung for an instant to trailing rigging or broken dory, but few clung long in that mad breaking sea.

David, as the sea engulfed him, caught the trailing end of a dory's painter, whipped it twice around his body beneath the armpits, and tied it fast with a double net hitch. Then, as a sea drove the dory near him, he wormed his great right hand through the loop, at the dory's stem, and let himself hang limply by the wrist. He kicked off his rubber boots, tore loose the shoulder straps of his oil pants, and wriggled his legs free. He gasped for breath when his face was clear; he was bewildered but not afraid. This was the Tempest without the saving magic. A pleasant numbness beginning at his feet stole over him. He saw Gershom, half naked in the rockweed, cursing the triumphant ram on the cliff's edge above him, and almost laughed . . . his back doorstep was sagging, he must put a beach rock under it when he got home . . . perhaps a new sill . . . he had a piece of spruce in his building that would do . . . Jennie Run-over chased him with a stick to make him hurry with the wood, and the load was more than his right arm could bear. . . .

On Tuesday, Uriah walked along the bar of

sou'west cove to see what harm the storm had done his island. Big seas were still running violently against the red cliffs; the beach was strewn with marine plants and mollusks from the sea floor. Deep-water mussels, torn from their tough moorings, were scattered by thousands in beds of rose-coloured sea moss. Upon rock and sand lay tons of eel grass, rockweed, and long streamers of broad-leafed kelp. Uriah looked with delight upon these piles of sea dung. When rotted and spread it would give growing power to his Rockbound soil. "Dere's nuttin'," he thought, "like rotten sea dung, 'specially kelp, mixed wid barn manure, fur forcin' cabbage. If de nets is gone, we got dis."

As he stood there, Casper and Joseph came running across the island toward the beach.

"De *Sylvia Westner's* lost wid all hands," Joseph shouted. "An' de *Sadie Oxner*, too." News of disaster travels fast in the islands.

"Is it sure true? How come ye hear?" asked the old man.

"Alan Slaughenwhite's boat jus' brung de word from de main."

Uriah turned from them and said nothing. For some five minutes he gazed seaward, his eyes shifting from the rolling waves and misty horizon to the big piles of kelp upon the shore. Suddenly he twirled on his heel and shouted savagely at Casper and Joseph:

"What fur ye stand idlin' here? Wessels is always lost, boats is always lost—ain't dat our life? Now, wid Martin an' David gone, ye'll have to drive harder an' work like real mens. Go yoke up de cattle an' haul off dis sea dung what de Lord sent us 'fore it git mixed up wid sand an' too heavy fur to fork."

CHAPTER X

THE roaring southeaster drove the dory, to which David was lashed, shoreward. Life guards, who had seen the last flicker of the *Sylvia Westner's* lights, patrolled the beaches through the night, and one caught a glimpse of yellow dory in the white water. Wading into the surf waist deep, they dragged it ashore. To their astonishment a man was fast to the painter, his right hand, black and cruelly swollen, wedged in the dory's loop. They cut the ropes clear, carried him beyond the reach of breakers that yelled for their prey, and laid him in the lee of a steep sand dune. There they built a fire of driftwood, cut his soaked clothing from him, and wrapped him in warm wool blankets. His right arm, broken above the elbow by the barging of the sodden dory in the surf, hung limp and distorted. He seemed dead as a stone. Still, as there was some warmth in his body, they prized open his clenched teeth and poured brandy in his mouth. They pulled his tongue forward, jerked the sea water from him, and by relays inflated and deflated his lungs by a mechanical process. Yes, there was a flicker of life in him. They strove to restore him with all their vigour, so careful are men of life nigh lost, so careless of it in full flush. When breathing was restored they carried him on a stretcher to the life-saving station and laid him in a warm bed.

The name on the dory told them the name of the vessel lost, but there was nothing in David's clothing to identify him save a sea-soaked book on the flyleaf of which appeared the name Dauphiny. "One o' dem Dauphinys down La Tuque way," they conjectured, and sent word to the main that the *Sylvia Westner* had been lost, and a man named Dauphiny washed ashore, living. It was only at the end of two days that David was able to whisper: "I'se David Jung from Rockbound."

The government cutter fetched a doctor from

the main, who withdrew the sharp bone from the torn muscles and set the compound fracture. He shook his head gravely over the chafed and blackened forearm as he watched by David through days and nights. "Blood poisoning," he said. "Best amputate, best cut the arm off and save his life."

But David, who overheard, settled that argument: "No, I'se 'll die wid my arm on if I has to; dere's no place fur a one-armed man on Rockbound."

For a time it seemed impossible that he could live, but he was well nursed by doctor and guardsmen, and his vitality and giant strength prevailed. Destiny turned an upward thumb; he had yet something to endure and accomplish in the world. Dull blacks and ugly purples in his forearm turned to healthy pinks. He began to eat and drink—how good cold water tasted— and to have some interest in living. One day he asked for his book and turned over the sea-stained pages detached from the broken cover.

"Dem poets is de bunk," he said grinning at the tattered volume. "Dere ain't no magic nur enchanted islands! But de feller what wrote it knowed what a tempest was, jus' de same."

When he was strong enough the cutter took him to the main, and by easy stages he worked

his way to Sanford, and from there a friend's
boat carried him to Rockbound. He approached
the island on a lowering autumn afternoon, his
heart as low as on the day he had first landed in
his salvaged dory. As he had rested for a few
days in Sanford and the news of his advent had
reached the island before him, all Rockbound
was on the launch as his boat's prow took the
logs. Joseph offered a shoulder to help him from
the gunwale, but David shook his head. "No,
t'anks," he said. "I still got my left arm and no
dunnage wid." Uriah, Casper, and the Jung
women spoke no word of greeting, but stared at
him reproachfully, as if he had murdered young
Martin. "Ye can't drown dat David," thought
Uriah. "Why does dis bad penny turn up an'
my boy Martin gone?" But Mary Dauphiny
stepped forward with glowing eyes and, seizing
his left hand in both hers, cried: "Welcome home,
David Jung, welcome home! We're glad the sea
spared you."

David looked at her with singular equanimity.
In his struggle with death, in the wash of the sea,
he had seen reality stripped bare and caught a
glimpse of the heart of things.

"I seen de Tempest all right," he said grinning
at her.

Then he turned sharply on Uriah. "You guv

me no greetin', an' I takes it I'se not welcome.
I'se sorry young Martin's gone, but I could do
naught to help him, nor air anoder man. 'Twas
no wish nor fault o' mine dat de sea drove me
ashore."

Then Anapest began to cry and pushed forward with tears trickling down her wrinkled
brown face. "You is welcome, David, you is
welcome from bein' washed to and fro in de cruel
sea. Yur boy's well an' hearty, an' it's come an'
stay wid, ye will, in my house, till ye gits yur
stren'th back." So David went across the fields
to Anapest's house, the old woman's arm about
him.

Anapest kept him at her house for some weeks
and dressed his arm daily. From the first he was
able to make the round of the island, and on such
walks he frequently met Uriah. There was always the same query from the old king, the
same reply from David: "When is ye comin'
back to work?" We'se short-handed now—ain't
dat arm healed yit?"

"No, it ain't healed yit. De Doctor said I
could do nair a stroke o' work till spring. I'se 'll
let ye know when I'se fit to work."

But he was less worried during this period by
Uriah's nagging than by the bewildered state of

Mary's mind. She came almost daily to Anapest's house to talk with him; she had a troubled look and had lost the serenity that had been such an important part of her charm. Seeing her distress, he lost all the ground he had gained and fell more hopelessly in love with her than before. He could not fathom her trouble, for he was ignorant of many things that had happened in his absence.

This was Mary's second year of teaching on Rockbound. Though she had been offered better schools on the main at higher rates of pay, some irresistible attraction, which she herself could not understand, had drawn her back to the island. The summer she had spent with her father in Bay of God's Mercy, and as they had laboured together at fish flake or in hayfield, he had pressed the suit of Casper Jung upon her. Yet he had not done this tactlessly nor without cunning. The burden of his talk was: Casper is safe, Casper is the eldest living son, and when Uriah dies, he will be the richest man in the islands. Mary used to defend herself by replying that she did not want to marry for ever so long, that she must first make her mark as a teacher.

"An' when ye've made yur mark as a teacher, what den?" old Jean used to rejoin. "Does ye

want to be an old maid an' wither up? No, a
healthy lass like ye ought to have a man an'
kids. Marriage is de t'ing fur ye, my girl."

One day Mary, goaded beyond endurance,
had said to her father: "I don't want to marry
now, but if I must, why not David Jung or
Gershom Born?"

"David Jung's jus' lost his wife a year gone,
ye can't t'ink on him. Besides, he's got naught but
a sliver o' land an' no gear to speak on. Why
marry a poor man when ye kin git a rich one an'
eberyt'ing to yur hand? As fur Gershom Born,
he's a strong man, but he's too foolish bold. He'd
have a woman in a steady stew an' fotch her a
peck o' trouble. How many times has he had
boats ashore or upsot dem after drinkin' in
Liscomb? Onct he had to swim half a mile to de
Outposts an' landed wid one foot froze, an' de
women was afeerd to let him in dere houses wid
de men away, so bad was de fame o' him. An'
what's life on Barren Island fur a woman? No,
Gershom Born's no man fur a wife. Take Casper,
he's safe, he's got house an' land an' money in de
Liscomb bank, an' more he'll have when de old
man dies."

So in early September, Mary had come back
to teach in the Rockbound school with a troubled
mind. In that primitive community a father's

wish in regard to a suitable husband was almost
an order that must be obeyed, though the fact
that she was earning her own living allowed her
in some small measure to escape his whole man-
datory influence. One part of old Jean's argument
had struck home: it was better to marry and bear
children than to remain single and become the
best of teachers. She loved little children; perhaps nothing in life was finer than to bear children to some of these great-limbed fishermen.
She even sympathized with Fanny's point of
view.

She tried hard to obey her father and like
Casper, and sometimes of a Sunday walked the
round of the island with him. But she could not
think of him as a lover; something mean and
calculating in Casper's nature pushed her away
from him. He was never quite himself, his arti-
ficial smile, a mere wrinkling of the lips, faded
when no one was looking, his laugh was hollow
and insincere. Why had not her father chosen
David for her? Almost daily she sought his company and talked with him as he lay on Anapest's
kitchen sofa. Yes, he was the best to talk with.
Over and over she made him tell her the story
of the storm and the loss of the *Sylvia Westner*.
Her imagination exalted the tale into an epic.
Their former relations were reversed: she was no

longer the teacher but the learner. She asked
for the tales of the islands and of Gershom, but
there were few of these that could be told a
woman. Those few David related with a quaint
humour, and Mary watched his sly eyes twinkle
and the corners of his mouth twitch in the shadow
of a smile. Yes, it was tedious of her father not
to have chosen David.

These visits of Mary's were not matters of
pure joy for David. Hardship and suffering had
taught him restraint, but one day, when she left
him, he groaned so deeply that Anapest came
running in with: "Is dat arm hurtin' ye so bad
to-day? Here, I'se 'll put a new dressin' on it."

But it was Gershom who eventually became
Mary's accepted lover. Marriage and children
she had decided upon—the rhythm of the sea has
a magic effect upon women—and if she could
not have David the widower, Gershom the giant
was vastly preferable to Casper. True, she would
invoke her father's anger, but she could not take
Casper nor, unmarried, endure another summer
of the old man's nagging.

From Anapest's kitchen window David daily
saw Gershom's boat make the launch and his
great figure stride up the logs and along the lane
to spend the noon hour with Mary. Then David
suffered. When the bell called the children to

afternoon school Gershom would come to Anapest's house to visit his friend and, if they were
alone, to talk of Mary. As Gershom recounted
the progress of his courtship David's heart
burned within him. Sometimes he feared that his
friend would see the pain in his face, and he
would turn away from Gershom, under the pretext that it eased his arm to turn toward the
window. From these conversations with Gershom, who opened all his heart to his friend, from
Mary's furtive remarks, from the memory of a
thousand commonplaces, a glance, an attitude,
a movement of the hand, David, by reflection in
later life, was able to piece together the fragments of their tragic story, in which he was by
turn actor, unheeded prompter, a mute and disregarded spectator.

Certainly Gershom was madly in love with
Mary. Old Gershom Born had made it a rule to
stay on his island when the Bull was breaking,
but in that autumn of his courtship young Gershom used to push off on days when the furious
Bull snorted columns of spray heavenward.
Giant-strong, he could alone turn his boat on the
ways and point her seaward; then, with staring
blue eyes, he used to study the seas; usually three
big rollers came together, smashing into the rock
cleft and rattling the beach rocks. These three,

he knew, would be followed by lesser waves, and when the third big roller had spent its violence he used to launch his boat with catlike quickness into the swirling undertow. A great push from the last log, a swift leap over the gunwale, and he seized an oar to fend her off the cliffs and work her clear of the passage; a swift dart astern, and he started the engine he had primed and tried on the launch. When clear of the breakers on the open sea, he used to stand gripping the tiller, his eager eyes sweeping the red cliffs of Rockbound. He always steered for the eastern end, round Lynch's Hole and Whale Cove, where he remembered having seen, as a boy, flaring torches by night as the islanders tore strips of blubber from a stranded whale, for by this eastern route he came more quickly near Mary, who sat teaching the children in her one-roomed schoolhouse.

Mary, in truth, used to look forward to Gershom's coming as a relief against the pressing attentions of Casper. In vain Uriah stamped his feet in the fish house and cursed his laggard son whenever he heard Gershom's prow take the logs of the launch. Casper could make no progress with his love affairs. Mary would hurry through her lunch and walk with Gershom through the wood to the eastern end, where, at the foot of an

old stargon, they used to sit on the soft matting
of crowberry vines that grew along the cliff's
edge. Below them a giant symphony of seas came
roaring in; before them, the ocean stretched to a
misty infinity.

One morning in November, when Gershom
launched his boat into the surf, he felt a strange
sinking at heart. He tried to make himself believe that his depression was caused by his having
eaten too heartily of corned herring, and by having forgotten, in his haste to be off, his morning
draught of rum, but in his heart he knew that it
was because the tingling nip in the air told him
that winter was close at hand. Winter, when he
could see Mary but seldom, while Casper could
be with her daily! Winter, that meant biting
cold, ice, mountainous seas, and, worst of all,
thick mists and driving snow.

Every fisherman has something that he fears;
for Gershom it was fog or snow that shut out his
landmarks. Uriah used to say of him scornfully:
"He's a blind man come fog or snow." Now,
David or Joseph could drive their boats through
fog straight as homing birds and slow down their
engines to hear the roar of Rockbound surf, but
Gershom was always in a panic when fog or snow
shut down around him. Twice during old Gershom's lifetime he had started from Liscomb,

salt laden—true he had had a few friendly drinks in Maurer's bar—missed Barren Island in the snow, and in a lost man's panic stood in for the main. Once, sleep-drunk, he ran his boat high and dry on the sand above Sou'west Gutter. Let him but catch, through rifts, glimpses of rock, tree, or fish house, and he could thread his way among the three hundred islands, and their thrice three hundred shoals, but with the blanket of gray came panic. He had little or no confidence in the box compass that lay under his amidship thwart.

So, on that November morning Gershom's heart sank at the thought of his coming imprisonment through winter's ice and snow. Casper, backed by Uriah, might, in his absence, wear Mary down by persistent entreaty. He must ask her and get her promise that very day. Hatred for Casper burned in his heart. Casper was a cunning craven who liked tilling the soil or shooting nets close inshore, who in bad weather had to be driven by his father's jibes to fish on the outer banks. Still, Casper had a fine white house and twelve thousand dollars, cash money, in the Liscomb bank. That would mean a lot to a woman or a man like old Jean Dauphiny. He had naught but the light house as a dwelling, and his salary as keeper, and would a woman like Mary Dauphiny choose to live on Barren Island? He would give up the light if Mary wished it, and build her a house on the main. Curse Casper Jung! He was a better man than Casper; he could catch more fish, pull harder on a halliard, and drive a boat through seas that Casper dare not venture out in. He could sing, make ballads against his enemies, and knock the hat off any man in the islands. He had crowds of friends in Liscomb, Dover, and Polly's Point, whereas Casper, with all his money, had none. All these angry thoughts rushed through his head that November morning as he rounded the eastern end, passed inside the sulking Bull, and made the Jungs' landing.

The Jungs were packing herrings in the fish house, but David stood at the head of the launch to welcome his friend. He was discouraged, for his arm had swollen again and was paining him more than formerly. They greeted each other in fisherman fashion, and David did what he could to help Gershom drag out his boat. Partner though he was in the Jung firm, he dared not hook the landing cable into Gershom's stem ring without Uriah's order.

The old king, in yellow oil skins, came wadling to the fish-house door. "Air a halibut on yur trawl lately?" he queried.

"Ay, plenty. I got a whole school buoyed off de natural pier," replied Gershom scornfully.

"What's de matter, is ye short-handed dis-mornin'?"

"De boys is busy a packin' herrin' fur de Liscomb market to-morrow. Herrin' is riz."

"Too busy fur to give a man a hand wid his boat, hey?"

The old king kept silent. He wanted Gershom to know that he was an unwelcome visitor. Of all his numerous reasons for disliking Gershom, none was greater than that Gershom had seen his retreat before Anapest's shameful attack.

"P'r'aps de price o' gasoline is ris wid de herrin's, an' ye poor fellers can't afford fur to start yur engine. Well, maybe ye'll be wantin' a drag out on Barren Island some day. T'ank God, I kin still haul a boat good as any two Jungs' David excepted," and with that bitter retort Gershom went whistling up the lane to the school house.

David's ear caught some sneer about loafers from the fish house as his eyes followed Gershom up the lane. The children were just flocking out of school, and Gershom met them.

"Hello, Gershom!" they cried merrily; the cunning rogues knew that Gershom bought hard candies by the bucketful and that his pockets were always stuffed with them.

"Want some net rocks picked up?" they shrilled.

Now, while Barren Island is nothing but a projecting cliff over which a mat of turf is laid, the rock formation there does not split into long narrow slivers that fishermen can tie with a double hitch as sinkers to the foot of their nets. So when Gershom wanted net rocks he used to hire the urchins of Rockbound to gather him a bushel and pay them in candies.

"Git along wid ye," said Gershom, giving each child a hard and highly coloured candy. "I don't want no net rocks to-day."

"He wants naught but teacher," cried Nathan Kraus, a bandy-legged brat, who from the age of two had walked swaying like a fisherman balancing in a wave-tossed boat.

The children sent up a shout of laughter at this retort. Gershom, in pretended anger, made a dive to catch the offender, but little Nathan slid under the fence pole and danced away through the pasture with cries of derision.

"You're naught but a passel o' young rogues," David heard Gershom cry with his great voice. Then he hurried up the ledgy lane from which all turf and soil had been worn by a century of grinding cart wheels.

Mary, her red cap drawn over her ears against

the nip in the air, was waiting for him at the door
of the schoolhouse. As he approached with long
rolling strides, his giant strength seemed to over-
whelm her. A woman could face life with such a
man and bear children to him gladly. She felt a
pang of regret as she saw far off the sea-mauled
David standing in the attitude of dejection at the
launch's head, but that was forgotten when she
caught a glimpse of Casper peeping from the
back door of the fish house.

"Hurry up wid yur lunch, Mary," Gershom
called gaily.

"I'll be with you in fifteen minutes," she replied, setting off in the direction of Christian's
house.

Gershom kept on up the lane and halted near
the fixed light that Uriah had tended for forty
years. He lighted his pipe, smoked furiously,
hummed a tune, and stamped his feet in im-
patience, till he saw Mary's red cap twinkle
through the trees. Then his heart rose in his
throat; he broke out in a perspiration; he would
decide his fate that day. Mary joined him, and
they walked through the wood to their favourite
place on the cliff's edge.

"I seen Casper peekin' as ye come up de lane."

"He watches me wherever I go."

"Are ye wid him much, Mary?"

"He walks home with me after school. He won't enter Christian Kraus's house, but when I call round to see the folks of an evening he comes along."

"Do ye like him, Mary?"

"My father thinks he's a grand man, but I like David better; he's had to endure so much from everyone. Uriah nags him now that he's sick, and he's eating his heart out."

"But ye likes me best, Mary."

"I don't know, Gershom, I don't know."

"You got to marry me, Mary darlin'," Gershom blurted out. "I'se wild about ye. You're goin' to marry me, ain't it?"

"My father says I've got to marry Casper Jung."

"Dat stingy coward! Don't take him."

"You're too wild and desperate, Gershom. People think you'll come to ill."

"I'm none so bad, Mary."

"Yes, you know you're reckless in boats, and you've lots of fights."

"I'se 'll change all dat an' be as quiet as a woolly lamb, if ye'll have me."

"And you drink rum, Gershom, something awful."

"I'se 'll stop dat too when we's married."

"Why not stop now?"

"Dat I'se 'll do if ye says de word, lass. I had nair a drop o' liquor this day. I plumb furgot to have my draught, I was dat wild fur to see ye."

"Then there's Nettie Langille on Big Outpost, and folks say you're often seen in Jennie Runover's place."

"It's true, it's true, but I'se 'll go dere no more; I'se 'll be true to you, lass, an' drink no more rum neider, an ye'll have me. Dough mind, Mary, what I tell's ye; it's awful lonesome on dat light wid nair a drink, an' strange yellin' goin' on t'rough de night."

"The Jungs say you've got no religion, Gershom."

"Dat I can't change nur help, Mary. Would ye want fur to make a long-faced hypocrite out o' me? Dat's de way a man's born, an' I'se like my fader. Religion's well an' good fur dem as kin believe. You don't want me to purtend, does ye, Mary?"

"No, I don't want you to pretend, but people tell such awful tales about you, Gershom. Johnny Souter says you talk with the devil."

"I talks wid myself, any man alone learns to do dat, and when Johnny Souter comes out to mend my boots he hears me at it. He's full o' ghosts and devils. Half my time, when he's dere peggin' away, I pull down dish pans wid strings to fright him, an' he goes back to de Outposts wid a mess o' ghost stories. He's naught but a wisp of a man wid no guts in him. He won't eben leave de light buildin' after sundown, and when he goes out in broad daylight he's forever peerin' about an' lookin' ober his shoulder. Why listen to his chatter? Don't believe what Uriah and Casper says, eider; dey's got an ax fur to grind: Uriah wants you fur Casper. Ask David about me, he'll speak me fair. I loves ye, Mary, dat I does."

"I know you do, Gershom."

"Look here, snow and mist and mountainous seas come soon, an' maybe drift ice. I don't fear no seas nor ice, I'd drive a boat t'rough hell fur ye, Mary, but, try as I kin, dere'll be days an' weeks, maybe, when I can't git off, ain't it?"

"That's true, Gershom. I'll be sorry when the winter and the strong cold set in."

"But will ye have me, Mary?"

"I can't say yet, Gershom. I'll wait and see how you keep your promises. I like you, but maybe I'd be safer with Casper. That's what my dad says, anyway. If you only weren't so wild and would save your money!"

"Mary, I'll change an' take a bearin' on de opposite point o' de compass. I gits eighty dollars a mont' fur keepin' de light—dat's a fortune on Barren Island—an' nex' summer come I'll set t'ree halibut trawls and mackerel and herrin' nets. I kin easy make five hundred dollars in a summer's fishin'. I'll work dese hands off fur you, Mary, an' I'm de strongest man in all dese islands."

"That you are, Gershom."

"Look here, Mary, you wait fur me dis winter, an' see if I don't keep off rum an' women. I won't drink no rum, nur I won't go nigh de Outposts or de main."

"How will I know that?"

"I'll give you my word, lass, and, look here, every day I'm storm- or ice-stayed, I'se 'll fly ye a signal flag, an' you, Mary, fly a signal back to let me know you've seed mine. Here on dis stargon or 'gainst de spruce or agin de granite boulder. Will ye do it fur me, Mary, if I'se ice-bound?"

"Yes, I will."

"And look, lass, fly a different colour ebery day so I'se 'll know you've changed dem an' dat you're t'inkin' o' me. I kin see dem right well wid my glasses. Fly a white or green 'gainst the granite boulder, de red 'gainst de scrub spruce. When ye sees my flag it means I'se keepin' off rum an' t'inkin' o' you, an' when I sees yur signal I'se 'll know ye understands."

"I'll put up a signal every day, Gershom, I've got to go now, it's time for school."

"An' ye'll have me in de spring if I sticks it out?"

"Yes, but keep it a secret."

"I kin tell David, maybe."

"Yes, tell David."

"Come close till I kiss ye den, Mary."

They walked back arm in arm through the spruces, to the door of the schoolhouse, where Gershom said good-bye and strode joyfully down the ledgy road. He said not a word to the Jungs in the fish house as he passed, but held straight on to Anapest's house to tell David the good news.

"Mary's agoin' to marry me in de spring if I keeps off liquor t'rough de winter."

"You'se a lucky man, Gershom," said the generous David, holding out his sound hand to be gripped by Gershom's paw. "I'se right glad dat Casper's not agoin' fur to git her."

"An' it's a secret, man. Mary said to tell you and jus' you."

David turned pale as Gershom spoke these words, and cast his eyes upon the ground. Gershom noted his friend's pallor and distress, but mistook the cause.

"You'se lookin' awful, Dave. Is it yur arm a-hurtin' or is de old man worryin' ye?"

"He nags away an' says dere's no place fur a sick man on Rockbound."

"De ole hound! Say, boy, why not git away from here? Come out an' stay wid me on de light till ye gits yur stren'th an' yur arm heals."

David was indeed ready for a new venture; any place would be better than Rockbound with the nagging of Uriah and his heartache for Mary.

"I'se 'll go wid, Gershom," he said. "Dat's a good idea. I kin do a little cookin' an' sechlike wid my left hand, but furst we'll have to see what Anapest an' de ole man says."

Gershom snorted his great laugh.

"Dat ole woman tries fur to run eberyt'ing, but she's a good soul. I spose you'se under petticoat government now. I'se 'll soon conwert de ole woman. As fur Uriah, to hell wid his opinion."

Anapest at first protested violently against David's departure, but in the end she yielded to Gershom's blandishments and David's desires.

"See dat de hand is dressed ebery day an' dat David don't ketch no cold. He's wort' two o' you, Gershom Born."

Uriah gave a grudging consent, and for a second time David set out with Gershom for Barren Island.

One morning of the week before Christmas, when Gershom climbed to the tower to put out the light, he gave a start of surprise on looking down upon the sea; the whole surface was a rough jumble of dull grays and glistening whites; the drift ice had come in the night. Southward as far toward the open sea as the eye could reach there was no patch of blue; northward, the drift was jammed between Barren Island, Rockbound, the Outposts, and the Sanford main. Spruce-clad Rockbound, in its new setting of drift, looked like an emerald laid on a white cloth. He and David were prisoners. His heart sank as he realized that he could not see Mary for many a day, and he longed for a glass of rum. He descended to the downstairs bedroom, where David slept because of its warmth, and gave him the melancholy news. David, who knew the secret of the signals, said: "Well, you kin try yur signallin' now, Gershom."

"Yes," thought Gershom, as he stirred up the porridge in his untidy kitchen. "Mary'll see de ice too, an' set her flag at noon, an' I'se 'll fly my signal back. Dat's somet'in'."

Breakfast finished, David stretched out on the kitchen couch. His arm was worse rather than better, he felt weak and tired, and as he spoke but seldom he was poor company for the sanguine Gershom. Gershom sat down to mend a torn net, a three-weeks-old newspaper propped up before him. Old Gershom had solaced his loneliness with books, and his son had inherited a love for reading. He wove a few meshes and then glanced up to read an item of news which he retailed to David. Presently a passage on temperance set him off on a line of thought.

"Shakespeare's fellers was always fornicatin' and drinkin' and carousin'. Dey seemed to git on all right. I wonders why women's so set agin it now."

"I don't know," said David feebly. "I can't make dem out. No man kin faddom de mind o' a woman. Dat's what I t'inks."

"De ole man used to say dat Byron an' his gang an' lots o' great mens was hellians fur women."

David closed his eyes and offered no comment.

Then Gershom became impatient, the morning seemed interminably long, the newspaper bored him, he could get no conversation out of David, he was sick of mending nets. At ten he went out-of-doors and hoisted his red ensign, although he knew that Mary could not see his flag nor set hers in position before the noon hour. He dawdled about and attended to various odd jobs to pass the time. Presently he started up from his tinkering and ran at top speed the quarter mile from light to boathouse, scattering the frosty snow in glittering clouds as he ran. There he watched for a little the drift-ice churn and grind against the logs of his launch; as yet the ice had done no damage to his landing place. He prized up the loose plank of his boathouse floor, lifted out and with moist lips looked longingly at a hidden rum keg. Reluctantly he replaced it on its rock cradle and, running back to the light, went up into the tower to peer and peer for Mary's signal. In vain he swept tree and cliff wall with his glasses.

Then at half-past twelve, as he was beginning to despair, he caught a flicker of green against the gray stargon. He even imagined he could make out the red speck that was her stocking cap, and he shouted till the whole light tower rang. He rushed down the two flights of stairs to tell David.

"She's signalled, she's signalled. I seed her green flag."

"Ay," sighed David. "Now ye'se happy. Ye need have no fear she'll break her word."

For a week, in response to his wind-tossed pennant, Gershom saw Mary's signal daily. For the change of her flag at the noon hour he spent the rest of the day in expectation. The imprisoning ice made both Gershom and David restless

and unhappy. When they made the round of
the cliff, they spoke less and less; the sight of that
endless ice field was depressing. North, east,
south, west, there was no flash of blue, nothing
but vast stretches of white, yellow, and dull gray.
The field was formed of old ice from the Far North
broken into spheres, cubes, cylinders, and pyra-
mids, and eroded by the wash of a thousand tides.

Gershom talked of nothing but the signals,
and was often irritable and ill-tempered without
a draught of rum that he craved hourly. His
energy was boundless, he was as restless as a
caged tiger. While David lay on the couch trying
to get back his strength Gersham paced to and
fro, read furtively at his father's books, which he
already knew well-nigh by heart, mended his
nets, overhauled and rehooked his tubs of trawl,
painted his boat, laid a new plank floor in his
boathouse, and on cold afternoons shot brant
and sea duck from the north ledge till his
shoulder ached from the kick of his heavy duck
gun.

If his days were bad, his nights were twice as
dreary. David, the invalid, went to bed early
in the warm bedroom off the kitchen, while
Gershom sat alone in the light tower, listening
to the wind cries, thinking of Mary and wondering if Casper were with her. Often in these dark

lonely hours he climbed to the glass dome and sat by the light for company. As it revolved quietly, telling off the minutes, it seemed a living and friendly thing. Outside the winter wind shrieked, floes bumped and snarled against the natural pier, sea birds came blundering against the glass, but the light flashed out with calm and quiet dignity.

It was comforting to think that far out at sea some captain on a dark sharply tilted deck was saying to his mate:

"There's a flashing light, watch it and count," and the mate, stooping to get the binnacle light on his watch face, would call out: "Five seconds flash, five seconds occult, five seconds flash, five seconds occult, twenty-one seconds flash, nineteen seconds occult." And the captain would back down the companionway, look at his lights almanac, pop his head up again, and say to the mate: "Yes, I thought so, that's Barren Island. We're about ten miles off. That twinkle inside is fixed, isn't it? That's Minden Rockbound. We ought to see Lubeck Island Light soon, and in an hour Little Hope."

Yes, it was a great comfort for the lonely giant to sit by the light that blinked faithfully, and to imagine these conversations far out at sea, and to know that captain and mate were glad to pick up his light and read his light's language. Perhaps it was a liner with row upon row of flashing portholes the light spoke to, perhaps a lumber-laden Norwegian barque, or perhaps one of the Liscomb fleet, his own friends aboard, homing from Turk's Island with a load of salt.

Some nights, when he left the light and went into the room below, where he slept and kept his records, the shrieks and howls of the wind about the light were awful. He longed for a drink, but he had promised Mary that he would keep off rum, and he drank none. His pipe was his great solace; he smoked continually throughout the day and in the intervals of the night, when he woke and ran aloft to see that the light was flashing clear. He wrote pages upon pages of ballads and love verses to Mary, though he could never get any rhyme for "Mary" but "fairy," and that was silly. None of his verses seemed right to him, and not at all like those of the great poets.

Of course, his chief occupation was watching daily for Mary's signal. For the first week of their imprisonment all went well, and he saw her flag every day, either white, green, or red. In the second week came sea mists and driving snow-storms, and it was only by watching through every rift in mist banks and every lull of the snow squalls, that he caught short glimpses of his sweetheart's flag. But in the third week, when the weather was comparatively clear, Mary's signal was missing. Sometimes he fancied he saw it for a moment at about twelve-thirty, but when he looked again it was gone; it was neither against gray boulder nor dark spruce. On the clearest days he could make out the gray stargon, at the foot of which Mary and he had sat on the crowberry vines, and where she had given her promise, but certainly Mary's flag was not flying.

In his despair Gershom flung a thousand questions at David, variations of a single theme. Was she sick? Was she false? Had she so soon forgotten him? Had she taken up with Casper Jung? By God, if she had, they would both pay dear for it. David, himself sick in heart and body, did his best to comfort his half-crazed friend. Sometimes Gershom in a maudlin mood would stand in mid-floor with tears streaming down his face.

"Yes, she must be sick," he would shout at David. "She's sick in bed, she's dyin' an' I can't git to her. Mary wouldn't break her word to a man imprisoned in the ice."

One day, in the depth of despair, he pulled on his sea boots and ventured out upon the ice, intent on making a passage to Rockbound by leaping from floe to floe. Before he had gone fifty yards a loose rounded block turned and threw him into the sea, and it was only by his greatest effort that he made the safety of his launch.

Still he flew his pennant and kept off rum. By turns anger, hope, and despair possessed him. In his angry moods he raged at David, forgetting his weakness. Uriah, the old fox, had been too cunning for her, she had gone to Casper, the doxy, she had lied to him, women had no bowels of compassion, they cared for nothing but money. He stormed about the light tower, struck his fists against the boarding till knuckles were skinned and bleeding, and cursed the ice prison, mankind, God, and the devil. In this mood of anger he hauled down his pennant at the end of the third week of imprisonment.

When the ice closed in, Mary's heart was full of pity for the imprisoned Gershom. She knew how restraint irked a man of Gershom's sanguine disposition, and had imagination enough to picture the awfulness of being hemmed in through winter storms on a lonely island. She was glad David was with him. Daily she watched for a rift in the sea ice through which he might drive a boat, but no rift showed its streak of blue;

instead, the intense cold cemented the inner ice, and for the first time in the memory of men living, people walked over the ice between Rockbound and the Sanford main. This gave both Mary and Uriah a sense of uneasiness, but for different reasons. Mary knew that it meant a long imprisonment for her lover; it irked the old king to have his island kingdom so closely knit to the main. Faithfully at noon hour of each day, she trudged through the snowy wood to place her flag in position against green spruce or gray stargon, and saw Gershom's answering pennant raised and lowered on his staff. In performing this simple act of faithfulness, she was very happy.

Now, Uriah, crafty king of Rockbound, who saw and pried into all that happened on his island, observed that Mary daily hurried through the crusted snow to the eastern end of the island. His curiosity was piqued; something was happening that he did not fully understand. One day he stealthily followed her, at a distance, and from the shelter of a thick spruce watched her place her flag in position and look intently toward Barren Island. His sharp old eyes, which had stared through many a fog for his island's shape, followed hers to Barren Island, and he saw Gershom's pennant dipped and raised.

"Signallin', is it! Dat's dere game!" thought Uriah. "I'se 'll stop dat quick, ain't it?"

He had no pity in his heart for the lonely men imprisoned by the ice.

"I got him and David in de place where I wants dem now!"

While the thought of the inner solid ice disquieted him, the sight of the outer loose-floating ice that imprisoned David and Gershom filled him with joy. He waited patiently till Mary started back through the wood, then advanced cautiously in the shadow of the bushes, took down her flag, wrapped it up, and stuck it in a cleft of the rock. Next day he was near the signal rock well before Mary, and when he heard her far off brushing through the trees, he replaced her flag, so that she might think it had been in position during her absence. On the instant of her departure—it was too cold to linger long—he removed the flag and hid it as before. Day after day the patient old fox repeated this manœuvre, until at the end of three weeks he saw that Gershom no longer flew his pennant. The old man was delighted with the success of his stratagem; without him his son Casper would be a sorry wooer.

When Mary observed that Gershom's pennant was missing she was bewildered and sick at heart.

Was he sick, or had he broken his promise and gone back to rum? He could not be sick, for on every clear night she could see his light flashing, and even if he were bedridden he could get David to fly the pennant. One of them would make a smoke if either were in dire peril, though naught but a government ice breaker could reach them. She racked her brain for an answer; there was but one: Gershom had broken his promise, gone back to rum, and forgotten her. He and David were carousing together and making women a matter of jest. For a week after the disappearance of Gershom's signal she faithfully set her flag in position, and just as faithfully the cunning Uriah removed and hid it. Then, in despair, convinced that Gershom had broken faith, she gave up and visited the eastern end no more.

Meanwhile, Casper was eagerly pressing his suit. Every afternoon he was waiting to walk home with her from school. In the evenings he followed her as she called from house to house. To his credit he knew nothing of his father's stratagem; that secret the old man kept locked in his breast. Nor did Casper speak unkindly of Gershom and David; he was cunning enough to know that slander and gossip displeased Mary. Once she asked timidly: "How do you suppose

Gershom and David are getting on all this time?"
His reply, "Oh dey're all right. Dey got plenty
o' coal an' meat an' drink. Dey's a great pair
when togedder fur laughin' an' drinkin'," confirmed her worst fears. Piqued and hurt in pride,
she tried to see desirable qualities in Casper.
Though he was not quite the man to be the
father of children she would bear, he was at
any rate strong, sober, and patient. After all,
would life on Barren Island be endurable? What
if she were imprisoned by the ice—could she
endure for weeks, alone, Gershom's boisterous
strength? Her hurt mind turned more and more
toward Casper, though to his frequent solicita-
tions she refused a promise of marriage. She
would wait, she resolved, and see what happened
when the ice broke.

But Uriah was impatient. Was all his labour
to be fruitless? Daily he rated Casper in the fish
house for his lack of enterprise and he rarely
passed Mary without calling after her: "When is
ye agoin' to tell us de good news, lass?" This
was no time for sluggard lovers, and the old king
decided to play his trump card. One bitter
morning at break of day he set out, crossed the
ice to the main, crunched through the snows of
a wooded peninsula, and before nightfall was at
Jean Dauphiny's house on the Bay of God's

Mercy. In the kitchen that night the two old men sat long in muttering conference, and when Uriah came back next day to Rockbound old Jean was with him.

Old Dauphiny greeted his daughter and without delay began to urge her immediate marriage with Casper. He had been frightened by the story Uriah had told him of his daughter's intrigue with Gershom. A father's wish, he reminded her, is usually obeyed by dutiful children, and scolded her severely for having taken up with Gershom. Shame upon her, did she wish to spend her life on a lonely island with a reckless drunkard? Upon Casper's virtues he dwelt at great length: he was a good man and a safe one, a man who could read and write, well versed in the Bible, a rich man among fishermen, who would become richer when his father died. Casper was his choice, and he made angry threats should she disobey him.

In her distress she turned to old Anapest and to Fanny, the potato girl, the only disinterested persons on the island. Anapest's views, she felt, might be coloured by a desire to oppose anything that Uriah promoted. To her astonishment, Anapest said, after some thought: "Casper Jung's a poor fish, as is all dose Jungs, an' o' course I favours Gershom; still, ye better think a

long while, lass, 'fore ye go agin yur fader's will."
Anapest gave this advice thinking of the necessity of retaining a guiding hand in the affairs of
her own empire. Like the absolute monarch, she
was fearful of the establishment of a republic on
the fringe of her kingdom.

Fanny, the potato girl, who had tasted bitterly
of the meanness of the Jungs during her years on
Rockbound, ended her advice by saying: "Gershom Born's a better man dan Casper Jung, an'
a more generous, but if I was you, Mary, I'd wait
an' take David. He likes ye, too, dough he says
naught. He's de kindest o' all an' would wear
best."

But Mary had no desire to introduce a new
element into her troubles; she had put the
thought of David as a husband out of her mind.
It seemed strange to her, however, that in this
crisis of her life she yearned for David's counsel
and advice. He was the only person in the world,
she felt, who could tell her rightly what to do.
Nightly she knelt in her chilly bedroom and
prayed the good God to open a sea lane so that
David might come and counsel her. It seemed
strange that she never prayed that Gershom
might come. Gershom's coming would mean
fierce, boisterous quarrels; it would be his way to
fight them all and carry her off by force. She

prayed fervently for that sea lane, but no sea lane opened. Instead, the devil jammed the ice tighter in the bay, and the Lord God could not push it out. Intenser cold came that cemented ice blocks outside of Rockbound, despite the heave of the open sea.

Finally, Mary's resistance was broken, and under cumulative pressure she consented to marry Casper. Uriah dispatched Joseph across the ice to fetch the Reverend Green, minister on the Outposts. The old king knew that the ice would not stay in the bay forever, and that if his plans were to be crowned with success the wedding must be held without delay.

The wedding, celebrated in the seventh week of David's and Gershom's imprisonment, was a great social event on Rockbound. Of course, no Kraus was asked, but old Jean Dauphiny was there, and every soul of the Jungs and their dependent sharesmen was invited. In Uriah's chilly parlour, from the walls of which a row of ghastly carboned ancestors looked grimly down, the Reverend Green mumbled through the ritual, and Mary, in low, soulless tones, promised to love, honour, and obey the apple-faced Casper. Her thoughts were on Barren Island: Gershom, though he had broken troth, would be savage with rage, and what would David think? He

might think that she cared only for money and
that Casper Jung had bought her. He would
never know how she had suffered or what force
had been put upon her. Uriah went about with
a beaming face, for he had arranged the destinies
of his subjects and shown himself a true king.

The long table was laid in the kitchen; Uriah
and Jean Dauphiny, patriarchs, sat side by side
at the upper end; Fanny, the potato girl, and
Nat Levy, the lowest paid sharesman, at the
lower end; along the sides were ranged the
Jungs in strict accordance with their feudal
ranks. On the table were platters of roasted
brant and sea duck, piles of kraut and potatoes,
pumpkin pies, pitchers of hot brown rum, red
apples, candies, and at Uriah's end a joint of
roasted veal. The old man had intended to rear
his bull calf for an ox, but in his delight at Casper's lucky marriage had sacrificed it to the
occasion. In the brick fireplace the spruce logs
roared, cracked, and shot out glowing sparks
upon the floor. When Uriah, red-faced patriarch,
stood up to whet his long knife and carve the
joint of fatted calf he shouted to everyone:
"Eat and drink hearty." He and old Jean
pledged each other in hot rum, and all drank the
health of bride and groom. Hot rum loosened
their tongues; they began to talk freely; rude

jokes brought shouts of laughter; in the midst of this babble Mary sat silent, pale but comely in the gray dress Martin's widow had made for her. She alone thought of the men on Barren Island: Gershom had forsaken her, but what would David think? Casper did little but grin and fix his narrow eyes greedily upon his bride.

Dinner over, Nat Levy was ordered to play jigs on the fiddle, and dish pans on the walls and hams hung from the rafters danced with the dancing feet. Uriah, who believed in the propriety of drunkenness at a wedding, saw that the rum jugs were placed at strategic points and refilled as soon as emptied. With the dancing the Reverend Green withdrew; it was not seemly, he thought, to be in a room where both drinking and dancing were being carried on. He was glad, however, that Uriah's wife followed him into his fireless bedroom with a warming pan and a steaming glass of rum.

Joseph and Ned Slaughenwhite fell sound asleep in corners before the evening was spent, and had to be carried home on stretchers by sharesmen who lurched and swayed as they crunched through the snow. As the party came to an end and these drunken ones were carried off, Mary thought: "And I cut poor Gershom off his glass of rum on that lonely island!" Then she walked with Casper to his dark house, with as much dread in her heart as had the Athenian girls handed over to the Minotaur. At that moment David was turning restlessly upon his bed, and Gershom in the light tower was adjusting the mantle and cursing the ice that held him prisoner.

CHAPTER XI

ONE day in the eighth week of imprisonment a sea lane opened between Rockbound and Barren Island, and the half-crazed Gershom pushed off with fast-beating heart and drove his boat through the ice to see what had happened to Mary. David stood by to tend the light in case the ice closed and cut Gershom off. From safe cover, Uriah and Joseph watched him as he zigzagged from floe to floe. He was a desperate man, they knew; how would he take the news? Fear was in Joseph's heart. Certainly he had better not learn from them; he would go straight to Anapest's house, they reckoned.

Gershom could pass round neither eastern nor western end to reach a landing, but as the pack kept all surf down, he ran straight into Sou'-west Cove, beached his boat upon the frozen sands, and hauled her out as best he could.

Just across the bar, from the point on the beach where he had landed his boat, the rosy-cheeked Rockbound children were making a skating place by clearing Nigger Pond of snow. They had not seen Gershom's approach through the sea lane, for Nigger Pond is set low, and the winter seas had piled the bar high with beach rocks, but as his head and shoulders appeared over the barrier they rushed toward him with shouts of joy.

"Hello, Gershom, hello, Gershom!" they called. "We'se right glad ye got off Barren Island."

"What a pity ye couldn't git in fur de weddin'."

"Us had ducks, an' roast calf, an' heaps o' kraut."

"Whose weddin'?" he asked faintly.

"Teacher's an' Uncle Casper's, o' course. An' we was allowed to stay up late, an' had cakes, an' candy, an' preserves."

"An' Nathan an' Caleb was sick."

"When was all dis?" he stammered.

"Oh, a long time ago. An' Uncle Joe an' Nat Levy was awful drunk, an' Nat Levy played de fiddle, an' dey all danced in Gran'pa's kitchen."

"An' we all danced, an' de minister, he said it were wicked, an' we kep' on dancin' jus' de same."

"Where'd de minister come from?" asked Gershom, hoping to get the truth by detail.

"Uncle Joe went ober de ice an' fotched Mr. Green from Big Outpost, yes, he did."

Gershom was stunned and turned to stagger away. Yes, she had been false to him and broken her promise to wait till spring.

"Ain't ye got no candy in yur pockets to-day?" the children shrieked at him.

Gershom turned and fished out a candy for each of them from his deep pockets, then staggered across the bar toward his boat. His knees felt weak, his face was as white as a new sail, he wrung his hands together in his agony. When he topped the bar he met Christian Kraus face to face.

"Hello, Gershom."

"Hello, Christian."

"Glad ye got off de island. Eberyt'ing all right?"

"All right. De children tells me ye've had a weddin' on Rockbound. Is dat true?"

"Dat's true, Gershom."

Then Gershom began to cry, half in rage, half in anguish. The tears ran down his cheeks as he bellowed with anger and stamped his feet upon the beach rocks.

"I'se agoin' fur to kill dat bugger Casper."

Christian kept silence; he was sorry for Gershom.

"Where is dey now?" asked Gershom, mopping his face.

"De inside ice holds, an' dey've went off to wisit her folks in Bay of God's Mercy up to de west'ard."

"Dey was some dirty trick somewhere. Mary promised to wait till spring. By God, I'll be revenged on de Jungs o' Rockbound. By God, dey'll rue de day dey stole my woman from me an' me froze in on de light."

Christian said nothing, there was nothing to say; he did not know of Uriah's ruse, and even if he had known, he would hardly have dared tell Gershom in such a rage. The man was half crazy with grief and loneliness. Despite his hatred of the Jungs, he did not wish to have murder on Rockbound.

"I got to be gettin' back to de light now, 'fore de lane closes. You tell Uriah, damn him, he ain't t'rough wid me yet. I'se'll be back to square accounts wid Mr. Casper."

"De ice shuts in quick on an ebb tide," said Christian, anxious to speed Gershom's departure, "an' it's jus' de top o' de flood now."

Christian helped Gershom off with his boat, and, flinging a curse at Uriah and the Jungs of Rockbound, Gershom jumped aboard and was off through the channel, already half full of bobbing ice floes. He was numbed at what seemed Mary's treachery, but he had little time to think about it on the outward voyage, for the blue lane began to narrow with the first of the ebb. What if it closed and he could not get back? David would light the lamp, but Uriah would report his absence, for he had always coveted Barren Island as a post for one of his retainers. Gershom's outward journey, in fact, was a succession of swift advances and returns from stem to stern. He set the tiller in a notch to keep the boat on a certain course; then, oar in hand, darted to the bows to ward off a block of ice, then swiftly back to the stern to set the tiller in another notch. Between him and Rockbound the ice was closing fast. He had no time to think of Mary, the whole of his mind was concentrated on a struggle to make Barren Island. Sometimes he had a choice of two or even three channels, and then he slowed down his engine and, standing forward by the spar, surveyed the route with a swift glance and selected that most free from big cakes.

David, on the shore of Barren Island, stood for a long time watching Gershom's slow progress through the floes. Would he make the passage or have to return to Rockbound? He wished he had lit the lamp at midday and gone with him in the boat. When he was certain that Gershom would get through, he walked back to the light, shivering with the cold that shot fierce twinges of pain through his arm.

Gershom was not caught in the ice jam; in two hours he made the passage, hooked on the cable to his boat's stem, and, with the windlass, hauled her up well clear of the grinding ice. That done, he prized up the loose planking of his boathouse and, stooping, lifted out a five-gallon keg of rum. He broached it and drank deeply of the raw liquor. Now he had time to think of the injustice done him, and his anger began to grow. As he drank, he cursed all men, and swore by all the gods he knew that he would destroy the Jungs of Rockbound and the whole world, if it lay in his power. He drank more rum, and then, swinging the keg on his shoulder, staggered across the turfy path toward the lighthouse.

Twilight was already coming; in another half hour it would be time to light the lamp. To hell with the light! Let the ships run on the rocks and men's bodies be bashed to pieces! What cared he for men! Uriah and Casper and Mary had somehow cheated him of life; he would cheat the world of life!

He burst into the lighthouse kitchen, his eyes bulging with rage and drink.

"She's married!" he screamed at David.

"Married!" echoed David, his head drooping to his knees.

"Ay, married to that bloody Casper, damn him!"

David groaned deeply.

"How'd ye learn that?" he asked faintly.

"From de children on Nigger Pond and Christian what I met on de bar. By God, she'll rue de day. Dey's gone to Dauphiny's now. I'se'll twist de fat head off dat bloody Casper when I meets him."

"Ye can't do dat, Gershom."

"Dat I kin and will."

"Den ye'll be hunged."

"Who de hell cares? I'se'll have my revenge, anyhow," shouted Gershom, tossing off another glass of raw rum. "I'se'll beat hell outer all Jungs, 'cept you, Dave, dat I will. I'se'll devote

my life to beatin' hell outer Jungs whenever an'
wherever I finds dem." Then, in an altered mood,
he shouted: "Oh, Mary, how could ye play me
false?" with a bitterness that pierced David to
the heart and made him forget his own sorrow.
Then Gershom began to cry; without restraint
he howled and blubbered like a great schoolboy
beaten by a teacher.

"De sun's low on de Ragged cliffs, Gershom,"
said David, hoping to divert him from his
wretchedness. "It's time fur to light de lamp."

"I ain't agoin' to light de lamp no more, dis
night nor no oder night," shouted the tearful
giant.

"What if a wessel goes ashore, wid no light
burnin'?"

"Let de bloody wessels go ashore, an' de
bloody mens in dem. Dey's all rotten. All mens
and womens, too, is rotten. Let dem perish on de
cliffs in de freezin' winter sea. Let de ice grind de
Jungs to bits, way it did the flittin' nigger! I
lights dis lamp no more."

"Den ye'll lose yur job as light keeper, and
maybe Casper'll git it. Uriah's tried fur years
to git dis light."

That sobered Gershom and brought a cunning
leer into his drunken eye. "You'se right, Dave,
by God, you'se right! Dey'd steal my light from

me if dey could"; and half crazed with
drink and anger he staggered up the tower stair-
way to light the mantle and wind the revolving
mechanism. The mantle flared up, and, cursing
and swearing, he applied the hand crank to the
shaft that wound the revolving apparatus, and
gave a savage heave. There came a tearing crack
followed by a confused buzzing; he had broken
the mainspring.

That sobered him thoroughly; now the clock-
work would not revolve, and the light would
appear as a fixed one! God, what if some
vessel making Duren Bay would mistake his
light for Rockbound and run hard on the northeast shoal! Then he would lose the post, and
Casper Jung would get it, and old Uriah
would chuckle. Neither they nor the devil should
cheat him of his light. They had stolen Mary,
but they could not steal away his friend to whom
he talked on long winter nights. There was only
one thing to do: to turn the crank by hand
through all that night, and through every night,
till the supply boat ploughed through the ice
and came to him in answer to his emergency
signal.

He ran downstairs to tell David of his pre-
dicament, and, returning, began to grind,
his watch before him, timing each complete

revolution of the occulting apparatus to sixty seconds. It was wearisome work, but it helped him to forget his sorrow. He had no time to think of women, as for two hours he ground, cursing quietly. David climbed the stairs wearily to offer help, but Gershom declined curtly; it was no job, he said, for a sick man with one arm. David went back to his bed and Gershom continued to grind alone.

Then, suddenly, for no apparent reason, there flashed into his mind a sharply outlined picture of his grandfather's clock in the old house on Big Outpost. It was a tall clock, he remembered, and when he had stood before it as a child it had seemed to tower up into the darkness of the rafters. It had been brought with the first shipload of immigrants, the old folks said, and had been made by some cunning old clockmaker of Frankfurt am Main. It had not been run by a spring, but by big weights hung on chains. Then came his grand idea: why not run the light mechanism by a weight? Fired by this idea, he stopped grinding: Barren Island must appear as a fixed light for a while; after all, he thought, the inside and outside ice is so heavy, no vessel can make the bay, only vessels far out at sea might be misled.

He dashed downstairs and, without pausing

to tell David where he was going, ran out into the yard to get a small block of dried maple he had left on the edge of the wood pile. As he stooped to pick up the stick, the ghost yelled at him, "Ahoy, there, ahoy!" in its unearthly voice. Gershom straightened up and shouted back: "Go to hell, ghos'. I'se too busy to fool wid de likes o' you dis night, an' I ain't skeered o' nuttin' dat walks de eart' or de wind." Whereupon the ghost replied, "Ahoy, there, ahoy," and from the cliff there came a noise like the crash of a broken boat and the clatter of oars.

Gershom secured an auger and a couple of small chisels from the oil house, and with these climbed back to the tower. There he bored a hole in the end of his maple block, squared it with the chisels, and fitted it tightly over the end of his crank shaft. Down again he darted for a coil of half-inch rope and a single block pulley. Lantern in hand, he ventured out on the sloping face of the natural pier in search of a beach rock. It must be a rock of peculiar size and shape, larger at each end than in the middle, so that a rope made fast to it could not slip. By daylight he could have found quickly a score of such rocks, but it was no easy task in the darkness.

The ice ground and snarled against the cliff,

and spray driven by a rising southeast gale
drenched him through and through; the blown
spume in the white ray from the light made
unearthly iridescent colours. The ledge was sloping and slippery; a single misstep, and he would
be in deep water among the ice floes. Over his
head squawked the careys by thousands, like
minor demons, glorying in such a night.

He peered about him in the small circle of
light his lantern shed, and at last espied the very
rock he needed, a granite of some twenty pounds,
worn small in the middle by being trundled
about in the seas. He slid his feet cautiously
along the sloping surface, but, as he stooped to
grasp his stone, a sly, treacherous roller slipped
in under the ice, broke on the pier, and flushed
the great shelf. Out went Gershom's lantern.
He was knee and elbow deep in icy water, but he
held fast to his stone, and when the wave receded
worked his way up the shelf, the lightless lantern
hooked over his left arm and the rock between
his big hands.

Then he was back in the light tower, dripping
but warm. He made fast and wound the rope
with many turns about the maple block that was
wedged fast to the crank shaft, attached the
pulley with a stout iron staple to the casing of
the window, rove the free end of the rope through

the pulley, made fast the granite rock with three good turns and two net hitches, and lowered the rock gently from the window. As soon as the weight came on the rope, the occulting apparatus began to revolve. Gershom clapped his hands, bellowed like a bull let loose in a spring pasture, and roared out his full-hearted laugh. In his excitement over the mechanism he had forgotten the treachery of Mary, Casper, and Uriah. But at what speed she ran! He pulled out his watch. God, it was midnight! She was making a revolution in thirty seconds—twice too fast. He must rig a brake. But he found a brake unnecessary, for, by adjusting the timer, he could run the occulting mechanism fast or slow. He turned the adjusting screw till he got a revolution in exactly sixty seconds. By God, it was perfect! Looking out the window, he saw that his granite rock had not lowered perceptibly; there was a fifty-foot drop, and she would run all night. "Nuttin' to do but h'ist up de rock in de mornin' to run anoder night." He gazed in wonder and admiration at the work of his hands. "Nair a one o' de Rockbound Jungs could do dat."

He went below, pulled off his wet sea boots, and tried to sleep, but it was no go: he was too excited and exultant. Then came a relapse, as he

began to think of Mary at that very moment
lying in Casper's arms. To whom could he
now recite his epic struggle with the light? Once
Mary had listened with glowing eyes to the story
of his adventures. The glory of his achievement,
now that he could not tell it to Mary, turned to
bitterness and despair. He had almost forgotten
the existence of David, who in the room below
heard his deep groans and mad trampling to and
fro.

There was but one cure for his sorrow, and he
sprang up and drank draught after draught of
rum. His spirits rose again, and he began to shout
and sing. He picked up the Bible and began to
read from the Book of Job in a loud chanting
voice: "Why is light given to a man whose way
is hid, and whom God hath hedged in?" That
line, "Why is light given to a man whose way
is hid," must mean him. He drank more rum and
became maudlin and sentimental. God had
allowed the devil to afflict Job with boils and the
loss of all his cattle and children that in the end
he might bless him with great possessions. Perhaps God meant something like that for him;
perhaps God had sent him that trouble with the
light to save him from madness. He fell on his
knees, clasped his hands, and cried aloud: "O
God, t'ank ye fur breakin' dat spring."

"God didn't break that spring, I broke it," said a deep voice behind him.

Gershom pivoted on his knees and saw an obscure burly form in the dark corner by the desk. It looked like the figure of Uriah Jung. Every hair of his flesh prickled.

"Who is ye?"

"Don't you know me?"

"Dat I don't."

"I'm the devil, and I broke that spring to keep you from pressing the trigger of your duck gun with your toe, or drinking yourself to death like your father."

"Is you de devil?"

"I am."

Gershom plucked up courage.

"Come out where I kin see you."

Out in mid-floor stepped the devil, clad in sea boots, blue dungaree pants and jacket, a sou'-wester on his head, and no trace of tail or cloven foot. He certainly looked like a Rockbounder, for he had the big nose and jaw of the Jungs and the rounded cut-up nostrils of the Levys.

"An' what might ye be wantin' wid me?"

"I've come to save you."

"Save me fur what, fur Christ's sake? I'm not wantin' to be saved. Ye talks like a **damn** preacher."

"I'll save you to get revenge on the Jungs."

"Now you'se talkin', dat sounds good. How kin I git my revenge on Uriah and de damn stinkin' Jungs? By Christ, I'll kill de lot o' dem, David excepted."

"I'll tell you how to get a good revenge," and he crossed the room, stooped, and whispered something in Gershom's ear. His eyes bulged in terror and amazement. It is no light thing to have the devil whisper in your ear.

"Are you game?" asked the devil.

"I is," replied Gershom, "but don't forgit yur part o' de promise."

"The devil never forgets."

"Here, drink hearty to de bargain from dis island lovin' cup." He raised the rum pitcher to take a hearty draught himself, swilled mouthful after mouthful, but when he lowered the jug the devil was gone. The jug dropped from his fingers and crashed to the floor, he made three swaying lurches across the room and sprawled upon his bed. The light burned next day till David climbed the tower and extinguished it.

As long as the ice imprisoned him, Gershom went about with the text of the devil's revenge humming through his brain. He was a changed man; he seldom spoke to David, and, absorbed by his own thoughts and plans, almost ignored his existence. By times he cursed and swore, by times his lips curled in a cunning grin. To keep himself from entire madness, he jacked up the west side of the oil house and put a new sill under it; with every blow he struck he knocked a Jung upon the head: "Dere's one fur Uriah, dere's one fur Joe, dere's one fur Casper, and dere's a lot o' little ones fur de scum dey've bred." Sometimes he stood up, put his thumb to his nose, and twiddled his fingers at his enemy the sea, and cried in derision, "Dere, I'll take yur picture, ragin' winter sea."

Every night he drank heavily and invited the devil to visit him, but the devil never returned. However, he had lots of company; one night swarms of little gray men about four inches high came from under the old walnut desk, where he, and his father before him, had made up the meteorological reports for the government. These little men had bulgy popping eyes, and wide mouths like sculpins, their lower lips drooping on their chests. They danced and bowed and twirled their legs; then, forming platoons and companies, marched and countermarched, a little captain in yellow at their head twirling a gold stick longer than himself.

Another night came a flock of careys; in a second the room, which stank with their nasty

fetid odour of fish liver, was full of them, fluttering and squawking. That was a hideous night.
Gershom, lashing at the obscene birds with a
stick, broke a Sanford-made chair and cracked
the top of his walnut desk. He knocked down
scores of them, but as soon as they touched the
floor they sprang up fluttering. They tangled
their claws in his hair, perched on the rim of his
rum glass, and smothered him with their horrid
stink. By a great effort he got across the room,
stumbled down two flights of stairs, and, leaving
the careys in possession of the light tower, rushed
out into the open air.

At last the ice broke, and a succession of ebb
tides carried it out to sea. The supply boat, in
answer to Gershom's distress signal, came puffing
up to the island. She launched her stout jollyboat
to land oil and supplies, and Gershom proudly
led the inspector to the tower, to show him the
mechanism he had devised. A new spring was
fitted, and over a friendly glass of rum the inspector said:

"Uriah Jung reported that one night your
light did not flash from eight to midnight and
burned next day till midday."

"Dat was de night my spring bust an' I rigged
my stone," explained Gershom. "How could she
flash? I groun' her by hand fur two hours. De

damn Jungs, dey see ebert'ing. What de hell would dey o' done if dey'd bruk a spring!"

The fact that Uriah had reported on him rankled in Gershom's bosom and deepened a hate already deep as hell. Gershom gave the inspector a quart of brandy got from a friendly rum runner, and on his arrival in Liscomb he wrote a long report on the gallantry and re-sourcefulness of the keeper of Barren Island Light, and that report rests in some dusty pigeonhole to this day.

CHAPTER XII

Tragedie is noon oother maner thyng;
Ne kan in syngyng crie ne biwaille
But for that Fortune alwey wole assaile
With unwar strook the regnes that been proude;
For when men trusteth hire, thanne wol she faille,
And covere hire brighte face with a cloude.

CANTERBURY TALES.

HE breaking of the pack enabled David to escape Barren Island and the hateful company of a man who was no longer Gershom. Grief and anger over Mary's apparent treachery had completely changed his nature. In his anxiety for Gershom, David had almost forgotten his own troubles. His hand and arm were healed, at any rate, and he felt ready to go about light work. It was a glad day for David when he set out in Gershom's boat for Rockbound.

Uriah, fox with a lion's heart, was at the launch's head to meet them. To David's astonishment, Gershom showed no sign of rage or violence, but greeted the old man with an affability that seemed sincere. He shook Uriah's hand, and when questioned gave an entirely false account of their imprisonment. He had mended all his nets, cleared up all his chores, and had a grand time to read and loaf. He even went into the loft and passed the time of day with Casper and Joseph, who were putting new twine into a seine spiller. He smiled upon them with a strange glitter in his eye that only David noted. There was no mention of the marriage, of course, but much talk of the hard winter, the ice, and the likelihood of big flocks of spring sea ducks bedding near the rock. Gershom went no farther than the loft, and made no attempt to see or speak to Mary.

"De cold's tamed him," said Casper to his father one day, on Gershom's departure.

"Maybe, maybe," replied the old king, "but he'll bear watchin' jus' de same."

As David went about light jobs in the fish house, he often caught glimpses of Mary, as she hung out her washing in the yard or fetched wood from the wood pile. He saw unhappiness in her attitudes; there was no joy in her movements. Like Gershom, he made no effort to speak with her and she now spent all her hours in the school or Casper's house. Even if he had spoken with

her, he would have asked nothing, and he knew
she was too proud to volunteer information.
Why had she married Casper? That problem he
continually revolved in his brain as he went
about his work. Of course, Anapest had told him
all she knew; but Anapest only knew in part.
Her version was that old Jean Dauphiny had
come and forced his daughter into marriage.
There must be something more than that, but
the mystery of her choice he could not fathom.

Now that he was strong, he could no longer
live with Anapest, but returned to his lonely
house, though he often crossed the fields to talk
with the old woman and look at the boy. They
were his only friends; Gershom and Mary were
lost to him. No sunshine came with the spring
weather; again he was seized with the obsession
to sell house and land and go far away, yet he
could not. In his boat at sea he had often sensed
an impending tempest by languid air and sullen
lowering cloud, and it seemed to him now that such
a cloud hung over Rockbound, and that Gershom
was the cloud from which a storm might break.

On almost every day of fine weather Gershom
came to Rockbound to hang about the fish house.
David he ignored, but he smiled and smiled
upon Casper, Joseph, and Uriah. The Jungs
seemed completely disarmed. Sometimes, to-

ward noon, he would set off for the Outposts, waving his hand to Uriah and calling as he slipped his boat down the launch: "Dis is my day fur sinful pleasure."

One day in mid-March, as he loitered thus in the Jung's fish house, he heard what he wanted to hear. Uriah, the general, was laying out the work for the boys and issuing his orders.

"To-morrow, Joe an' Dave, take de big boat wid herrin' to Liscomb an' bring back salt an' barrels."

Into his eyes came a leer of triumph; at last Uriah and Casper would be the only Jung men on Rockbound; the Krauses' and the Jungs' sharesmen he need not worry about.

Next morning Gershom on Barren Island watched with his glasses till he saw the big boat, abreast of Bib Duck, on its way to Liscomb. Then, with a mad grin, he ran to his launch, long duck gun in hand, and pushed his boat into the surf. He drove straight in for Rockbound and ran his boat up on Uriah's launch.

"Git yur guns an' duck tub quick. Dere's t'ousands upon t'ousands o' sea ducks bedded round de Rock," he cried from his boat to Casper and Uriah, who were fitting some new logs to the head of the launch. Gershom knew that he could appeal to Uriah's greed, who could not resist getting a boatload of sea ducks. Moreover, the old man, though no shot, liked to tend the tubs with his dory and pick up cripples. Uriah and Casper straightened up from their work. To go ducking with Gershom, next to David the best shot on the islands, was too great a temptation to resist. Still, the old man thought he must show proper reluctance.

"What's dat you say, Gershom—t'ousands o' sea ducks bedded on de Rock?"

"T'ousands, more like millions. Come on quick."

"Casper an' me was figurin' on fixin' de launch to-day, where de ice gnawed her."

"All right! It's a shame ye'll miss all dose ducks. I'll git two o' de Krauses to go wid."

"Don't do dat. We'll go wid. Git de duck tub down, Casper. Ye kin tow our dory, Gershom, ain't it?"

"Dat I kin."

They were soon off, and passed the eastern end, the dory in tow, the duck tub amidships, Gershom at the tiller and Uriah and Casper together on the low bow thwart. Now that Gershom had them in his power, he grinned at them with a sinister flash in his staring blue eyes and hummed a ballad as he steered for the Rock.

Now, Gershom had neither looked for sea

ducks feeding in the shoals around the Rock,
nor did he care two straws if none were there.
This was their season of migration, and if they
found no birds he could say to Uriah that the
great flock must have rested and taken the next
hitch on their northward flight.

As a matter of fact, sea ducks were there in
thousands. They got over the duck tub weighed
down with rocks, threw out the strings of decoy
tollers, and the old man and Casper took off the
boats to a safe distance to tend and pick up. How
Gershom shot that day! Bang went his long gun
as the sea ducks planed and fluttered to light
among the decoys; bang again as they struggled
to rise to windward. When he signalled Casper to
take his place in the tub, he had dropped eighty-
three dead ones on the water, along with a number of cripples, which the old man had gaffed
with his sharp boat hook.

By the time Casper had shot twenty-three,
the afternoon was well advanced, a sea was beginning to get up, and a ragged scrap of white
showed on the top of rollers going over the Rock.

"Time to be gettin' in," called Uriah, "if yur
goin' to make de light by sundown. Dough it's a
pity we can't take a few more." The old king was
never satisfied.

"Yes," said Gershom, "by de time I sets ye in,

dere'll be little daylight to spare. We'd best be startin'."

They set off homeward, dory a-tow with the duck tub aboard it this time. Gershom was at the helm, Uriah and Casper in the shelter of the bows, a tarpaulin about their shoulders, and fluffy eiderdown ducks piled high about their legs and feet. A wind had risen, blowing cold from the northwest, and a big sea was rising. In the west over Sacrifice were heavy bars of black cloud through which the red disk of the sun glimmered. The three duck guns were piled aft by Gershom; he had seen to that.

Casper nodded off to sleep—Rockbounders who worked long hours and took little rest in bed slept when they could; in a boat when one was awake at the tiller the others drowsed with head against thwart or fish pen—but Uriah had his eyes half-open, at least one eye, for his left eye always drooped and squinted. He was busy calculating how many sea ducks he and Casper could claim. True, Gershom had shot nearly all, but he and Casper had picked up the dead ones and gaffed the cripples; yes, there should be an even division; that would give him and Casper eighty ducks between them. He felt them over, picked out a dozen birds with thick breasts, and worked them into the corner of the bow as part of his own share. They could freeze them solid at night and hang them in the big ice house to last through the spring and early summer.

The sea was running big now with a long swell; aft, where the streak of white water left the screw, the stern was almost flush with the sea. Gershom turned for a moment as if to look at Barren Island, drew a flash of straight rum from his inside pocket, and emptied it in three gulps. Presently Uriah, still pondering on a division of the ducks that would accrue to his advantage, felt beneath his buttocks that short, dull, compressed heave, betokening to any experienced sailor or fisherman that a boat has passed from deep to shoal water. The old man threw the tarpaulin from his shoulders, raised himself, and glanced around: they were headed straight for the Bull and almost on it.

"Quick, Gershom, sheer off quick, you'se steerin' over de Bull," yelled the old man. Casper started up shouting: "Look out, man, look out, de Bull's breakin'!"

"Ay," said Gershom calmly, a triumphant grin of madness on his face, "yes, de Bull's breakin', and we'se goin' ober it. Me and you wid."

Uriah and Casper started toward him, terror in their eyes.

"Stay forrad," yelled Gershom, picking up his double-barrelled gun, his grinning mask dropped off to reveal satanic rage. "I'se got a charge here fur each o' you if ye comes a step nigher."

"De Bull's breakin', can't ye see? Ye'll swamp her," screamed Uriah.

"I knows de Bull's breakin'. I bin a-watchin' him. Us is goin' ober him, an' to hell togedder. Now pray—pray, ye damn bloody Jungs. Ye stole my Mary from me by some trick. No Jung eber got ahead of a Born wid a woman by fair means. Pray, Uriah, ye old fox. See if yur lovin' God will come down an' save ye now."

Casper cowered in the eyes, but Uriah sprang toward the steersman, a ballast rock clutched in his old hand. "Sheer off, ye crazy loon," he yelled.

A mountainous roller carried them onto the Bull, which, snorting savagely with both nostrils, shot two streams of spray high into the air. Down came the crest of the wave, filling the boat flush from gunwale to gunwale. Down she dived beneath the seas, dory and duck tub dragged with her by the weight of ballast and engine. None of the three could swim far in that chaos of breaking sea; a few choking screams drowned in the Bull's roar, a flash of yellow oilskinned arms, and they were gone, to be trundled over jagged cliff bottom or tangled in long streamers of kelp. Loose boards came to the surface, and sea ducks, floating belly up, made a circle of white in the Bull's foam.

Gershom went down triumphant, the devil's promise in his mind. "You will land on Rockbound when Uriah an' Casper are washed to and fro on the sea floor." He clutched an oar for a moment, but it slipped from his grasp. The dory's painter had tangled about his feet and dragged him down. Nevertheless, the devil spoke true, for, while Casper's and Uriah's bodies were never found, David, searching along the shore with Mary, found poor Gershom's great body, battered and torn, among the boulders of Southeast Cove.

CHAPTER XIII

He was a verray parfit, gentil knyght.

CANTERBURY TALES.

HEN Joseph and David got back from Liscomb with their load of salt and barrels on the day of the disaster, they were surprised that Uriah was not at the launch to haul out their boat and help them unload. In sixty-odd years he had never missed meeting a homing Rockbound boat; in the old days he used to be at the launch with his cattle, and when the cattle were superseded by cable and stationary engine, he used to stand on the lower logs, cable in hand and slip the hook into the stem ring so quickly that the boat slid up the launch scarcely losing her seaway. From the sharesmen they learned that Uriah and Casper had gone ducking to the Rock with Gershom. No one felt anxiety about them, for it was a day of moderate weather, and it was a matter of common knowledge that

sea ducks settled best among decoys when the
beginning twilight hid boats and duck tub.

No one on Rockbound had seen the disaster to
Gershom's boat, for the Bull is hidden from the
dwellings and fish house by the eastern wooded
knoll, but one of the watching women had seen
some boat far to the eastward of Barren Island,
making in from the Rock. As twilight fell and
deepened into dusk, the women stared seaward
and waited and waited for Casper and Uriah.
They made all kinds of conjectures, none of
which were satisfactory. Perhaps they had stood
in for Minden or Sanford, to sell their ducks, but
against that it was highly improbable that any
boat could cross the wide stretch of water between Rockbound and Sanford without being
seen by some soul on their island. Perhaps they
had landed on Barren Island for shelter, for the
sea was rising, but that hope died when night
settled down and no light twinkled from the
Barren Island light tower. Joseph lit the fixed
light on Rockbound, as he always did when the
old man was away, and although the sea was
rough and a wind blowing up, David made ready
his boat to go out to Barren Island. With him it
was a principle of faith that the great lights, on
whose guidance rested the safety of the fishermen, must always be lit. Above all, his friend's

light must flash its ray out through the night. Moreover, David hoped that on the island he might get some bit of information that would explain the whereabouts of Gershom, Casper, and the old man. Though it was always dangerous around the Rock, there was no reason why a stout boat should be lost there on such a day. It was just possible that the light in the tower was broken beyond immediate repair, though that did not explain the unlighted lamp, for David knew right well that Gershom kept two or three emergency paraffin lamps.

Just as he laid his hand upon his boat's stem to push her into the sea, Mary came suddenly out of the darkness and caught him by the arm.

"Where are they, David?"

These were the first words she had spoken to him in months.

"I don't know, Mary, p'r'aps in Sanford, p'r'aps on Barren Island."

"They never crossed the bay to Sanford."

"Den dey's on de island."

"Why doesn't the light burn?"

"P'r'aps de light's busted."

"I know where they are," she said solemnly. "They're lost."

"Don't say dat, Mary, don't say dat till we hunts. Dey was all good mens in boats."

"They're lost, I'm sure, I feel it inside me; still, if you're going to hunt, I'm going with you."

"Not dis night," said David gently. "Not dis night, Mary. De sea's rough."

"I've been out in rougher seas; I've been with my father on Matt's bank. I'm going with you to hunt," and with that she climbed aboard and sat stolidly on the amidship thwart. David, seeing that he could not dissuade her, ran up to the fish house to fetch her an oil coat and to send word by one of the sharesmen to Joseph and Martin's wife that Mary had gone with him to Barren Island.

They pushed off in the rising sea and rounded the western end guided by the white of the breakers. Then David had to steer a course, for there was no flash of light to guide him. Mary gave what aid she could by holding a hooded lantern over the compass box. Thus they ploughed through the night-black sea on their quest, spray flung from the bows, a streak of white water astern. When David heard the roar of Barren Island surf, he slowed down his engine and, giving the tiller to Mary, ran forward, hooked an arm about the spar, and stared ahead into the ring of white. Then shouting by turns "port" or "starboard" to Mary at the tiller, they made the cleft in safety, and David sprang out upon the logs, painter in hand. Even as he did so, a big sea swilled into the cleft, at the moment of their greatest danger, and half-filled the boat. Mary was drenched, but she ran forward, scrambled over the bows, and with the windlass they hauled the boat to safety.

No answer came to their shouts. Save for the careys squawking overhead and the tireless rhythm of surf, Barren Island was silent as death. As they approached the spectral form of the lighthouse, looming sudden and gray through the night, David half feared to find there some evidence of tragedy. He thought of the night when he and Gershom had found old Gershom's body on the kitchen floor. But the lighthouse was empty and returned naught to their cries but mocking echoes.

David at once went aloft to the tower, adjusted and lit the mantle, wound the mechanism, and the light began to talk to boats and ships at sea. Then he hurried out into the yard to run up emergency lantern and pennant: that should bring the cutter in two days, at the latest. He made a complete round of the cliffs, calling down into every cove and cleft in the rocks.

When David returned to the light after an hour's search, he found that Mary had built up a fire in the kitchen stove, dried her clothing, and boiled some coffee. He could search no more that night, and he had eaten little since morning. They sat down in silence to their meal of coffee, tinned beef, and thick round biscuit from Gershom's cupboard.

Once David ventured, "Dey mus' be on de Sanford main, dere warn't no sea to-day to lose a stout boat wid t'ree such mens." But to this Mary made no answer.

After supper, Mary cleared up the dishes and lay down on the kitchen sofa. David went aloft to see that the light was burning fair, then sat by the kitchen fire and smoked Gershom's pipe. It was a blowy night, but not a wild one.

Once, after midnight, he asked softly: "Are ye warm enough, lass?" and Mary replied at once, "Warm enough, thanks." Except for that they spoke no word throughout the night.

When gray dawn glimmered through the windows, David put a pot of oatmeal upon the stove and went up to put out the light. They breakfasted, tidied up Gershom's kitchen, and set out for Rockbound.

On their arrival they found that no word of Casper, Uriah, or Gershom had come from the Sanford main. In little groups the islanders began a search of the Rockbound shore, peering into every rock cleft and turning over piles of kelp and seaweed on the sand bar. David and Mary, searching together, made the entire round of the island. A little before noon of that day, as they walked along the cliff's brink above the Whale Cove, David's quick eye caught a glimpse of some boards nailed together in a triangular shape that were banging against the rocks at the cliff's base. He clambered down and looked at them closely. His head swam, he was sick at heart as he drew the boards from the water; they told him the story; now he knew.

"What is it?" called Mary from the cliff.

"Naught but some bits o' boards," called back David.

He put the wet boards upon his shoulder and climbed the face of the cliff to reach her.

"Dey're lost, Mary," he said simply, laying the pieces at her feet. "It's de bow floor boards from Gershom's boat. I knows dem well. Yes, dey're lost, Mary. Dey must o' run ober de Bull."

Mary stood mute and tearless, staring at the wet boards. What thoughts ran through her brain! A rejected, half-crazed lover, marriage with a man she did not love, and death within a six-month.

"Don't grieve, lass, don't grieve too much,"

said David gently, putting his arm around her. "Dat's de way wid us fishermen, as ye knows well: one day livin' an' well, de nex' day de sea gits us."

David led her back through the woods toward the houses, but before they emerged from the shadow of the trees, Mary clutched his arm and said, "Come and talk to me often, David. You're kind, you're the only one can give me comfort. And, say, for my sake, take the *Mary* on the banks from this on. She's mine now. You take her. She's not so fast as your *Phœbe*, but a stauncher boat."

David spread the melancholy news among the Jungs and went to Anapest's house to tell her what he'd found.

"We oughter give ober dis fightin' on Rockbound, Aunt Anapest, what wid dese childer a-growin' up. Yes, we oughter quit fightin' twix' de Krauses and de Jungs."

"I were ready to quit long since," said Anapest, "but de old man, he were dat hard. He'd 'a' done me out o' my rights on dis island if I hadn't 'a' fought him—dough I don't wish to speak ill o' de dead."

"My rights, too," said David. "He were dat mean, it's true. He learned dat meanness, I guess, from de hard times de old Jungs had in de old days. Still, he were a hellian to git work done, ye can't deny him dat, an' in a kind o' rough way he kep' his bargain."

"Ay, if ye watched him close," said the old woman.

"An' who'll mend de nets an' seines fur de Jungs, nets what's ripped and mangled wid albacore? De ol' man gloried in dat work, an' he done it fine. De ol' feller had his good p'ints. Life's short fur a fisherman. Yes, us oughter quit dis fightin' an' discord on Rockbound."

"Won't dat Joseph keep on jus' like his fader? He's de spawn o' de ol' man."

"I hopes not. I can't say what Joe'll do, but as fur me, I lives in peace. I won't quarrel wid Kraus, Jung, nur Outposter."

"Joseph's boss now, we'll see how he carries on wid my boys," was Anapest's last word as he departed.

Nat Levy, the sharesman, went out to light Barren Island that night, and to stand by till the cutter came. Next morning, soon after daybreak, when the ebb was at its lowest, David found Gershom's body in the sou'west gutter, tangled in long streamers of kelp. They carried the body from the shore and laid it in state on the parlour table of David's house, where the

women and children came to stare at it mutely.
David fashioned him a coffin of white boards,
carried him to Big Outpost in his boat, and stood
bareheaded beside his grave. Casper's and Uriah's
bodies never came ashore.

CHAPTER XIV

For I have seyn of a ful misty morwe
Folwen ful ofte a merie somer's day;
And after winter folweth grene May.

TROILUS AND CRISEYDE.

BUT the world moves, work goes on, children must be taught, and hungry mouths fed; one cannot live upon regrets and sorrow. Within a few weeks of the island tragedy Mary was back teaching the children in the Rockbound school; David, in his new boat, the *Mary*, was setting halibut trawls on the bank beyond the Rock, and Joseph had brought green sharesmen from Sanford to labour in place of Casper and Uriah. The old man's demise made a sad gap in the island life. He had been a real king, who alone and without counsel had shaped affairs of state. Joseph had as much greed but less character and deep cunning.

One day, when David came in from fishing,

he found that a Sanford boat had brought him a
letter in a long envelope franked by the government. He had never received a letter before, and
surmising that this strange thing portended evil
his hand shook a little as he took it. He weighed
the letter in his great hand and stared at it
blankly. There was his name and address right
enough, printed on the envelope: "David Jung,
Rockbound, Sanford Post Office."

"Why doesn't ye see what's in her—you'se a
risin' scholard, ain't it?" said Joseph in a ferment
of envious curiosity.

David tore the letter open and made what he
could of the contents, but he was vague about
the printed word when he got outside the realm
of dissyllables. He left the curious Joseph unsatisfied and carried the letter to Mary, who read
it to him. Its purport was as follows:

The officials of the Department of Marine and
Fisheries had consulted with the people of the
islands and neighbouring main, and they had
been unanimous in their opinion that David Jung
of Rockbound was the fittest man in all the bay
to tend the Barren Island Light, which meant so
much to their safety. Acting on their suggestion,
the Department offered David the light. The
temporary keeper would stay for a month, and
he would have that time to think the matter

over, and make his business arrangements, if he accepted.

"What you t'ink o' dat, now, Mary?" he gasped in surprise. To have her know that the islanders trusted him gave him a glow of pleasure.

Mary did not hesitate in her decision. "Of course, you must take it. It's the first light in the islands. And you're the right kind of man to keep an important light."

"I couldn't make out nair a government report."

"Nonsense. I'll teach you. Call in at Barren Island some day as you come in from the Rock and get some of the forms. They're naught but reports on wind and weather, and who knows wind and weather better than you? I'll teach you how to fill them in."

"An' me wid a handwritin' like a fly creepin' ober a page."

"I'll start you at writing again, and you can go on yourself with copybooks. You must take the light. You and Joseph will never agree on Rockbound. Already I can see the old quarrels with the Krauses flaring up."

"I'd be right lonesome dere. De place's full o' haunts an' ghosts."

"Why does a strong man like you talk of

ghosts? Ghosts are stuff made of ignorance and fear."

"It's right lonesome dere, Mary, on a windy night."

"Then you must marry again some day and have a wife with you."

"It's none so easy to get the kind o' woman ye wants to live wid on a place like Barren Island," said David, wishing in his heart he could say something quite different.

"Then change Barren Island. That's what I'd do if I were a man. Barren Island soil is as deep as Rockbound's, and see what the old Jungs made of this island."

"De sea spray blows on de land dere an' salts it."

"Trees would stop the sea spray," said Mary with her honest brown eyes looking straight into David's. "I own land here now, a house, and a fourth interest in the firm. I'm going to look after my property, and Joseph will bear watching. Take the light, David. It'll be good to have a friend near me. I'll never marry again, but I may live here always. Yes, take the light, David, and come and see me whenever the sea is smooth."

David went that night to his old place of meditation on the cliffs above the dog holes, where he could watch the light blink, and thought the whole matter over. Joseph and he could never agree, he knew, for Joseph had all the concentrated greed of the old Jungs and was already back to a round of baiting the sharesmen, minor cheatings, and quarrels with the Kraus men, who had tried to show some friendliness after the loss of Casper and the old man. Martin's and Joseph's boys were growing up and in a few years could fish off Rockbound. Barren Island would be his own—he could be king there, though not such a king as Uriah—for he had found by inquiry that, with the exception of the acre on which the light stood, he could buy for a small sum the whole of Barren Island from Gershom's estate. Here on Rockbound, with Joseph, he felt cramped and confined. He hated to leave the old place that had been his mother's, but he could retain the ownership and rent it to some married sharesman; in turn, it could go to Tamar's boy, little Ralph.

David decided then and there to take the light, and before the allotted month was up he stood one day on the launch, his boat piled high with household goods, ready to set off for his kingdom. Mary, who was herself on the eve of departure to pay a visit to her parents in Bay of God's Mercy, stood by him to say good-bye. Anapest came swaying down the pathway, little Ralph in her arms; the Kraus boys shook him by the hand, but Joseph was too busy goading the sharesmen in the fish house to waste time in farewells. He pushed off into a sea as smooth as that on which he had floated from the Outposts on the day he had first dared to face Uriah. Mary waved her hand to him till his boat rounded West Head, and when he looked back to Rockbound from the open sea, he found she had crossed the island to Southeast Cove and was still waving to him.

Now David had great dreams about Barren Island, and he was no idle dreamer. He dreamed of making his island a garden; perhaps he had got the suggestion from Mary. For the first weeks after his arrival he drove his boat every day to the Sanford main and brought it back loaded with little spruces. The island must be reforested, as the underwater stumps showed it had been in old time, and spruces are quick growing and stand up best against wind and weather. He planted his spruces in a double row all about the cliff edge of Barren Island. This was his first labour.

This accomplished, he began his second: war upon Gershom's enemies, the careys. This involved a journey to Minden to purchase a pair of oxen and a heavy breaking-up plough. He

and Nat Levy, who had gladly come to him as
sharesman, hoisted the cattle into his big boat
and lashed them to poles, one on either side of
the centreboard. He had waited for a smooth
day for this enterprise. When they arrived back
at Barren Island, a derrick had to be rigged, and
the frightened, bellowing oxen hoisted out with
broad slings of canvas beneath their bellies.

Next day they began to plough the turf,
Nathan Levy driving the oxen with great shout-
ings and twirling of whip, while David gripped
the helves. At his heels followed two big dogs of
the Rockbound breed, that pounced upon the
careys as they fluttered from the furrows, and
destroyed them with one crunching bite. It was
necessary to plough deep, to plough and cross-
plough, but in a fortnight of steady labour it was
done, and the loose stones were gathered into
heaps, hauled on the drag, and dumped over the
cliff. No more was Barren Island the home of the
careys; those that fluttered in the air and escaped
the dogs sought other islands, where no plough
cut the turf.

After the conquest of the careys David and
his sharesman set about digging a well, blasting
out fragments from the rock, for the soil was
soon sweet with the evil birds gone. He had al-

ways dreaded that Gershom might be imprisoned on the island and the cellar tank run dry.

Next he declared war upon the herring gulls that bred and nested among the rocks on the western side. David hated this job, for the herring gull, with its snowy body, gray wings, and scarlet bill, is a beautiful bird. He liked birds, and in spite of himself admired the daring of these small gulls. But they drove off the island all other birds except swallows, and he wanted birds to come to his island, each kind marking a season: long-legged curlew, yellow-billed black robins, golden plover, and swift-winged checkerbacks. Moreover, the herring gulls were a continual source of annoyance: they swooped close to one's face with ceaseless shriek and chatter, they protested forever the ownership of the island, they might even, he feared, pick out the eyes of children, and children he hoped some day to have on Barren Island.

So he and Nat Levy set about the ugly job remorselessly, smashing the nests, breaking the eggs, destroying the fledglings, and knocking down with stick or gun the old birds that hovered about their heads in hundreds. It took much to discourage the tenacious herring gulls, which had doubtless laid their eggs and reared their young on Barren Island for centuries, but at last they gave up the struggle, and, migrating to Big Duck, took that island for a breeding place. Then, to David's great joy other birds began to come to his island; one morning he discovered that a pair of robins had nested in his spruce hedge.

Next came the labour of enriching the soil with rotted sea dung. David and his man gathered all kelp and seaweed that drove upon the shore, piled it in heaps above the cliff, and covered it with turf and manure. But Barren Island is a poor place to get sea dung; there is no beach on which it is rolled in tangled masses after a storm. So, when he had time, he took his big boat to Sacrifice, where he and Nat cut rockweed and came home gunwale-laden.

David's last great labour was a sentimental one. On the sloping shelf above the natural pier David and Nat set up a derrick of three logs, lashed together at their tops and firmly guyed at their bottoms. On this derrick they rigged tackles, and, with the oxen hitched to the fall, moved and cross-piled some of Pharaoh's coffins into a rough pyramid. On the very top David set a square stone upright, upon its end, and upon this rock, north, east, south, and west, David and Nat rudely graved the name "Gershom."

It stands there to this day as a memorial to his friend, and fishermen far up and down the coast know it as Gershom's beacon.

For two years David and his sharesman laboured in the intervals between fishing seasons to make Barren Island a garden. The hedge of spruces grew thick, cowering close to the ground on the southward and seaward side, but keeping off, nevertheless, the salt-water spray that had theretofore stunted the grasses.

David fetched fence poles from the main, and divided his kingdom into hayfields, pasture lot, and kitchen garden. Soon he could grow cabbages and potatoes as large and fine as those of Rockbound. He even set out a tiny apple orchard. No longer the ghost cried, "Ahoy, there, ahoy," as he stepped from the lighthouse door on foggy nights, nor was there any sound of broken boats and clattering oars from the cliff's edge. With the careys and herring gulls, the ghosts sought other haunts.

In fact, it had become so fine an island that one day the inspector of lights, on his round of visits, said to David: "Barren Island's a fit name for this island no more. The government's having a new chart of the bay made; what shall we name this island on the new chart?"

And David, after a moment's reflection, replied: "Name it Gershom's Island, arter de great mens dat once kep' dis light."

"Why not Jung's Island?" asked the inspector. "You made it what it is."

"No," said David, "dere's a Jung's Island inside a'ready. Name it Gershom's Island after de two Gershoms." And thus the island was named on the new chart.

One summer day in the third year of his occupancy of the island he saw a boat heading in for his landing stage. He ran across the island and waited at the head of the launch. The boat drew nearer: Christian Kraus was at the tiller, and amidships were Mary, old Anapest, and little Ralph.

"We come fur to visit ye an' hold a picnic," called Anapest as the boat's prow took the logs. "Yure glad to see us, ain't it?"

"Dat I is," said David. "You'se right welcome."

"An' she's cum fur to marry ye," said Anapest abruptly. "An' here's a start fur a family," and she put the little boy's hand into his father's great paw.

David was dumbfounded, but Mary smiled serenely.

"I talked her into it," went on Anapest. "Says I to her, 'Ain't it a shame fur to leave dat strong man alone on Barren Island an' him a-lovin' ye to death, an' ye a stout lass wid no man an' nair a kid? Ain't dat a pretty kettle o' fish?' says I to her, an' in de end she sees de p'int. She wants ye, too, she's been a-wantin' ye all along. Ain't dat de complete foolishness now, to be young an' livin' alone an' missin' de good years, 'cause ye lost yur woman, an' her, her man, t'ree years gone?"

Then Anapest, empress of all the Krauses, turned to Christian in the boat. "Ye, Christian, steam ye back to Big Outpost an' fetch de Reverend Green dis day, an' if he hums an' haws about comin', say dat Anapest Kraus bid him come."

So the minister was fetched, and that very afternoon David and Mary were married upon the cliff's edge, near the spot where Gershom had had his adventure with the ram. In fact, a memory of this incident came so vividly to David's mind that he almost laughed in the face of the parson droning through the service. Below them, the rhythmic sea played a grand wedding march. When the preacher closed his book and shook the hands of the married pair, Anapest unpacked her hamper and spread the wedding feast upon the grass. To test reality, David pinched himself hard and often: surely a great wave would sweep in to bear off beauty in its undertow, leaving naught but the gravel and beach rock of sordid reality; surely this was the magic of the Tempest.

At last they were left alone: little Ralph, wrapped in a warm blanket, slept in the shelter of the spruces. Arms about each other, they watched the boat vanish into mist and twilight. Then it seemed to David that he had fulfilled his destiny, and that all the burden of weariness had rolled from his shoulders. Life was worth enduring if only for such an hour. He picked up the sleeping child and, still holding Mary close to him, turned toward the light, along the turfy path. But it was no turfy path: it was a way of gold, full of flowers, not of this earth, but like to those with which mediæval painters adorned their foregrounds.

THE END

1 Detail from *Portrait of Frank Parker Day*, c. 1935
by Mabel Killam Day
Oil on canvas, 57.5 × 45.4 cm

AFTERWORD

Gwendolyn Davies

On 20 February 1929 an outraged letter appeared in the *Progress-Enterprise* of Lunenburg, Nova Scotia. Signed by the "Offended Citizens of Rockbound," the letter reappeared in untempered form in the *Halifax Herald* on 26 February.[1] Charging that author Frank Parker Day had visited the island of Ironbound off the South Shore of the province "last summer...collecting material" for his "ridiculous" and "notorious" novel *Rockbound*, the letter went on to accuse the writer of portraying "us humble inhabitants of our little island, as ignorant, immoral and superstitious." The image was unjustified, argued the Ironbounders, for "Our Island can boast of three school teachers, and there isn't a child who cannot read and write. We earn our livelihood by honest toil, from Father Neptune and Old Mother Earth." Why, then, "Mr. Day put such a ridiculous book on the market, belittling the inhabitants of his native province, and those who befriended him," was beyond their conception, but they could only suppose that he might "accumulate quite a bit of money" from his enterprise. So too "did Judas Iscariot when he betrayed his Master," they pointed out, and so too did "Castelreigh [sic] who sold his country, and yet in the end cut his throat." Such, they predicted, was "the ending of all ill-gotten gains," and of all those "who betray their country-men."

The target of the Ironbounders' wrath was at the height of a distinguished career as a scholar, writer, sometime military officer, and president of Union College in Schenectady, New York, at the time that *Rockbound* appeared. Born in the Methodist parsonage in Shubenacadie, Nova Scotia, on 9 May 1881, Frank Parker Day has left vivid impressions of his childhood in "Apology of an Egoist" and *The Autobiography of a Fisherman*. Descended from Irishmen who had immigrated to the Maritimes from Straban, Day early recognized in his clerical father a man more at ease with "trout-fishing, curing horses, making models of boats and schooners and mixing up Asthma Cure" than with preparing sermons and preaching:

Father was a kind of missionary person who had had some slight training in medicine. He had the obsession that he could cure asthma, a disease prevalent among the fishermen. He was a big powerful, dogmatic man, and his parishioners dared do nothing but get well, after they had swallowed two bottles of his Cure. Certainly the colour, blackish purple, and the smell, rotten eggs, gave testimony to its efficiency. Some of the ingredients were expensive and it was because of the Asthma Cure and a succession of trotting horses, Palmer, Evangeline and Israel Junior, that we endured the life of poverty and often debt. "Christians should be poor," the old man used to say.[2]

Father and son shared a common bond in their love of fishing, and as the family travelled around Nova Scotia from parish to parish the young Day developed the appreciation of outdoor life and knowledge of the province's waterways that were to inform his writing and bring to it an almost spiritual respect for the restorative powers of nature. Moving to Mahone Bay at the age of fourteen and attending school in Lunenburg gave Day an introduction to the South Shore fishery that was to stand him in good stead when he later turned to the writing of *Rockbound*, for it was on the South Shore that he first became interested in "the fleet of vessels that sailed every spring to the Grand Banks and the Labrador to fish for cod."[3] His friendship with Captain Enoch Mason of "the stout schooner 'Nova Zembla'" found expression more than thirty years later in the text of *Rockbound* when the captain of the *Sylvia Westner* self-consciously vies to "be home earlier and with a bigger fare than the *Springwood*, the *Nova Zembla*, or the *Sadie Oxner*" (192).[4] It was Captain Mason who also introduced Day to the life of the inshore fisherman by taking the teenager "with him to fish on Green Bank, off our coast." "How happy and miserable I was then!" recalled Day in 1927. "I was seasick most of the time. There was not the slightest convenience, and bobstays are cold and slippery when seas slop around your knees of a brisk morning, but I was learning to be tough and a sailor."[5]

After graduating from Lunenburg and Pictou Academies, Day worked on coastal vessels in the summers and taught in Acacia Villa, Lower Horton, in the winters ("the dreariest of boarding schools ... well-run by a heavy-handed, old-fashioned schoolmaster"). In 1900, Day entered Mount Allison University. Here he revelled in the stimulation of sports, friendships, and academic studies, remembering years later that "I used to feel that my brain was growing, as I sat at my little deal table and tried to solve in my mind some complicated syllogism in the back of Jevon's *Logic*."[6] The result of the Mount Allison years was not only an abiding affection for his *alma mater* and its strong sense of fellowship but also a Rhodes Scholarship to Oxford in 1905. Entering Christ Church as a candidate in literature, Day approached this experience with the same thirst for life that seemed characteristic of all his endeavours. "Oxford," he was to write later, "is a glorious place to loaf and think and learn slowly ... I had a wonderful time there; servants, luxury, theatres, beautiful buildings, pictures, music, burst upon me all at once."[7] In the next two years, he rowed for Christ Church, won the Oxford-Cambridge heavyweight boxing championship, became a lieutenant in the King's Colonials Light Horse, and graduated with honours in English after work with Walter Raleigh, then completing his "English Men of Letters" book on Shakespeare. The year 1907–8 was spent at Berlin University as an assistant to Professor Alois Brandl, but Day returned to Oxford the following year to work on an MA and to take up a post as an instructor in English at Bristol University. By the fall of 1909 he was back in Canada as a member of the English Department at the University of New Brunswick. In 1910 he married Yarmouth-born artist and Mount Allison graduate Mabel Killam, who later provided the cover design for his novel, *River of Strangers*. The outbreak of war interrupted an appointment to the English Department at the Carnegie Institute of Technology in Pittsburgh, and during the next five years Day served with the 85th Canadian Infantry Battalion, raised and commanded the 185th Cape Breton Highlanders, and in France commanded the 25th Battalion of the 5th Brigade, Second Division. Promoted a colonel on the field of battle at Amiens, he later integrated some of his war experiences into the *Roses of Mercatel*, "The Iroquois," *The Autobiography of a Fisherman*, and the unpublished "Apology of an Egoist."[8] Described by his son as an illustration of the well-known adage "Old soldiers never die but simply fade away,"[9] Day was to call upon his military background again in the Second World War when he organized a COTC Command Office at Mount Allison, helped plan a POW camp in New Brunswick, and wrote a series of books on basic English for Canadian servicemen.

After returning to North America in 1919, Day re-entered academic life, becoming director of the Division of General Studies at the Carnegie Institute (1919–26), professor of English at Swarthmore College (1926–8), and eventually president of Union College, Schenectady (1928–33). In 1927 Mount Allison awarded him an honorary Doctor of Laws degree and in 1929 New York University followed suit by making him a Doctor of Literature. In spite of his busy academic schedule Day retained an ongoing relationship with his native Nova Scotia throughout this period, often making summer visits or fishing expeditions to the province. By the time *Rockbound* appeared in 1928, it was clear that Nova Scotia was central to his literary imagination. "An Epic of Marble Mountain" (1923) and *River of Strangers* (1926) both drew on the Cape Breton background that Day had come to know so well in his wartime training and experience, and *The Autobiography of a Fisherman* (1927) integrated Day's Nova Scotian experiences with his exploration of man's place in the natural and social scheme of things:

As for me, I endure the city in winter in order that I may live through three long summer months. In the city, I write endless letters in my office, I am busy over executive work, I rush about day and night getting only half enough sleep, my mind full of ambitious and often angry thoughts. But in summer, all is different: in a country almost untouched by man, I get up fresh and clear-eyed to watch the sun rise out of the forest and chase the mist wraiths from the lake, I take my canoe and paddle over to the still-water for trout, I swim in the cool clean water, I gather pond lilies and berries in season, I cut wood or hoe my garden or drive back the forest of alders that is forever encroaching. I explore some new part of the forest, boil my kettle by some singing brook, and lie in the sun for hours. A lazy life, you say, yet life, after all, with one's head full of sweet dreams and fancies. At night, I build up a log fire, for it is always a little chilly in the evenings, and by the light of a shaded oil lamp settle down in my armchair with a book I love.[10]

Moments of relaxation like these were few for Day. As he wrote Nella Broddy of Doubleday, Page & Company in 1923, he could find little time in his busy academic schedule for writing the stories and novels so important to him.[11] None the less, surviving notes, letters, and drafts all indicate that he was working on *Rockbound* in the mid-1920s even as his first novel, *River of Strangers*, was still with the publishers. Day had vivid memories of the rugged coast of Nova Scotia's South Shore from his two years of living there as a youth, and his periods of fishing with Captain Enoch Mason had provided him with an introduction to the rigours of a fisherman's life. These first-hand experiences clearly played a part in the shape and design of *Rockbound* as Day began to work on the novel, and manuscript stories like "The Footless Nigger" and "The Ghost-Catcher"[12] indicate his experimentation with South Shore folk tales that might be incorporated into the text of the narrative. However, the key element in filling in the background of Rockbound, Barren Island, and the Outposts in the novel lay in Day's visit to Ironbound, Pearl Island, and the Tancooks in the summer of 1926. Here he began to scribble descriptive notes, names of people, ghost stories, island gossip, and interesting expressions ("to rutch up") into a working journal and text begun on 30 July 1926 on Ironbound. The ballad sung by Gershom in the fish house scene in the novel is copied into the notes under the title "How Israel's Prayer Was Answered." A visit to the Smith's Cove cemetery to check the accuracy of local names introduced him to "Gershom" and eventually led to his changing the name of the "blonde Viking" from "Mather" in one working draft to Gershom in the final version. He also made lists of books that light keepers had read on Pearl (Barren) Island, researched the bird life existing in the offshore islands, and consulted Mather Byles DesBrisay's *History of Lunenburg County* (1870) for background information.[13]

Nowhere is Day's on-the-spot integration of South Shore life into the novel better illustrated, however, than in his response to the tragic events of 7–9 August 1926, when a Caribbean storm swept up the Atlantic and battered schooners of the Lunenburg fleet fishing off the coast of Sable Island. Headlines and articles from the *Halifax Herald*, the *Halifax Morning Chronicle*, and the *Yarmouth Telegram* from 11–19 August were clipped out and glued into Day's draft of "The Summer Storm" in *Rockbound* as the tragic fate of the *Sylvia Mosher* and the *Sadie Knickle* unfolded in the newspapers.[14] Day's *Sylvia Westner* in the novel is a fictional ship, but her captain, crew, and destiny find close parallel to those of the *Sylvia Mosher* described in the *Herald* and the *Morning Chronicle*. Like the *Sylvia Mosher*'s Captain John D. Mosher, memorialized by the newspaper as "one of the youngest skippers in the Lunenburg fleet and high-liner for the last three years," Day's Captain Johnny Westner is the "smartest young skipper on all the coast" with a schooner that "had been for three seasons high-line of all the Liscomb fleet."[15] The crew, as one newspaper noted, had been carefully selected, for "the Sylvia Mosher being a hand liner, took the pick of the young men, 'the brightest, ablest, finest men of the community.'"[16] In the novel, Uriah takes great pride in his Rockbounders being asked to serve on the *Sylvia Westner*, for "Johnny Westner, smartest young skipper on all the coast, picked only the most skilled hand-liners and ablest men for his crews" (174). In at least one case, Day made no distinction between a factual and fictional crew member, for Caleb Baker of the LaHave Islands appears in the newspaper as a missing member of the *Sylvia Mosher* complement and in the novel as a helmsman from the La Tuque Islands.[17] The most striking example of the integration of documentary into fiction, however, lies in the description of the *Sylvia Mosher/Sylvia Westner* sinking off Sable Island. The *Mosher* was at anchor some thirty miles south of Sable when the storm broke, according to the *Halifax Herald*, and from the evidence it seems that Captain Mosher decided to run with light canvas before the wind and head toward the western end of the island:

It would only require a flying jib sail to send the craft bowling along at a fast rate before such a wind. The island was rapidly approaching. West Light was showing up on the port bow. Stygian blackness and only the flashing hope of the sailors' friend as a guide. Hauling off before such a wind might send her into the vortex of raging breakers ahead, broadside on to certain destruction. She had crossed this western bar before. There were numerous channels. It was high water. Anyway to turn back now was impossible. Through the hissing foam-lashed breakers she must go – and through the other side to safety and shelter in the lee of the island on the northern side. But the doomed vessel did not win through.

With the hurricane driving her sheer hull through the spume-drift and tempest-lashed shallow water over the bar at a speed calculated to be anything between twelve to sixteen knots, she grounded on a shoal, her whole bottom was ripped asunder in one fell sweep and she turned over and over, her masts wrenched completely from their holdings in the keelson and everything movable, living and inanimate gone in one catastrophic crash that could have taken but moments to happen.[18]

The vividness of the *Halifax Herald* account obviously fuelled Day's imagination as he plotted the last minutes of the *Sylvia Westner*'s voyage. In the novel, Captain Johnny decides that "the only chance was to drive straight on before the gale." Knowing that when "the tide was at the top of the flood, there were deep channels through the sand," he tries to run the *Sylvia Westner* over the western bar of Sable Island:

Wind furies shrieked, stays and halliards groaned with the straining spars, piled dories tugged at their lashings, a water butt broke loose and went booming along the deck to crash into the forecastle hatch. A mountain of white water gathered behind the *Sylvia Westner*, rose with slow, malicious dignity, and crashed down upon her poop ...

At that moment the *Sylvia Westner* struck; Hand-line Johnny had no luck that night. All was over in the twinkling of an eye. The vessel, deep-laden, was travelling at the rate of twenty knots, and a tooth of black bottom rock whipped bottom and keelson from her as cleanly as a boy with a sharp jackknife slits a shaving from a pine stick. Two thousand quintals of split fish and the unwetted salt dropped down upon the yellow sands; out came the spars with a rending crash, and deck and upper hull turned over. Within ten seconds of her striking, every man of the crew was in the sea. (195–6)

The malignancy of the storm, the reference to the Sable Island light, the hope of channels through the bar, the moment when rock lacerates the hull, and the image of men and fish tossed to the sand and the sea all link Day's imaginative depiction of the sinking to the *Halifax Herald*'s reconstruction of actual events. Episodes like this one prompted Archibald MacMechan to write Day on 27 October 1928 to congratulate him on "bringing realism into Canadian fiction." "You have got rid of convention and polite periphrasis," noted the Dalhousie professor and critic. "You have given us life, in the raw actuality."[19] MacMechan's claim may have been somewhat dramatic, but the working manuscripts of *Rockbound* and the surviving letters and notes surrounding the composition of the novel leave no doubt of Day's search for authenticity. A sketch of Pearl Island, the model for Barren Island in the novel, reveals the location of buildings, fishing grounds, net, trawl, and even a "groaner" or bellows buoy to the south of the island. The detail on a mock-up of Ironbound (Rockbound) includes trees, pastures, houses, and the place where a "whale ran ashore in the olden days." And a working map of Mahone Bay includes actual place names of mainland and island locations appearing in the novel with Day's fictional adaptation of those names. Thus, Ironbound becomes Rockbound, Big Tancook becomes Big Outpost, Blandford is

Sandford, Chester is Minden, and Lunenburg becomes Liscomb. Sacrifice Island, Big Duck, Little Duck, and the Bull remain unchanged in the transition from geographical fact to fiction. Even specific buildings seem to be thoroughly researched by Day as he develops a visual sense in his novel. A sketch of the lighthouse on Pearl Island reveals it to be the inspiration of Gershom's lighthouse on Barren Island in the novel. Integrated into a draft text of *Rockbound*, the sketch reveals everything from the placement of guy ropes on the outside of the structure to the location of a bookcase in the interior. That Day was actually working with a first-hand knowledge of the building emerges in his manuscript notes, for number 19 on his sketch is marked "Upper room where Mather & I drank rum & talked till 1:30 after the women slept" and number "3 = 6" includes the note, "Table where I wrote on the sly pretending I was preparing Shakespeare lecture."[20]

It was Day's discretion in gathering realistic detail for his novel that no doubt escalated the tension between the Ironbounders and Day after the publication of *Rockbound* and further precipitated the letter to the Lunenburg *Progress-Enterprise* from the "Offended Citizens of Rockbound." Certainly, surviving correspondence from local residents after the summer of 1926 does not give any indication that people were aware of Day's research intent when he visited the islands. Writing to Day on 22 September 1926, one lighthouse keeper thanked him for sending a copy of H.G. Wells's *The Outline of History*, noted that he had caught "a 200 lb. Halibut" the "next day after you left," and observed that "It is lovely out

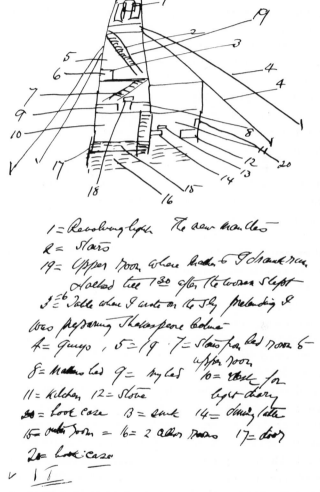

1 = Revolving light   The new mantles
2 = Stairs
19 = Upper room where ladder → I drank rum
      I slept till 7:30 after the women slept
3 = Table where I wrote on the Sky pretending I
was performing Shakespeare below
4 = Guys , 5 = [?] 7 = Stairs from bed room to
                                upper room
8 = Mathers bed 9 = My bed   10 = stove for
11 = Kitchen 12 = Stove   light chart
20 = book case   13 = sink 14 = dining table
15 = outer room = 16 = 2 other rooms 17 = door
20 = book case

Sketch of the Pearl Island lighthouse, the model for Gershom's
lighthouse on Barren Island

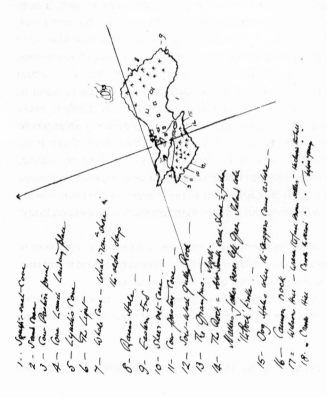

Day's mock-up of Ironbound (Rockbound)

here at this time of year cool days and lots of sport – good rum and brandy & wine. I was ashore for a week and had a change." Similarly, three letters from an islander in the Blandford post office district are filled with news of people Day knew, acknowledgments for seeds that he had sent after visiting, and a request that Day purchase a "10 gage hammer gun" on his behalf "when you come down" next. In a letter dated 31 January 1927, the correspondent remarked: "I have heard you have written a book and we would all like very much to read it, would you tell me where to buy it. I would be verry much interested in new book of eny kind and especially the one you wrote."[21] Given the fact that Day was still negotiating with Doubleday, Page & Company for the publication of *Rockbound* as late as the following summer, it seems likely that the book being discussed is either *River of Strangers* or *The Autobiography of a Fisherman*. However, there is no question that it is *Rockbound* to which a former islander referred when he wrote to Day on 2 May 1929, two months after the Ironbound letter in the *Progress-Enterprise*. Noting that he had recently moved to the mainland, he went on to say:

My object in writing is to see if you can secure for me a copy of your book (Rockbound). I've been trying to get hold of it ever since it came on the market but seemingly cannot.

They have it at Ironbound but will not send it no doubt they blame me altho I am not sure for spilling myself to you at any rate they are wild about it.

In responding on 18 May 1929, Day apologized for not

forwarding a copy of *Rockbound* but explained that he had none available. "I am very sorry that the people of Ironbound have been in any way offended," he said, "as the story is not intended to be about them nor did I get any information whatsoever from you. The story refers to a time long ago not to present-day conditions and I learned many of the stories when I was a little boy before I had ever heard of Ironbound."[22] In spite of Day's denials, feelings against him did not die easily on the islands, as author Thomas H. Raddall pointed out in his 1976 autobiography *In My Time*. Engaged by *Maclean's Magazine* in 1946 to do an article on Tancook Island, Raddall chatted to a local doctor in Chester as he prepared to board the ferry to Tancook:

He warned me not to reveal myself as a writer. In the mid-1920s a literary professor named Frank Parker Day had spent two or three summers on Tancook's small neighbour, Ironbound Island, whose people are all close blood relations of the Tancookers. In 1928 he published a pseudo-novel called *Rockbound*, portraying the Iron-bounders as a backward folk, the result of generations of inter-marriage, speaking English with a thick Old German accent, and lusty in their quarrels and amours. According to the doctor, Day never returned to Ironbound. The Tancookers and Ironbounders would have hanged him if he did.[23]

As late as 1980 there were still elderly residents of the South Shore who spoke disparagingly of Day's novel and of the impression of Ironbounders and Tancookers that it had created.[24]

Ironically, Day's early draft of *Rockbound* contained little of the material that was to offend Ironbound residents in 1929. A short typescript version found in Day's papers at the Dalhousie University Archives has a cast of islanders named Harris, Uriah, and Mary Mader. There is no Gershom Born figure in this story, possibly the one submitted to Doubleday, Page & Company in 1925 or early 1926 to test the publisher's interest.[25] In it, a New York artist named Antriquet comes to the island, wins Mary from Harris, and goes off to New York with her at the end. References to daily life and to the rugged individualism of the islanders do provide some sense of local colour in this working text, but there is none of the rich, regional dialect that was to bring verbal vitality to *Rockbound*. When Uriah and the young Harris (later David) meet for the first time on Ironbound in the draft, their conversation is in conventional English:

At eighteen when he heard that his great great Uncle Uriah, the rich king of Ironbound wanted a man, he rowed out in a dory and applied for the job.

"We work here on Ironbound," said the old man.

"I know how to work."

"Know how to work and from Tancook," said Uriah scornfully. "We've half a day's work done here before the Tancookers begin to rub their eyes."

"Try me," replied the boy.

"Where's your gear and clothes?"

"I got all my gear and clothes with me," said Harris, grinning down at his ragged trousers. "I own yon dory, I salvaged from the sea and beat the man who tried to take her from me." Uriah's eyes showed a glint of interest.[26]

Between the writing of this draft version entitled "Iron-bound" and the submission of the work to Doubleday, Page & Company in the spring of 1927, Day seems to have revised the novel to capture the distinctive flavour of the "Lunenburg Dutch" spoken along the South Shore of the province. A form of English that evolved amongst the descendants of the German settlers who immigrated to the area in the eighteenth century, Lunenburg Dutch retains some of the syntactical and phonological features of German speech. The result, as Kirsten Stevens has pointed out, is that Uriah will say "I'se'll let him go wid as a favour" instead of "I will let him go with you as a favour." "Ain't" or "ain't it" often end statements seeking confirmation, "v" becomes "w" in words like "wery" and "wisit," and consonants like "d" and "t" become substitutes for the "th" sound ("He had dat wery audacious Sanford Ghos'" 120). It is this distinctive speech pattern that Mary Dauphiny tries to correct when she begins to teach Fanny, David, and the children in the new school on Rockbound. "You and Fanny have got to stop saying 'wid' and 'dat,'" she tells David, as she "put her tongue between her closed teeth and showed them how to say 'th' ... Then David and Fanny each had to say 'that' and 'with' fifty times with much spluttering, spitting, and suppressed laughter" (163).[27]

In practical terms, Mary's attempts to homogenize Rockbound speech are part of a process of social change on the island that also sees engines replacing oxen at the launch and Casper's going out west on a harvest excursion. In literary terms, however, Mary's educated speech lacks the uniqueness of idiom and syntax found in the oral tradition. Day's self-conscious effort to make a record of expressions, pronunciations, and names when he visited the islands in the summer of 1926 and his integration of that research into scenes like the opening Uriah-David confrontation reveal the painstaking diligence with which he revised the manuscript to make it as dramatic and as authentic as possible. As Stevens has noted, instead of the "we work here on Ironbound" structures of the early draft, the reader of the final version has a sense of the rugged isolation that has preserved the originality of both character and speech on the island:

"An' what might ye be wantin'?" said the old man, the king of Rockbound.

"I wants fur to be yur sharesman," answered David.

"Us works here on Rockbound."

"I knows how to work."

"Knows how to work an' brung up on de Outposts!" jeered Uriah. "Us has half a day's work done 'fore de Outposters rub de sleep out o' dere eyes, ain't it!"

"I knows how to work," repeated the boy stubbornly.

"Where's yur gear an' clothes at?"

"I'se got all my gear an' clothes on me," said David, grinning down at his buttonless shirt, ragged trousers, and bare, horny feet, "but I owns yon dory: I salvaged her from de sea an' beat de man what tried to steal her from me."

Uriah's eyes showed a glint of interest. (4–5)

By the time that Day submitted the novel to Doubleday, Page & Company in the spring of 1927, it had gone through a number of drafts and had been read by at least two discerning friends.[28] Referred to at various points in Doubleday's correspondence as "The Devil's in the Sea," "The Devil's Island," and "The Islanders," the novel was initially returned to Day on 1 June 1927 with the suggestion that he tighten the point of view. The scene with the sinking of the *Sylvia Westner* was praised by the editors although Day was encouraged to expand or delete the confrontation between Gershom and the devil.[29] In letters of 2 March and 15 March 1928, Doubleday, Doran & Company enthusiastically accepted Day's re-submitted manuscript, offering him a royalty of "10% until our plant account is paid, $12\frac{1}{2}$% on the next 2500, and 15% thereafter."[30] There were suggestions that Day might make the sinking of the *Sylvia Westner* even more vivid and that he might reconsider his use of Shakespeare's *The Tempest* in the text, but publication was none the less assured. A follow-up letter from Beecher Stowe of Doubleday on 30 April 1928 explained somewhat apologetically that the publisher had "taken the liberty of slightly modifying certain words and phrases in your manuscrip which it seemed to us might give unnecessary offense to a considerable number of readers ... For example, where you say 'God Damn' I have cut out the 'God.'" Correspondence about editorial changes and the title continued until the end of June when publisher and author both decided to change the name to *Rockbound* even though the dies for another title had already been cast and the book was in galleys.[31]

By the late fall of 1928, *Rockbound* was being reviewed in a number of American newspapers. Responses were favourable if misguided, often placing the novel on the Grand Banks or identifying Day as a Newfoundlander who returned to his native area "every summer to fish and sail." Commentators frequently confused Day's nationality as much as they did his geography, describing him as a Rhodes Scholar from the United States, or, in the words of the Dallas *Times-Herald*, "an Englishman who has spent much of his scholastic life in London, Berlin and Heidelberg" but "likes best to live and work in America and feels that he would not be content anywhere else." The *New York Herald-Tribune* of 9 December confirmed the Ironbounders' worst fears by noting that "A woman with the morals of a mink is pictured as the dear chum of the school teacher" and that "It is true that there are people of rabbit morals living on the outer islands of Maine and Canada ..."[32]

In his native Canada, Day fared somewhat better in the accuracy accorded both his book and his background, but his distance from literary circles in Toronto militated against his receiving much national attention. In a review in *Saturday Night* entitled "Heroic Mould," author Raymond Knister set his discussion of *Rockbound* in the context of Day's previous fiction, praising the story "An Epic of Marble Mountain" published in *Harper's Magazine* in September 1923 and describing the novel *River of Strangers* as "distinctly a cut above the average." The mores and the conversation of the Rockbounders struck Knister as being "very crude," but he praised Day for being an author who "does not blink them."

"There is nothing here of the evangelical or the idyllic," he noted. "Rather does the story, its swift telling, and the full-lunged men and women call for the word epic. Epic breadth of material and of language."[33]

The mythic or epic proportions of the tale also caught the attention of two other Canadian reviewers. Detecting an almost naturalistic relationship between "the crass superstition, the low moral standards ... The ignorance and quarrelsomeness" of Day's characters and the restrictedness and harshness of their living conditions, Eliza Ritchie of the *Dalhousie Review* none the less praised the "unfailing courage and intense laboriousness" of "the Atlantic fishermen's heritage" depicted in the novel. A Wellesley College professor who had returned to her native Nova Scotia, Ritchie was not uncritical of the "commonplace" love interest and ending of the book. On the whole, however, she found "With no sentimentality, and but little romance, there is an almost epic strength and largeness in the atmosphere of the story."[34]

The other major Canadian review also responded to the "stark realism" and epic sweep of the tale, introducing into its text such phrases as "turbulent epic," "Viking pioneers," "Norse hero," and "supremacy of man ... working with Destiny." Written by J.D. Robins of the *Canadian Forum*, it countered Eliza Ritchie's implications of naturalism in the novel by declaring that "Back of Rockbound ... is the sense of the supremacy of man again, working with Destiny if you will, but achieving by means of an indomitable will which can send even Destiny to its purpose."[35] Robins was particularly drawn to the fish-shed scene during the herring run when "on an unimaginably fatiguing Saturday night" the "blood and filth and sweat are cleansed away from the reader's mind by the old hymn of Fanny the fish-girl." It was this realism that Mazo de la Roche praised when she noted the "fine simplicity" of *Rockbound*'s "hard bitten fishermen."[36] The novel was "without sugar and without rose-pink," added Archibald MacMechan in a letter to literary historian Ray Palmer Baker: "He [Day] has caught the life of Lunenburg. Absolutely. Enter Realism on the amateur stage of Canadian fiction."[37]

MacMechan's reference to the "amateur stage of Canadian fiction" reflects his consciousness of literary change in the 1920s. James Joyce had published *Ulysses* in 1922. Gertrude Stein had uncategorically proclaimed her generation lost. And there was an explosion of literary and publishing energy throughout North America and Europe that saw Day's titles competing in bookstores with those of F. Scott Fitzgerald, D.H. Lawrence, Ernest Hemingway, and Sinclair Lewis. In Canada the Group of Seven, the *Canadian Forum*, and the McGill Group were challenging old shibboleths; while in the United States a decade of rapid social development had found literary expression in a new emphasis on form and irony.

For Day, like many others, this period was one of enormous cultural shift. Raised in a rural Nova Scotian environment that saw the novel "as something depraved if not essentially wicked," Day harkened back to values, virtues, and codes that made him a forceful leader among his peers but a reluctant catalyst for literary change. Thus, his ideal in fiction still lay with the great classics of Richardson, Eliot,

Meredith, Dickens, and the other novelists of character. The two significant developments in the history of the genre, as Day argued them, were a growing democratization of character in the eighteenth and nineteenth centuries and a shift in emphasis from outward life to inward life. "We do insist on knowing about hero and heroine," he noted as he addressed his audiences of the 1920s in a lecture entitled "Some Aspects of Modern Fiction": "what they think and feel; we insist on knowing their ideas – if they have any – we want to get their point of view in regard to the world and life. Thus the psychological novel has arisen in the hands of great artists like Eliot and Meredith, and these artists have laid bare to us the souls of their characters. The psychological treatment of characters has in fact gone over to all novelists and influenced them."[38]

In spite of Day's statements on the importance of interiority in the novel and his own attempts to develop that emphasis in *John Paul's Rock* in 1932, he remained comparatively untouched by the modernist tendency to make ethical considerations secondary to those of form, language, and style. By contrast, the novel "that lifts one from the dull grey world in which we live, a grey world full of incompatibility, divorce and the thousand ills that flesh is heir to," was the novel that Day admired. "Surely the function of the artist is not to depict life photographically," he argued, "but to help us to interpret the beauty of life as it may be, to present to us romance, adventure, idealism, and to reveal the nobility lying latent in every human breast."[39]

Romance, adventure, idealism, and latent nobility underlie

David Jung's struggle in *Rockbound* and ensure that after a period of testing he can forego a "turfy path" for "a way of gold, full of flowers, not of this earth, but like to those with which mediæval painters adorned their foregrounds" (292). The Garden of Eden that David creates out of Barren Island, the fable-like story of the King, the Empress, the young trojan, and the Blond Giant, and the implacable confrontation of the devil, Gershom, and Uriah, all bring an element of romance to the work that place it in a continuum of story-telling from the Old Testament to the present. Day's classical allusions and literary references further enhance the universality of the novel, linking the elemental passions and straightforward heroism of the Rockbounders to a well of human emotion and experience. The timeless story patterns, Chaucerian headnotes, and analogies to Shakespeare's *The Tempest* were not enough to convince irate Ironbounders that Day intended the general rather than the specific, however. Nor is there any question that the appeal of the novel lies in the detail of its island life. Day-to-day rhythms linked to the sea and the weather, patterns of domestic routine and gossip, intricacies of land feuding, lighthouse-tending, and the herring run, and the islanders' pragmatic mingling of Old Testament theology and superstition all give *Rockbound* a distinctive texture of local colour. Moreover, more than any other English-Canadian novel of its period, *Rockbound* conveys a sense of the folk-life of its constituency, particularly in its integration of tale-telling, balladry, and ghost stories into the pattern of the narration. Uriah understands his people well when at the height of the herring

320

scene he can offset their weariness by prevailing on Gershom to "Speak us a piece ... speak us one ye made yur own self" (59). The resulting ballad draws on irony, mock religious rhetoric,[40] and the appeal of hypocrisy, greed, and cuckoldry as enduring themes. Uriah pretends to be shocked, but he is as taken as are his followers with the audaciousness of Gershom's irreverence. Throughout the novel, Rockbounders take no chance with heaven, but they also exhibit an enduring belief in fate, destiny, and the supernatural as being potentially as powerful as their Old Testament God. Thus, it is perfectly natural that the devil should appear to Gershom in the guise of a fisherman, for whether it be the philosophical David, the romantic Gershom, or the grasping Uriah, all Rockbounders believe that "the devil" is "in the sea" (72). The "supernatural in Nova Scotia is not a subject talked about for the sole purpose of entertainment," Helen Creighton has pointed out in *Bluenose Ghosts*, "but for many of us," she adds, "it is part of our way of life."[41] Day's *Rockbound* acts as a gloss on Creighton's observations, for only the careys, "cursed birds of night" (108), or the threat "o' dem haunts" (102) can reduce the blond Viking, Gershom, to fear and trembling. He has inherited from Old Gershom a repertoire of stories, a healthy respect for haunts, and an ability to "present" a tale. In the ferocity of the storm on Barren Island, Gershom and David prepare for an evening of story-telling by boiling hot water for the rum, putting out lump sugar and lemon, and establishing the context of the narrative:

"Dere's somethin' queer on dis island, too," said Gershom, "dough

I don't understand rightly why, 'cause de Sanford folks tuk it away."

"How's dat?" asked David, though he knew the story well.

"You mind Johnny Publicover, de ghost catcher on Big Outpost?"

"I minds him well, 'cause I lived nigh him when I was a gaffer."
(115)

The tale is known to both men, as Debra Surette has pointed out in "Folklore in *Rockbound* and *John Paul's Rock*," but "they follow story-telling conventions, drawing comfort from the familiarity of the story and from the personal interaction the conventions provide." As the night progresses, the rum-drinking is part of the ritual, part of the measured presentation and anticipation of all the mysterious details. "The query and answer were made for no rhetorical effect," notes Day's speaker, "but for the purpose of allowing narrator and listener to pause long enough to take another draught of hot rum and hold it in the mouth a moment before letting the soul-kindling liquor trickle slowly down the gullet" (115–16).[42] It is long past midnight by the time Gershom has completed his tale, having embellished it with his own touches of comedy, opinion, and detail. Day further enriches the presentation through the vividness of Gershom's speech ("... de ghos' fetches de back o' de schoolhouse whang, whang" 118–19), and through the dramatic irony of Gershom's confusing "exorcising a ghost" with "exercising" one (117). The result is an episode of humour, drama, and local colour that brings the central characters and their culture vividly alive. By turning to folktales like this, notes Surette, Day found an effective tool for creating a strong sense of place and for developing an "holistic approach to community."[43]

In spite of a number of requests in 1929–30 that *Rockbound* be reprinted,[44] the novel was not re-issued until 1973 when the University of Toronto Press published it with an introduction by Allan Bevan of the Dalhousie University English Department. In the years following original publication, Day brought out *John Paul's Rock* (1932) and *A Good Citizen* (1947). Crippling arthritis forced his early retirement as president of Union College in 1933, and in the succeeding years Day moved back to the Maritimes and enjoyed a sometime association with his *alma mater*, Mount Allison University. He also continued to write short stories and novels, turning at times to Mount Allison graduate, poet, and novelist Charles Bruce for advice on honing his fiction and submitting it to Canadian publishers. "I should like to send you my novel 'What Happened to Rosalie' that failed to win the Ryerson award, and get a criticism from you that might help me to amend it," he wrote Bruce from Lake Annis in May 1948; "... there is no one down here to whom I can turn for a worthwhile criticism. I don't want *praise* or applesauce. Also can you tell me how to get hold of good literary agents in N.Y. Toronto and London. McLelland & Stuart [sic] are now reading my 'What The River Heard' which I wrote last year. It is very hard to judge one's own babies but both of these books seem to me to have some merit."[45]

In spite of the merits of these manuscripts, however,

novels like "What the River Heard," "What Happened to Rosalie," and "Victory Garden" failed as sustained, fully unified narratives and were rejected by Scribner's, McClelland and Stewart, and a variety of other publishing houses Day approached. Often too crippled by arthritis at the end of his life to leave his bed, Day concluded a letter to Charles Bruce on Christmas Day 1949 with ruminations on the obscurity of contemporary literature and on the strengths of Bruce's own work-in-progress. "You have much talent," he noted, "and I hope you'll have time to express more and more your nostalgia for our wind-swept coast, and that when you come home you may be able to express the joy of your return."[46] The note is both prophetic and revealing, coming as it does just four years before the publication of Bruce's Nova Scotian novel *The Channel Shore*, just seven months before Day's death on 30 July 1950,[47] and some thirty years after the appearance of *Rockbound*, Day's own novel of the "wind-swept coast."

NOTES

I would like to express my gratitude to Dr Charles Armour, University Archivist, Dalhousie University Archives, Halifax, for his assistance with my research. The references that follow to the Frank Parker Day Papers all appear in the archives under the heading Ms. 2.288; further direction to the source under this heading is given in the note concerned.

1 "Letter to the Editor," Lunenburg *Progress-Enterprise*, 20 Feb., "New Book Is 'Ridiculous,' Citizens Say," *Halifax Herald*, 26 Feb. 1929

2 Frank Parker Day Papers, typescript, "Apology of an Egoist," B(ib), p 14

3 Day, *The Autobiography of a Fisherman* (Garden City, NY: Doubleday, Page & Company 1927), 45

4 Day, *Rockbound* (Garden City, NY: Doubleday, Doran & Company 1928). Page numbers for references to *Rockbound* are given within parentheses in the text.

5 *Autobiography of a Fisherman*, 46

6 *Ibid.*, 67, 79

7 Day Papers, typescript, Biographical and Autobiographical Notes, B2, pp 1–2

8 *Roses of Mercatel*, with words by Frank P. Day and music by J. Vick O'Brien, was presented by the Carnegie Institute of Technology School of Music in Pittsburgh on 8 February 1920. The text and program can be found in *ibid.*, J82 and J86. "The Iroquois" was published in *The Forum*, LXXIV, 5 (Nov. 1925), 752–64.

9 Day Papers, Biographical and Autobiographical Notes, B2, p 3, Donald Day to Miss Lewis, 22 Nov. 1972

10 *Autobiography of a Fisherman*, 73–4

11 Day Papers, C60, Day to Miss Nella Broddy, 12 Dec. 1923

12 *Ibid.*, "The Footless Nigger" Ts.ss. G14, "The Ghost-Catcher" G15

13 *Ibid.*, Manuscript Rockbound (Ironbound), E4C (i) and (ii), pp 99–100, 161, 102–3, 210–14, 257–8

14 *Ibid.*, 176–81, 215–25

15 See "Lunenburg Schooner 'Sylvia Mosher' Total Loss on Sable Island Bar: No Trace of Fishing Captain and Crew," *Halifax Herald*, 11 Aug. 1926, and *Rockbound*, 174

16 "Sea Is Strewn with Wreckage, But There Is No Sign of Life," *Halifax Morning Chronicle*, 13 Aug. 1926

17 "Lunenburg Schooner," *Herald*, and *Rockbound*, 193

18 "'Sylvia Mosher' Is Battered Derelict," *Herald*, 19 Aug. 1926

19 Day Papers, C277, Archibald MacMechan to Day, 27 Oct. 1928

20 *Ibid.*, E4C (i), p 89e; E4C (ii), n.p.; E4j; E4C, p 96

21 *Ibid.*, C329, to Day, 22 Sept. [19]26; C455, to Day, 31 Jan. 1927

22 *Ibid.*, C240, to Day, 2 May [19]29; from Day, 18 May 1929

23 Raddall, *In My Time: A Memoir* (Toronto: McClelland and Stewart 1976), 255–6

24 Over the years a number of Nova Scotians have told me of the unfavourable response of South Shore residents to *Rockbound* when it appeared in 1928. Around 1980 I sat next to an elderly Lunenburg woman at the annual banquet of the Royal Nova Scotia Historical Society in Halifax. She expressed great dismay when she learned that I was teaching *Rockbound* to my students at Mount Allison University. Her family had come from Ironbound and Big Tancook and the novel was still an anathema to her.

25 Day Papers, c60, Day to Nella Broddy Henney, 28 Jan.
   1926. In this, Day says: "I am glad you think there is a
   book in 'Iron Bound' and I am going to work on that this
   summer." Writing to Day on 31 January 1927 Allan Davis, a
   Pittsburgh lawyer, refers to "the first Iron Bound sketch that
   you read at the Authors' Club a couple of years ago" (c100).
   In all likelihood, the typescript of "Ironbound" is the one read
   at the Authors' Club and possibly shown to Doubleday.
26 *Ibid.*, Ts. g27
27 Kirsten Allegra Stevens, "Speech in Selected Works of Three
   Maritime Authors," unpublished BA thesis, Mount Allison
   University, 1981, pp 35–6, also 40–1. Stevens quotes H.
   Rex Wilson, "Lunenburg Dutch: Fact and Folklore," in
   J.K. Chambers, ed., *Canadian English: Origins and Structures*
   (Toronto: Methuen 1975).
28 Friends wrote to Day on 31 January (c100) and 10 April
   1927 (c252) about the working versions of *Rockbound*.
   Allan Davis had obviously seen a version of the novel written
   between the "Ironbound" typescript (which may have been the
   draft he had heard Day read at the Authors' Club in Pittsburgh
   a couple of years before) and the final one: he advised Day
   to focus the book on one central character more than he had
   done and to eliminate an artist theme that he had included.
   The other friend had been reading a version of the novel not
   unlike the published one, and advised Day to tighten the
   point of view in the novel. Both urged Day to develop the
   psychology of the female character (Polly/ Mary) in greater
   depth. Both felt he was working with epic material and expressed their admiration for what he was writing.

29 *Ibid.*, c60, Nella B. Henney to Day, 1 June 1927

30 *Ibid.*, c60, Nella Broddy Henney to Day, 2 and 15 March 1928. Day agreed to the financial arrangements on 20 April 1928 (M3).

31 *Ibid.*, c401, Beecher Stowe to Day, 30 April, 8 May and 26 June 1928

32 *Ibid.*, Book Reviews, M2, Sacramento *Bee*, 26 Nov. 1926, and Dallas *Times-Herald*, 25 Nov. 1928; Wilbert Snow, "A Professor's Novel," *New York Herald-Tribune*, 9 Dec. 1928, Section XI, 21

33 Raymond Knister, "Heroic Mould," *Saturday Night* (Dec. 1928)

34 E.R., "New Books," *Dalhousie Review*, IX, 1 (April 1929), 129

35 J.D. Robins, "Viking Pioneers," *Canadian Forum*, IX, 103 (April 1929), 245

36 Day Papers, c87, A. Page Cooper to Day, 22 Nov. 1928

37 *Ibid.*, c277, Archibald MacMechan to Ray Palmer Baker

38 *Ibid.*, Essay, K10, "Some Aspects of Modern Fiction," pp 2, 7

39 *Ibid.*, Essays, K6, "Modern Novelists: John Masefield as a Representative of That Group," p 4

40 Debra A. Surette, "Folklore in *Rockbound* and *John Paul's Rock*," unpublished BA thesis, Mount Allison University, 1981, pp 18–19

41 Helen Creighton, *Bluenose Ghosts* (Toronto: Ryerson Press 1957), 280, quoted in Surette, *ibid.*, 4

42 Surette, *ibid.*, 8

43 *Ibid.*, 10, 38

44 Day wrote on 18 May 1929 that he had no copies of *Rock-bound* and hoped "some day that they will print another edition" (Day Papers, c240). In a letter to Day on 15 August 1930, Nella B. Henney of Doubleday, Doran & Company noted that the publisher had received a number of requests for *Rockbound* and *Autobiography of a Fisherman* but had no plans to republish the books. She offered to sell the plates for $100 a book (*Ibid.*, c).

45 Dalhousie University Archives, Charles Bruce Papers, Ms. 2.297.c38, Day to Bruce, 27 May 1948

46 *Ibid.*, Day to Bruce, 25 Dec. [1949]

47 "Soldier, Author, Educator Passes Away on Sunday," *Yarmouth Light*, 3 Aug. 1950; "Dr. Frank Parker Day," *Union Alumnus*, Day Papers, m66